I0557260

OUTCASTS, LIES, AND A LEGEND

Leonard Dawson

ISBN-13: 979-8-9891208-5-7

Cover design by: Leonard Dawson

Outcasts, Lies, and a Legend

By Leonard Dawson

Alabama 1961

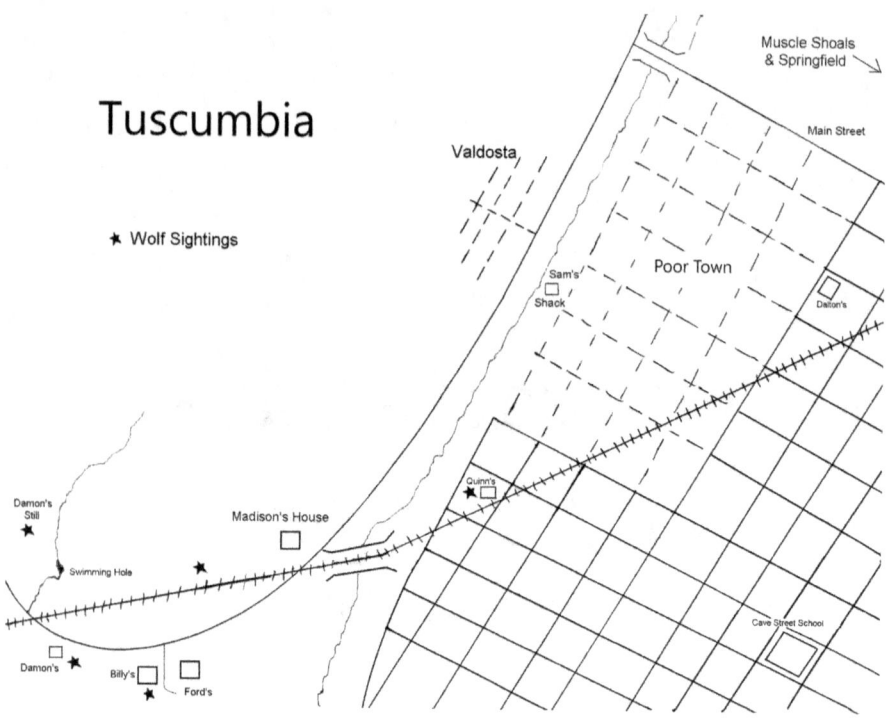

Tuscumbia

★ Wolf Sightings

Muscle Shoals & Springfield

Valdosta

Main Street

Poor Town

Sam's / Shack

Dalton's

Quinn's

Damon's Still

Madison's House

Swimming Hole

Cave Street School

Damon's

Billy's

Ford's

Table of Contents

3

A STOLEN CAR

Early on the morning of our first day in Tuscumbia, Alabama, a Monday in May of 1961, our new neighbor, Mr. Ford, told my sister and me, "If them bootleggers come around when your folks are gone, you call me and I'll run 'em off with the shotgun."

Kneeling down so close to us I could smell his aftershave and the pipe smoke on his breath he told us, "Don't let 'em in the house, no matter what, ya hear?"

The way my mother said, "Oh, dear," she sounded scared, her voice all shaky and weak, the way women in the monster movies sound right before they faint. Putting her hand on her chest as though she couldn't get her breath back, she said, "Maybe I shouldn't leave the kids home by themselves when I go pick up their father."

If I ever wanted to see Mr. Ford chase the bootleggers away with his shotgun I'd have to convince my mother that Sis and I could stay home by ourselves, and I'd need Sis' help for that. Thing was, she wouldn't mind the long boring ride all the way to Florence to get Dad because she could read her book in the car.

And if that wasn't bad enough, Mr. Ford nodded at me and told my dad, "The boy here shouldn't be in out in the woods alone."

Mom asked him why.

"Man up the road told me something killed his dog, really tore it up. Big old dog too."

Looking out beyond the farm fields around our house, at the woods that went as far as I could see in every direction, I hoped that whatever had killed the dog wasn't out there anymore because, by hook or by crook, I was going exploring in those woods.

Mom asked Mr. Ford, "What if it comes around here?"

"You see anything that doesn't belong here you call me. I'll get rid of it."

If he thought that would make my mom feel better, boy was he mistaken. She had turned white as a ghost.

* * * *

Everyone called me Billy back then, except my parents who called me Buster when I made them angry. I had just turned ten years old and we had come all the way from Central New York to live in a little town in Alabama because my father had taken a temporary job there with TVA.

For three long days I'd been trapped in the back seat of the family car with our full-grown collie, Star, and my sister, Lisa, who's a year and a half older than me. That made three of us in the back of the car with only two windows.

Sis and I tried to make Star sit between us. But whenever we passed something Star thought was interesting, which was just about everything, she'd climb over whoever had that window seat. And if you didn't let her have it she'd drool in your lap and blow hot, stinky, dog breath in your face. So, after three days with nothing to do but look for Burma Shave Signs and fight with Star and my sister, I'd had enough of traveling for a lifetime.

A stolen car left in our driveway caused the excitement that first day. When Mr. Ford came to see us, Dad was hidden behind a newspaper at the end of the kitchen table. Mother was making breakfast and Sis was making faces at me. She did it to annoy me, and she was so good at it that my parents almost never caught her.

6

None of us expected to hear a knock on the door at seven o'clock that morning. Dad lowered his newspaper and looked at Mom. She answered the door, stepping back after she opened it, as though something dangerous was standing on our doorstep.

It was a man my grandpa's age wearing clothes like the gas station guys wear. I figured he was probably a farmer or something because of his dark tan. When he took his cap off, I saw a thin ring of light-brown hair around his head.

Pointing back over his shoulder with his thumb he said, "I'm Mitch Ford from next door."

Mother invited him in but he shook his head and stayed outside on the step fumbling with his cap the way I do when I feel bashful. When she offered him coffee he didn't just say, "No," he said, "No, thank you, ma'am," which sounded really strange.

"I'm sorry to bother you so early," he said, "but I thought you'd want to know about that car parked in the driveway. It was most likely stolen and left there by the bootlegger who lives down the road."

The car would have been in his way too because we shared the driveway with the Fords, a driveway so long, that if we had a freak snowstorm and I had to shovel it, I wouldn't get to the end before I had to start over.

Leaning over the sink to look out the kitchen window Mother asked Mr. Ford, "That's a stolen car?"

"Yes, ma'am. But it's nothing to worry about."

Dad didn't say a thing. Mother said, "Oh, my," which is what she said when she didn't know what else to say.

Mr. Ford told my parents, "I already called the sheriff. I reckon I'll go out and wait for him."

As he was turning around to leave Dad asked him, "Why would a bootlegger leave a stolen car in our driveway?"

Mr. Ford put his cap on then seemed to think about his answer for a moment. "Most likely stole it to run bootleg whiskey. He couldn't very well drive it home for the sheriff to find, so he ditched it here and walked home."

While my parents looked at each other without speaking

I followed Mr. Ford outside to wait for the sheriff. Compared to the cold weather we'd left back in New York it felt like summer outside, so nice in fact, that if it hadn't been for Mr. Ford's warning about the neighbor's dog, Tuscumbia would've seemed like a great place to spend the summer.

Since we were going to be living in Tuscumbia for less than a year my parents had rented a house, a ranch-style brick house about fifteen miles outside of town. It had an open carport, the kind you never see up north because of the snow, and we shared a big, flat yard with the Fords.

The Fords' house, about as far from our house as second base is from home plate, was an old but neat-looking, one-story house with an open porch all the way across the front. The door on the one-car garage behind their house looked too small for the black Ford sedan parked in front of it.

The garage was painted white to match the siding on their house. They had lots of pansies growing in front of their house and along one side of their garage. I knew they were Pansies because Mom had some in her garden back home. I liked the way they had people faces and talked in the cartoons. An old barn in the field behind their house leaned so far over to the right I figured I could probably push it down.

Mr. Ford sat on his porch in a rocking chair while he waited for the sheriff. I stood under a tree near the driveway. After an eternity, a car with a round red light on the roof pulled into the driveway and stopped at the stolen car.

I'd never met a real sheriff. Assuming my parents, even my sister, would be as excited about seeing him as I was, I ran through the carport to our kitchen door. Gasping for breath as I opened it, I yelled, "Mom, Dad, he's here; the sheriff's here," before running back outside.

The sheriff got out of his car, and standing as straight and stiff as the creases in his pants, put his hat on, adjusting the big flat brim until it was level. While he looked over the stolen car Mr. Ford walked over to him. They shook hands and talked, and as they talked they watched me walking toward them.

The sheriff told me to go get my folks. Mr. Ford told me to get my sister too. Sis never did anything I told her to do, so I ran inside eagerly expecting to get her in trouble. When I told her she had to go outside, I made sure Mom and Dad heard me.

I figured she's get snooty about it and she did. "Says who?"

I was so excited about trapping her, I practically spit the answer out. "The sheriff, that's who."

"You can't make me," she said, sticking her tongue out.

"Let's go see what the sheriff wants," Mother said, wiping her hands on a towel.

Sis groaned and made a face but came with us. Mr. Ford introduced the sheriff to my parents. That got a smile from my mother, causing wrinkle lines to appear next to her eyes.

And that's when Mr. Ford came over to my sister and me, getting down on one knee so he was about my height, and told us, "If them bootleggers come around when your folks are gone, you call me and I'll run 'em off with the shotgun," and, "Don't you let 'em in the house, no matter what, ya hear?"

When Mom said, "Maybe I shouldn't leave the kids at home by themselves when I go to pick up their father," Mr. Ford told her he'd write his phone number down and bring it over to our house so Sis or I could call him if the bootleggers did come around.

After he told us about something killing the dog up the road he left us there with the sheriff who told my parents he'd have the stolen car towed away. I wanted to stay there with the sheriff, but Mother told Sis and me to go inside.

When I didn't move right away, my Dad said, in a voice that threatened a spanking, "What did your mother just tell you, Buster?"

One calm, quiet word from him scared me more than a whole string of threats from my mother, because by the time he reached for his belt it was too late, and you never knew for sure when he was going to do that.

Back in the kitchen, after the sheriff left, Dad hid behind his newspaper again, and Mother went back to cooking breakfast, but she looked confused, as though she couldn't remember what to do next.

While Sis and I waited for our food, I asked Dad what a bootlegger was.

He lowered his newspaper a little and looked over the top of it. "Someone who makes illegal whiskey."

"What's that?"

He raised his newspaper then said we'd talk about it some other time, but I knew we wouldn't because that was his way of telling me to forget about it. With nothing else to do, I wondered why Mr. Ford would need a shotgun to chase the neighbors away.

"ANTI WHAT?"

I couldn't very well tell my parents I hoped the bootleggers would come around, so I pretended to be worried about them. "Those people Mr. Ford told us about won't really come here, will they?"

Mother, who was just then cracking an egg into a frying pan, stopped mid-crack with the yoke oozing out of the shell. She rummaged through several drawers until she found a piece of paper and some scotch tape. As she taped the paper to the refrigerator she said, "I'll write Mr. Ford's phone number right here. If you need anything when your father and I aren't home you call him."

Dad lowered his magazine. He glanced at Sis then looked at me, real stern like. "You kids do what your mother says."

I wasn't so sure he even knew what she'd said, but I knew – and it meant she'd leave us home alone sometimes.

From the way Mother frowned when I said, "Okay," I knew I'd done something wrong but I couldn't imagine what.

She sat down at the table with us. "I want you kids to listen carefully. While we're in Tuscumbia you'll say, 'yes, sir' and 'no, sir' and 'yes, ma'am' and 'no, ma'am.' And you'd better get used to it, so you can start right now."

I knew it was going to be trouble for me but I told her "Okay" to end the lecture.

My mother always used the word "cross" instead of the word "angry," and I knew I'd made her cross because she said,

"Buster, what'd I just tell you?"

While I was thinking about my answer Sis said, "Yes, ma'am" then stuck her tongue out at me. When I returned the favor Sis said to me, "You're so dumb."

Mom gave Sis a stern look for saying that then looked at me. "Well, Buster?"

I said, "Yes, ma'am," but it felt strange, as though it wasn't even me saying it.

Dad went back to reading his newspaper, Sis went back to making faces at me, and Mother went back to making breakfast. She'd forgotten all about the eggs. When she saw them she swore. I went to see what had happened. The eggs were brown around the edges, just the way I like them but could never get Mom to cook them.

She opened the cupboard door under the sink to throw them in the garbage. I begged her to let me have them, saying, "Please, Mom," over and over until she made a face then slid them onto a plate for me. They were so rubbery I couldn't cut them with my fork, so picked one up with my fingers.

"Yuck," Sis said, scrunching up her face, "he's eating his eggs with his fingers."

Mom told me to use a fork. I tore them into pieces with my fingers then ate them with the fork.

Ever since talking with Mr. Ford, Mom had looked worried. Even Dad acted odd, adjusting his tie and his glasses over and over without changing the way they looked. Of course, Dad might have been nervous about his first day at work. I knew I'd be nervous my first day at my new school. Too bad for Dad we only had one car so he had to wait while Sis and I had our breakfast and got dressed. Too bad for me Mother planned to spend the day running errands after we dropped Dad off at work.

When I came out from getting dressed after breakfast everyone was waiting for me in the kitchen by the door to the carport. Mom was wearing a long white dress with big yellow flowers on it. She wore dresses with flowers on them a lot, and her hair fell down over her shoulders in big waves, like a golden

12

waterfall.

As usual, Dad had on a dark suit, white shirt, and plain dark tie for work. Even when he worked at home on Sunday afternoons, he'd sit at our folding card table wearing a white shirt and tie. And wherever he went, he wore his dark-gray Fedora. I knew the name because that's what he called it when he asked Mom where he'd left it.

After breakfast we piled into our seven-year-old Oldsmobile Eighty-Eight. I still remembered how excited I'd been when Dad brought it home, remembered how shiny the paint was, and how I could actually see myself in the big chrome bumpers even though it was a used car. Now it looked old, especially compared to the cars I saw advertised on television.

Because we'd arrived here after dark the night before, that morning was my first look at the country around Tuscumbia. Riding into town through stretches of woods so thick they felt claustrophobic, we passed a few clearings barely large enough for the little houses crowded into them.

A couple of minutes later we drove by a big pasture. I didn't see any cows, just one big tree, a tree so big it shaded an area the size of our whole front yard back home. And it had gray stuff hanging in it; stuff I'd never seen before, stuff that looked like a witch's hair.

Mother twisted around in her seat and pointed out the window as we sped past it. "Oh, look there kids, that's a live oak."

I asked her about the gray stuff.

Talking in a dreamy voice she said, "That's Spanish moss, dear."

"Is it bad for you?"

I guess she didn't hear me because, "There was one just like it growing outside my parents' house," was all the answer I got.

Alabama might feel like home to her, but to me it seemed like a foreign country. Of course, I'd never been to a foreign country, I just figured that's what it would feel like.

At the next break in the trees, I saw a village off to our left, which I found out later was called Valdosta by the locals. It was just a few rundown shacks where two dirt roads crossed. We'd passed places like it on our way to Tuscumbia, but they'd been so far off, and we'd gone past them so quickly, that they'd seemed like scenes from an old movie. But this place was different because the houses and people were up close and we'd probably be passing it every day on our way to school.

Most of the houses had roofs of curling shingles patched with sheets of rusty metal. I wondered if it rained inside when it rained outside. A few of the windows were boarded up. One had a piece of plastic over it that was torn and flapping in the breeze like the pennants you see at used car lots; it wouldn't do much to keep out the rain or the cold.

An old man was unloading crates from a pickup truck parked in front of the biggest building in the village; an old building with additions of all different sizes and shapes, and no two of them looked like they belonged together.

The only other man I saw was across the street lying under a car that had been put up on cinderblocks. With all four wheels missing and all sorts of rusty car parts sitting in the dirt nearby I figured that car would never leave that driveway again, as least not under its own power.

Three women were walking down the middle of the road, their long loose dresses fluttering in the breeze. They looked as old and rundown as the houses, and they were bent forward, as though they'd all just heard the same bad news. Some sand from the road, sent swirling into the air by a gust of wind, became a dust devil that followed the women for a few feet then dissolved.

I turned around to look out the back window, catching a last glimpse of the place. It looked as though the bricks were peeling off of some of the houses. I asked Dad about it. He said it was tarpaper made to look like brickwork.

"What's wrong with it?"

"The sun dries it out. After a few years it starts to peel around the edges."

"Then why do people use it?"

"Because those are poor people, Billy. That stuff is cheap and it keeps the rain out."

I doubted the part about keeping the rain out. A few minutes later, the woods on our right were replaced by pastures so big the bright white fences around them disappeared at the horizon. On the other side of the road, a huge two-story house with white columns all the way across the front, sat back on a long circular driveway lined with more of those big trees like the one that reminded Mom of home.

Sher turned around again to face Sis and me. "Did you see that, kids? That was an antebellum mansion."

I'd only half heard what she'd said. "Anti what?"

"Antebellum. It means the house was built before the Civil War."

I didn't understand what all the fuss was about, but Mom seemed more excited about that house than I'd ever seen her get over Christmas presents.

Dad turned right at the next intersection. Then we crossed a bridge over a stream and I craned my neck to get a good look at it. I wondered if it would be as good for hunting crayfish as the creeks back home. Unfortunately it was so far from our house that I'd have to sneak away if I wanted to explore it, because my parents would never let me go so far from home by myself.

As we came off the bridge we passed a sign welcoming people to Tuscumbia. A few minutes later we passed a small park in the center of town that had a large grassy lawn one block wide and several blocks long, with sidewalks crisscrossing it.

At one end of the park there was a big gray building with the word "courthouse" over the door. At the other end of the park I saw a low brick building. I knew it was the police station and jail because of the bars on the windows. A few blocks later we left Tuscumbia, passing through another small town called Muscle Shoals on our way to Florence where Dad would be working.

It seemed like a long, boring drive, but in a few days the drive into town would be a thousand times worse because

15

Mother would be dropping Sis and me off at school. I got queasy just thinking about it. Then I remembered our neighbor, Mr. Ford, warning us that the people down the road might come to our house, and that if they did he'd chase them away with his shotgun. I suppose I should have been worried about them, but nothing that exciting had ever happened to me before. And besides, my sister would be there and she was a year older, so if anything bad did happen it would be her problem.

Dad parked the car in front of a modern-looking, two-story steel and glass building. Behind it I saw a river so wide the buildings on the other side looked like the scale models on my toy train layout back home. Dad leaned over and gave Mom a peck on the check before getting out of the car. She slid across the front seat to get behind the steering wheel. As we drove away, I looked out the back window. Walking toward his new workplace carrying his briefcase, wearing a suit and fedora, Dad looked like one of the lawyers on the TV show Harrigan and Son. A boring show that had a catchy tune.

Mother and Sis and I spent most of the day shopping which put me in a really foul mood, but that was nothing compared to what happened on the way home. Mother turned off onto a side street and drove up to a long low brick building that looked so much like a school I felt queasy.

She parked the car then turned around in her seat to face us. "You kids wait here until I get back, and no fighting."

I guess she didn't think one warning was enough for me because she looked right at me. "I'd better not hear about you starting trouble."

Sis opened her book as soon as Mom left. Unlike my sister, who was actually eager to start school, a feeling of dread swept over me at the mere thought of it, so I waited nervously for my mother to return.

As soon as she was in the car Sis asked her the question I didn't dare ask. "Are we going to school here?"

Mother shook her head.

Lisa said, "How come? This looks like a nice school."

16

After Mother had turned the car around and headed back toward the highway, she glanced at us in the rearview mirror. "It's not a school for whites."

The way Sis sat up you'd have thought I'd poked her in the ribs. And she sounded not just surprised but confused too. "We can't go there because we're white?"

Mom said, "It's a school for Negroes," as though that explained everything.

Sis and I watched the news with my parents every night after dinner, mostly the show with Walter Cronkite. So I'd seen lots of stuff about segregation, but it was no more real for me than the man-in-the-moon or the tooth fairy. So I told Mom I didn't get it.

I knew right away I'd said the wrong thing and that we were going to get a serious talking to because Mom pulled the car over and parked it right there on the side of the road.

She twisted around to face Sis and me. "Negroes and whites don't go to school together in Tuscumbia, and they don't sit together in restaurants either. There are separate facilities for whites and coloreds, so when you're looking for a water fountain or public bathroom always look for a sign to be sure you're using the right one."

She looked at both of us, but especially me, without saying anything, as though she could tell just by looking at us whether or not we understood.

Then came the warning. "And don't you dare talk to anyone about this but me or your father. Is that understood?"

Even though I nodded my head 'yes,' she singled me out again. "Buster?"

Normally I would have complained about her calling me Buster, but I wanted to ask her something about the new rules before I forgot how to say it. "What's a 'fa' 'cilty'?"

"Never mind that. Just look for signs that say, 'Whites Only.' Do you understand?"

I had a bad habit of breaking rules I didn't understand or couldn't remember, so I always asked, "What if I forget?" because

17

I'd remember the rule if the punishment sounded bad enough.

When Mother said, "You'll be so sore you won't be able to sit down for a week," that settled it. I'd remember that rule for sure.

I knew she didn't want to talk about it anymore because she started pulling on her right earlobe with her thumb and forefinger. She did that when she got frustrated. It made a loud snapping sound. I've tried to do that with my ears, but I can't. Anyway, since that was something she only did when she was upset, I didn't ask her any more questions.

Before she turned around, Mother told us we could stay home for the rest of the week while we got settled. That meant I didn't have to go to school until the following Monday, which was a whole week away, and when you're ten years old a week is almost forever.

On Thursday, Mother got a fancy-looking card in the mail from Mrs. Madison, the lady who lived in the house with the big pillars we passed on the way into town; the one Mother told us was built before the Civil War. It was an invitation to a dinner party on Saturday night.

At dinner Mom told Dad she was thrilled about it, a word she only used when she was extra excited about something. But she didn't have to tell me that; I knew she was excited because she'd been singing all afternoon.

But as happy as the idea had made her, that's how upset it had made me, because she said us kids had to go too. I begged Mother to let Sis and me stay home by ourselves. I promised her that we wouldn't get into any trouble, but she wasn't having any of that, although she did leave Sis and me home alone the next afternoon while she went to pick up Dad at work.

Mother told us she'd be gone for about an hour. While we waited for her and Dad to get home, I sat at the kitchen table playing solitaire. Sis sat across from me reading a book. Mr. Ford's warning was just about the furthest thing from my mind when I heard a knock on the door.

Lisa stuck her tongue out at me and said, "I'll get it."

18

I was sure it was one of the Fords because I hadn't heard a car coming up the driveway. Boy was I wrong.

Sis pulled back the curtain on the window in the kitchen door to see who it was. Then, as she slammed the dead bolt home, she yelled, "Oh God, Billy. Go lock the front door." When I didn't move right away, she yelled, "Run, Billy, hurry."

Sis yelled, "Hurry," again, as I darted out of the kitchen and through the living room with Star chasing me, barking wildly and wagging her tail, as though it was a game.

After I flipped the bolt latch on the front door, I pulled back the curtain on the little window in it then almost screamed because a girl's face was just inches from mine through the glass. Too startled and scared to move I stared back at her with my heart pounding wildly.

The low, late-afternoon sun shining on her from the side made her face look as boney as a skeleton. I thought she looked older than me, maybe my sister's age, with limp, clumpy, shoulder-length straight hair. She had the kind of thin dark lines around her neck I get when sweat that's caught in the creases of my skin gets caked with dirt.

We stared at each other through the window until Sis, who had come up behind me, grabbed my shoulder, scaring the bejesus out of me.

When Sis said, "Don't you dare open that door, Billy," it was the first time I'd ever heard her sound scared.

I heard another knock on the kitchen door and a woman yell, "I just want to use your phone?"

As Sis pulled me away from the door, she whispered, "Come back in the kitchen with me."

I followed her to the kitchen and waited while she dialed Mr. Ford's phone number, which seemed to take forever. I could tell it had a lot of big numbers in it because I could hear the clicking of the phone dial each time it spun slowly back to zero.

After banging on the kitchen door again the woman in the carport yelled, "I can hear you in there."

Sis finally said into the phone, "Mr. Ford, those people are at the door."

Sis pulled the curtain back. I went and stood with her to look outside. A woman dressed in coveralls was standing in the carport looking in at us. Not much bigger than me, she had clumpy brown hair like the girl at the front door. I figured she was the girl's mother.

I couldn't see the Fords' house from that window, so I ran back to the front door. I got there in time to see Mr. Ford come out of his house carrying a gun. Looking in the direction of our carport he yelled something I couldn't hear.

The girl backed away from our front door then ran out of sight around the end of the house. As soon as she left, I ran out to the driveway, pretending I couldn't hear Sis yelling for me to get back in the house.

The woman in the carport didn't run away, not even when Mr. Ford fired his gun into the air. It sounded as loud as the thunder from nearby lightning. But she didn't move until Mr. Ford got within a few feet of her and pointed his gun right at her. She sneered at him then walked out the back of the carport toward the field behind our house.

Sis was waiting for Mitch at the kitchen door. He let me go inside first then stood in the doorway. Mr. Ford's gun smelled like someone had burned something nasty in the rubbish heap. Mom and Dad would smell it when they got home. Dad would recognize the smell. It would upset Mom for sure.

When Mr. Ford asked Sis if we were alright she told him, "That woman said she wanted to use our phone."

Mr. Ford shook his head. "Don't you believe it, Missy. That's a trick to get in the house. She wanted to look around, see if you had anything worth stealing."

He started to leave, but before he closed the door behind him, he told us, "I don't think they'll be back today, but you lock this door just the same, you hear?"

Mr. Ford was right; they didn't come back again that day. They didn't come back again for several weeks.

When our parents did finally get home, I could tell they

smelled the gunpowder as soon as they opened the door, because for a moment or two they looked confused. Then Dad asked us what had happened. Sis and I both started talking at the same time.

Dad held a hand up toward me. "Let your sister talk."

He let Sis tell them the whole story, which didn't seem at all fair.

The more Sis told them, the whiter Mother became. When Sis told them about Mr. Ford firing the shotgun at the woman, Mother said, "Oh my," then plopped down in a chair at the kitchen table.

When Mother got some color back in her face, and her breathing was steady again, she praised Sis for calling Mr. Ford and sent Dad over to thank him. Ignored again, as usual, I sat there wondering if Mr. Ford would really have shot the woman in the carport.

Sometime in the middle of the night the face of the girl I'd seen at the window appeared to me in a dream. I woke with a start, lying there for the longest time listening for a sound outside, too scared to sleep.

MY FIRST SIGHTING

Since my parents had nothing planned for me the next day, I expertly wasted it. After supper we all gathered in the living room to watch a TV show about a kid named Opie who lived in a little town called Mayberry. It was my favorite show, especially the beginning with Opie and his dad walking down a dusty road carrying fishing poles while someone whistled a catchy tune. When I was alone I sometimes whistled the tune and pretended it was my own memory.

Being a boy, and also the youngest kid, it was my job to take Star outside when she needed to make a mess in the yard. And it was my job to clean up after her. I had taken her outside and tied her to a bush at the corner of the house before the show started. I had closed the screen door but left the main door open so I could hear her. She'd bark up a storm when she wanted to come in.

Of course it was during the most exciting part of the show, when Opie was following some guy he thought was going to rob the bank, that Star began barking. She never looked or sounded vicious like some dogs, but she could make a lot of noise. That night her barking was extra loud and incessant. And it was mixed with whining, something she never did.

All Mother had to say was, "Buster." I knew that meant, "Go get the dog."

I wanted to wait for an ad so I could find out if Opie got caught by the bank robber, but the look I got from Dad told me

22

that would be a mistake. So I got up and headed for the front door, looking back to watch the TV as I went. I might have noticed Star was making more noise than usual if I hadn't been so upset about missing my TV show. And if I'd known what had frightened her so, I never would have gone outside by myself.

As far as we were concerned, her barking only meant one of two things – if she was outside and barking, she wanted to come in, or if she was inside and barking, she wanted to go out. I had never thought of her as a watchdog because there wasn't any need for one back home in sleepy Ithaca where no one even locked their doors at night.

The front of our house faced our driveway so one end of the house was toward the road, which was about as far away as I could throw a stone. I always tied Star's rope to a little evergreen bush at the corner of the house so she couldn't get near the front door, because Mother didn't want her leaving a mess where someone coming to visit might see it or smell it, or even step in it.

The light from the living room window didn't reach the corner of the house, and with no moon it was so dark beyond that the world seemed to end. In a hurry to get back to my TV show, I ran to the bush to untie Star's rope. By then she had pulled the rope so tight her collar was choking her. So instead of barking she just made gagging sounds.

Since I'd forgotten all of the knots I'd learned how to make when I was a Cub Scout, I always used a granny knot to tie her out. Even so, untying her wasn't usually a problem. But that night her frantic pulling had made the knot on the bush impossibly tight, and while I struggled with the knot she backed away from me toward the house, which made untying the knot even harder.

She was too strong for me to pull her back with my left hand to give me some slack in the rope while I worked on the knot with my right hand. So I gave up on the knot and looked to see what had her so spooked.

By then my eyes had adjusted to the darkness well enough

to make out the line of grass at the edge of the field, which was only about two car lengths from me. It hadn't been hayed in years so the wild grass was nearly as tall as me. In the darkness it looked like a solid black wall. In it I saw two small circles the size of quarters that were about shoulder high and glowing like gold coins in the sun.

As I tried to make sense of what I was seeing, they disappeared. When they reappeared I knew it was a pair of eyes, and that they had blinked, and that they were watching me, and that the thing was really big because its eyes were as high off the ground as mine.

Star started whimpering. I told her to shush. She wouldn't. I pulled on the rope to get some slack. She pulled on it so hard she began making choking sounds.

I yanked on the end of the rope tied to the bush as hard as I could with both hands. It gave a little, slipping a few inches up the trunk of the bush before it caught on a branch. I looked behind me to check on the thing in the field.

The bright yellow eyes were still there. They reminded me of what Mitch told us about one of the neighbor's dogs – that something had killed it, "really tore it up." All I could think about after that was a big ugly beast charging out of the field at me.

While I struggled with the rope and fought the urge to run and leave poor Star alone out there, a huge, shadowy, dog-like form, stepped out of the field with its head low to the ground and it's eyes locked on me.

In a panic I wrapped the rope around my wrist then ran for the house. Star lunged toward the house too. I was almost jerked off my feet when we ran out of slack, but it only lasted a moment before we broke free.

Star ran out ahead of me, which meant that thing from the field was closer to me and I knew anything that big could move really fast. I expected it to run me down and sink its teeth into me. I could almost feel them.

I cleared the front steps in a single leap then made the mistake of glancing behind me to look for the beast as I reached

24

for the doorknob. Whatever it was, it had come as far as the corner of the house, not far enough for the light from the living room window to reach it, so it was just a big, black, dog-shaped thing looking at me with glowing eyes. In the excitement my hand had missed the doorknob so I had to turn back around to find it. The scariest part was not knowing where it was when I turned away.

Star rushed in ahead of me when I opened the door, almost knocking me over as she pushed past me to get inside, and tangling her rope around my legs. Then she stopped, just inside the door, blocking it. I pushed her farther into the room so I could get inside then slammed the door before whatever it was out there could get me. The door closed with a very loud thump.

Frowning at me, Mom said, "What on earth?"

Sis told me to be quiet. Dad was frowning at me too. All I could do was sit on the floor and lean against the door until I stopped shaking.

Tangled in the rope hanging from the dog's collar I saw the branch that had held the rope on the bush. Still unable to untie the knot, I took Star's collar off instead. She trotted over to my mother then turned around in a circle half a dozen times before curling up by her feet. I saved her life and she sat with my mother. That didn't seem fair.

Mom eyed the rope with the branch tangled in it. "Buster, if you ruined that bush you'll be in serious trouble."

"But Mom, a giant scary dog with glowing yellow eyes came out of the field after us. It was as big as a horse and as black as coal, and I bet it's still out there."

She tipped her head and sighed, which was a bad sign. Then her shoulders drooped a little, which was an even worse sign. "Billy, what did we tell you about exaggerating?"

I didn't get into trouble because I said, "Aw Mom, I saw it, I really did." What got me in trouble was telling her that I wasn't exaggerating, which she considered back-talk.

Things really seemed unfair when Dad told me, "Go to bed right now, young man."

So unfair that I blurted out, "Aw, Dad," without thinking.

At the same time I got, "Don't make me come over there," from Dad, I got a singsong version of "Ha, ha, Billy. You have to go to bed early," from Lisa.

Dad scowled at her, which shut her up, but didn't wipe the smirk off her face. I jumped up and headed for the safety of the bedroom.

On my way I heard Mom tell Dad, "Maybe you should go out there and take a look."

He told her it was just my overactive imagination. By that time my show had ended, so I didn't care if I had to go to bed. And I was curious if I could see the big black what-ever-it-was was from our bedroom window. I left our bedroom light off so I'd be able to see outside, and put on my pajamas while I watched for the eyes. I waited as long as I dared before going to the bathroom to brush my teeth. My parents would know if I didn't - they could hear me.

The bathroom door was right across the hall from the double doorway into the living room. I stopped to look in on my way back to the bedroom. Normally Star would be sound asleep on the floor while my parents watched TV, but she was on a hair-trigger alert that night, her head popping up to sniff the air and look around when I stepped in the room. Mother asked me what I wanted.

I barely had time to say, "I saw what I saw," before Dad started to get up. I ran to the bedroom to avoid the belt.

I knew I wouldn't be able to sleep unless I made sure the bedroom window was locked. I must have set and reset and tested the latch ten times before jumping into bed. Sis came to get her pajamas a few minutes later. When she turned the light on I told her, "I really did see a monster dog."

She said, "Nobody cares" then left for the bathroom.

When she came back from the bathroom she left our light on. I knew she wanted to read. I told her I'd tell Mom if she didn't turn it off.

She made some angry sounds but got up and turned it off.

Lisa and I had gotten along okay in New York but our house in Alabama only had two bedrooms so Lisa and I had to share one, and if either of us was upset it usually resulted in an argument or a pillow fight, both of which ended up with me getting in trouble because she'd tell Mother I hit her, even though I hardly ever did.

The following Saturday evening was our dinner at the Madisons' house. Since I only owned one suit, Mother made me try it on that afternoon, before the party, to see if it still fit. Making boys wear dress clothes is a great way for their parents to torture them. I hadn't worn my suit for months. It was so tight in the armpits it cut off the circulation in my arms unless I held them up. I told Mother about it, but since it was the only suit I had she was happy with the fit.

My shirt was too small for my neck and too big everywhere else, so I looked like a clown with a red face from being strangled and had enough material stuffed into my pants for another shirt. I hadn't worn my dress shoes in a long time either. They pinched my toes something terrible just putting them on. But I knew if I complained about them I'd have to go shopping for shoes, and having my toes pinched was way better than shopping for shoes.

I didn't have one of the new clip-on ties, and had never learned how to tie a tie, so I had to stand still while my Dad tied it for me. It was about the only thing he and I did together. I didn't like it and I don't think he did either. Neither of us had figured out that I should just loosen the tie and leave it tied when I took it off.

And as if that wasn't bad enough, when the time came for us to get ready, Mother told me to dress in the kitchen so she could use the bathroom and Sis could dress in our bedroom. I told Mother it wasn't fair, that Sis always got the better deal. Mother told me Sis needed privacy more than I did. Dad told me to be shush.

I wadded my clothes into ball and took them to the kitchen. When I threw them on the floor I woke the dog, who

27

was curled up in the corner sleeping. She glanced at me, wagged her tail once, then went back to sleep. I really envied her never having wear clothes. Then I remembered that Dad dressed up every day, even Saturdays. I wondered if I'd have to do that when I grew up. Maybe being a kid wasn't so bad after all.

After I got my shirt and pants on I went to Dad for help with my tie. While we were suffering through that, Sis came out wearing a plain light-blue, short-sleeved dress and shiny black shoes. She was really, really tall for her age, as tall as mom. It made her look older. She didn't like that. I would've traded just about anything I owned to be taller so the mean kids wouldn't pick on me.

Mother blew through the house like a gust of wind several times, and each time she passed through the living room her outfit was a little more complete. By then Dad was sitting in his easy chair reading a newspaper. I joined Sis on the couch which turned out to be a mistake because she tried to tickle me, which I hated. I grabbed her hands so she couldn't touch me. Then the struggle was on. I told Sis she looked funny in a dress.

Dad put his newspaper down and told us, "Stop it, both of you."

As soon as Dad put his newspaper back up, Sis stuck her tongue out at me, so I did the same to her. Mother breezed through the room again just in time to catch me with my tongue out but too late to catch Sis.

She stopped in front of me and said, "You've just about earned yourself a spanking, young man."

That didn't scare me, but then Dad lowered his newspaper and said, "That was your last warning," which did scare me.

I wanted to tell them Sis had started it but I didn't dare. Sometimes that just made them madder and I got the belt even though Lisa had started the trouble. And it was an especially dangerous time to sass them because Mom had no patience when she was getting ready to go out. And Dad hated it when I got Mom upset.

Going to dinner was annoying enough without getting

blamed for trouble I didn't start, but to make things even worse, Sis stuck her tongue out at me again as soon as Mother left. Dad had already put his newspaper up so he didn't see her either.

Pretty soon Mother came back and made a grand entrance, swirling and twirling as she danced around the room like Cinderella at the ball, wearing a light-green dress with big orange and white flowers all over it. She had string of white balls around her neck, the smallest ones about the size of marbles, the largest ones almost as big as Ping-Pong balls, with big round white earrings to match.

The Madisons had sent us a formal invitation for the party. I guess Mother was really proud of it because she stood it up on the TV cabinet the way she did Christmas cards back home. The time for the party was printed on the card, but that didn't matter – we'd leave when Mom was "good and ready" and if I knew "what was good for me" I'd be ready when she said it was time to go.

I knew it was time to leave when she flipped a furry thing around her neck that looked like a giant squirrel's tail. She rushed us out to the car then. It was twenty minutes past the time on the invitation and that had made her frantic. I could tell because she was muttering something and making that snapping sound she made when she pulled on her earlobe.

It was in that state, when even the slightest irritation could push her over the edge, and only a fool would say something that might upset her, that I said, "This tie is choking me."

Mother snapped like a dry twig. "I don't want to hear another word out of you, young man. And if a grownup speaks to you, you will say 'ma'am' or 'sir', or you will be very, very sorry."

She had twisted around in her seat and was glaring at me. "Don't you dare embarrass me tonight."

Embarrassing my mother was about the only thing I did really well. I know because she'd told me so a million times. She thought I did it on purpose, but I didn't; it came naturally.

29

The Madisons' place was easy to spot in the dark because they had put spotlights in the yard shining up at the house, so many lights I saw the light through the trees long before we got there. When we pulled into their driveway and I saw their house it almost hurt to look at it, it was so white under the spotlights.

We were so late by then that the driveway was lined with cars and we had to park out on the road. I had just climbed out of the car when Mother grabbed me from behind by the shoulders and told me to stand still. I thought she wanted to straighten my shirt collar because Dad sometimes rumpled it when he helped me with my tie. But then I felt her wet hand on the back of my head. She had licked her hand to slick my cowlick down with her spit. I looked around to make sure no one had seen her. Moms do some really horrible things to their kids.

The branches of the big live oak trees on the sides of the driveway had grown together high above it, so it looked as though we were walking through a giant tunnel. The long curved driveway stopped near their front steps, which sat so high up on a foundation made out of big cut stones that the floor of their porch was higher than my head. Eight columns across the front of the house went all the way up to the third floor roof, each one of them as big around as the fifty-five gallon drum behind our house where I burned our garbage. And it had lots of windows, upstairs and down, all of them as tall as me, and every one of them with a lit candle on the windowsill.

Hanging from a pole on the left side of a balcony that went clear across the second floor of the house, was an American flag as big as a bed sheet. A Confederate flag that was just as big, hung from a pole at the other end of the balcony. And they had so many other buildings around their house with lights in them that the place looked like a small village.

As we neared the house I saw a colored man standing by the front door dressed in a black uniform with a white collar and white cuffs on the sleeves. It looked even more uncomfortable than my suit. Poor man. He opened the front door and held it for the people ahead of us even though they looked strong enough

30

to open it themselves.

I asked Mom why he was there.

"To hold the door for the guests."

"They don't look like they need help."

"Need help?" she said, in her far away voice, the voice she used whenever we went someplace where we had to dress up. She sounded like one of the pod people in the movie *Invasion of the Body Snatchers*.

I told her to forget it. She told me to behave myself for about the tenth time that night. But I didn't care because something had caught my eye. If I knew one thing really well it was cars, and almost every car parked in the Madisons' driveway that night was a Chrysler New Yorker, a Cadillac Deville, or a Lincoln Continental, the kinds of cars rich people drove. Our five-year-old Oldsmobile did not belong anywhere near them.

If a rich guy wanted a car he could show off, he bought a European sports car. If a sort-of-rich guy wanted a car he could show off he bought a Ford Thunderbird. They were hard to get, but convertible Thunderbirds were really hard to get, and I'd just seen a white one parked in the driveway next to the Madisons' house. I found out later it belonged to them and that it was the only one in Tuscumbia.

SAVED BY A GIRL

The colored man at the front door held it open for us. When I thanked him for holding the door Mother told me not to talk to anyone wearing a uniform. So there were rules I hadn't been told about; rules I could break without knowing, new opportunities to be punished.

I asked her, "How come?"

All I got was, "Because I said so," as she swept through the doorway.

Then we were standing in an entrance hall at the foot of two big staircases, one on each side of the room that made huge sweeping curves up to the second floor balcony. Women's heels clicked on the black and white ceramic tile floor. Above me, hundreds of glass crystals in the chandeliers hanging overhead sparkled like sunlight on a lake. When the crowd parted, 1 saw a fireplace in the next room so big I could've walked into it without ducking my head. Logs as big as my legs were piled on the andirons.

A man and woman came over to my parents and introduced themselves as Mr. and Mrs. Madison. My mother and Mrs. Madison smiled a lot. Dad and Mr. Madison shook hands but didn't smile. The Madisons asked about our trip and getting settled but didn't wait around for an answer before hurrying off to talk with some other people.

Dad followed Mom as she darted around the room introducing herself to other guests, like a honeybee flitting from flower to flower to collect nectar. Eventually another uniformed man gestured toward one of the doorways and announced that dinner was being served. Then he pointed to a different doorway at the back of the hall and announced that dinner was being served in there for us children.

As Mother gave Sis and me a gentle shove in that direction she said, "You two run along and enjoy yourselves," but I knew she really meant, "You two run along and behave yourselves."

A bunch of kids had gathered at the doors to the children's dining room, the kids bunching up as they pushed through the doorway, then spreading out again in the room beyond, like when I'm hunting crayfish and I pull out a rock out of the stream and the water rushes through the new opening. Lisa and I got separated going through the doorway and she was the closest thing I had to a friend at the party. I could see her because she was the tallest kid there, but by the time I got to the table, the seats on both sides of her were taken so I had to sit by myself.

And as luck would have it, I was sitting right across from a really cute girl. She smiled at me. I felt my face getting red and quickly looked away.

The room was bigger than our living room, with a ceiling as high as the ones at my school back home, except that this ceiling was clean and white and didn't have any cracks in the plaster. I'd eaten at kids' tables plenty of times, and all of them had been card tables, but this was a real table, so long it wouldn't fit in our living room, so long I couldn't hear what the kids at the other end of the table were saying.

And kid's tables usually had tablecloths with old food stains on them, but this one looked brand new, and each one of us had a neatly folded, cloth napkin on our plate with the initials 'JM' sewn into it. We also had a bewildering assortment of shiny silverware in front of us.

Except for eating, I didn't move or speak all during dinner for fear I'd knock over my drink or get food on my clothes, or say something stupid. I wanted desperately to make it through the evening without embarrassing myself. I didn't want to be noticed, especially not by the cute girl, especially not because I did or said something dumb.

Because the table was so big, I thought the food would get cold before it got to me, but the Madisons had solved that problem by having four uniformed people come to the table at different places holding big platters of food. I thought I had died and gone to heaven because I could take as much as I wanted, of whatever I wanted, and only what I wanted.

Just for fun, I put stuff on my plate I didn't recognize. Some of it was okay, but some of it made me gag and I worried about what to do with it. Luckily for me, the people wearing uniforms came around later and asked if we were done, even if we still had food on our plate. One of them took my plate away, yucky stuff and all. More than once my parents had sent me to bed early for leaving less food than that on my plate.

There was a skinny little girl with buck teeth sitting on my left who ignored me, which was alright with me because I had no idea what to say to a girl half my age. The boy sitting on my right was dressed in a suit that looked nicer than my Dad's. He had tonic in his hair and it was combed straight back on his head, the way older grown men combed their hair. At first he looked at me as though I was a curiosity. But then he made a smart-alecky face at me and I knew he was going to start trouble.

And he did, by saying, "You're not from around here, are ya, kid?" real snotty like.

Besides them knowing I wasn't from Alabama if they heard me talk, I was afraid of saying something that would make things worse, so I just nodded my head.

He raised his voice loud enough to be heard by all of the kids at the table. "What's the matter, kid? Too scared to talk?"

The kids all stopped what they were doing and stared at me. As I tried to think of a smart answer I felt my face getting hot and knew it was turning red. I heard some giggling.

"Leave him alone, Peter." It was the cute girl sitting across from me scolding the boy. I'm sure she meant well, but she made my embarrassment worse by making me look helpless.

34

The boy glared at her but backed down. He sulked after that, pushing food around on his plate, but not eating it. It got noisy again after that, conversations starting up then dying out then starting up again, like flames on a slow-burning log.

I suppose I should have thanked her, but she was much too pretty to talk to, especially in front of other kids. She smiled at me. I'd never had such a pretty girl smile at me. It embarrassed me something terrible. I smiled at her then quickly looked away so she wouldn't say anything to me.

Later, when most of the kids had finished eating, an older boy said, "That's the 'Wolf's-Head Man'," so loudly all of the kids stopping what they were doing to look at him.

The boy, probably a couple of years older than me, looked like the oldest kid at the table. Like me, his clothes didn't look as nice or fit as nice as the other kids' clothes, but that's about all we had in common. His features, like his nose, were big and rough looking. From four seats away I could see scars on his hands. He looked as out of place as I felt, but unlike me he sounded sure of himself.

The younger kids' eyes grew as big as quarters, as the boy told them, "He has the body of a man and he walks like a man, but he's got the head of a wolf and he's got big, long, sharp teeth. And no matter how fast you run, he'll catch you."

He looked around the table making eye contact with each of the little kids before telling them, "He'll sink his teeth into you and rip the meat right off your bones, and he'll do it while you're still alive."

"That's enough, Gary. You'll give them nightmares." It was the pretty girl again, the one that had smiled at me.

Gary backed down the way Peter had, but after he had frightened the little kids the noise at the table never did recover. By the time the servants came to take our dessert plates away, my belt was making me as uncomfortable as my tie. A uniformed man came into the room and said something about being received in the west parlor, which meant nothing to me, but when the kids funneled back out of the room, I followed them.

Most of the grown-ups were in one of the two huge front rooms, where five people sitting in a semicircle at the far end of the room were playing classical music I'd heard my mother try to play on our piano back home without much luck. Pictures painted on the ceiling of the room reminded me of ones I'd seen when my parents took us to an art museum.

The grownups had gathered in small groups, the way water settles in the low spots in our yard after a hard rain. My mother was standing in the middle of a group of women, all of them listening to her, as though she had something very important to tell them. She looked happier than I remembered seeing her in a long time. Mrs. Madison had a bunch of women standing around her too. I saw her and my mother glancing in each other's direction as though it was some kind of competition to see who had the biggest audience.

A group of men had gathered around Mr. Madison, and judging from the looks on their faces he was telling them a pretty good story. I spotted my dad standing near a different group of men, listening quietly to whoever was speaking. I never said more than I had to at parties. I guess I got that from Dad because he never said much either. But I never saw him get embarrassed like I do.

I was standing by myself feeling lost when I noticed the really cute girl looking at me. She started to walk toward me and I felt my cheeks getting hot again. The way her eyes stayed on me, I knew she was coming to talk to me. I couldn't imagine such a pretty girl being interested in me.

She walked right up to me and looked me in the eye and told me her name was Donna. She asked me my name. When she leaned close to me I realized she hadn't heard me when I told her my name.

Rising up on her tiptoes so her lips were close to my ear she said sweetly, "You don't have to be shy with me."

I'm sure she meant well, but she made me face my shyness and that made it worse, especially because she was so pretty.

36

I had never liked a girl. None of my friends back home had ever liked a girl. And even though the weekly Saturday night movies that my parents watched always had some romance junk in them, they were just movies. So I never expected it would happen to me.

Donna asked me if I liked living in a big city.

"I don't live in a big city."

She frowned. I told her I lived in a town about the same size as Tuscumbia; that I'd never been to New York City.

"Oh," she said, looking surprised at first then disappointed. Then she shrugged her shoulders and smiled and told me all about the party she planned to have when she turned sixteen. She went through the list of the people who would be there, as though I should know who they all were and would actually care if I did know who they were. Donna got all dreamy-eyed about it, just like my mother did when she talked about that kind of stuff.

First chance I got I asked her, "Do you always eat like that?"

She looked surprised by my question. "Why, whatever do you mean?"

"Do people wearing uniforms serve you your dinner every night?"

"Silly boy. Mother hired them for the party. How could we possibly feed all these people by ourselves?"

I blushed at the "silly boy" comment, but forgot that when she touched my hand, which made my skin tingle.

Donna, her voice as soft as falling snow, said, "Moonlit walks on snowy nights are so very romantic. Don't you think?"

I pictured Donna and me huddled together on a park bench with big puffy snowflakes swirling around us, like something I'd probably seen in a movie or maybe a snow globe. She asked me what I thought about it. I didn't know what to say, so I changed the subject.

I told her about sledding with my friends, something I was comfortable talking about. "I live at the top of a really steep hill, and cars are always getting stuck at the bottom when it snows.

37

They can't get up the hill because their tires just spin in the snow. So my friends and I wait at the bottom of the hill with our sleds. When someone gets stuck, we offer to sit in the trunk of their car to give them extra weight. The best part is we charge them fifty cents apiece, and we pull our sleds behind the car so we can sled back down the hill to wait for the next car to get stuck."

I was sure Donna would be impressed by how clever we were, but she told me she needed to do something and left me standing there wondering what I did wrong. As I watched her walk away I noticed two girls nearby talking to each other and staring at me. So I beat it out of there to find a safer spot. I found one behind the women surrounding Mrs. Madison.

I half-listened to them jabbering on about other people, two or three of them talking at a time, all of it rubbish which I ignored until I heard Mrs. Madison tell them, "Something killed one of our steers."

Wondering if it was the huge black dog-like thing I'd seen at our house I moved closer so I could hear them better. But then one of the other women mentioned last Sunday's church sermon and they all started talking about that, so I left them and spent the rest of the evening avoiding people.

The first good thing that happened was Sis coming to tell me, "Mom said we're leaving."

We found Mom and Dad in a line of guests waiting to say good-bye to the Madisons. With all of the hand-shaking and hugging and talking the line moved so slowly I thought we'd be there all night. I didn't see how they could possibly have anything left to talk about after talking all night.

Donna and Peter, the boy who had tried to bully me, were standing with Mr. and Mrs. Madison, so I figured Peter was Donna's brother. In a few moments I'd have a chance to talk to Donna, and I imagined myself saying all sorts of clever things, and I imagined her being very impressed. But when I found myself standing across from her my mind went blank.

Donna and Peter were both looking at me. He looked amused. She looked as though she expected me to say

38

something. I couldn't possibly tell her what I was thinking - that I liked her. So I shrugged my shoulders and wished Mother would shut her yap so we could leave. But then she wouldn't be my mom.

With Mr. Madison distracted by something my Dad was saying Mrs. Madison leaned in close to my mother, as though she was going to tell her a secret. But she didn't actually whisper, so I heard everything she said. "The bootlegger who lives in the shack down the road from your place has a still somewhere in the hills near there. We're going to look for it Saturday, and if we find it we'll have a grand old time busting it up. You should come with us."

"Oh my," Mother said, putting a hand on her chest and taking in a big breath, "won't that be dangerous?"

"Our foreman will be with us so there's nothing to worry about."

Mother seemed okay with that, but then Mrs. Madison shocked her again. "And do bring the kids."

At that suggestion my mother's eyebrows shot up and her head did a little jerk backwards. "You let the kids go with you?"

Mrs. Madison reached over and touched Mother's arm. "The kids have a marvelous time, and you'll get to meet some nice ladies from Tuscumbia."

I couldn't believe my mother agreed to go. My parents never did fun stuff like that. I'd have to find out what a still was, but busting stuff was always fun. The line finally moved and I escaped the party and feeling awkward around Donna. When I was safely in the back seat of our car, I told my parents what I heard Mrs. Madison say about something killing one of their steers.

"Now Billy," Mom said, "we warned you about telling stories."

"I bet it was the thing I saw behind our house."

"You know what I think? I think you need to take Star out to do her business as soon as we get home."

"I saw a monster dog, Mom. I really did."

Lisa, who was sitting next to me, and had been quiet until then, whispered, "Poor Billy, nobody ever believes him."

When Mother told her, "That's enough, young lady," Lisa kicked my leg.

I told Mom that Sis had kicked me.

Sis said, "Did not."

Mother spun around in her seat to face us. "Stop it, both of you."

When Mother turned back around Sis stuck her tongue out at me. I looked out my window to watch the eerie shapes in the scenery made by the car's headlights.

I thought again about what Mrs. Madison had said. I asked my parents what a still was.

It was Dad who answered me. "Bootleggers use them to make whiskey."

I asked him why I'd never heard of one back home.

"Because there aren't any".

"Why?"

"Because the county where we live back home isn't a dry county."

I asked him what a dry county was.

Dad, who was driving, turned his head up and toward me a little when he spoke, so it looked as though he was talking to the roof of the car, "They passed a law here that prohibits people from buying alcohol."

"Prohibit means you get in trouble if you do it, right?"

"That's right, son."

"But if people can't buy it, then why do the bootleggers make it?"

"You're just full of questions, aren't you?"

I asked him why again.

"Why what?"

"Why'd they prohibit it?"

"Because," he said, starting to sound annoyed, "some people think drinking liquor is a sin."

I'd seen my parents drinking it back home, and if that

made them sinners I wasn't about to pass up the chance to rub it in. "If it's a sin how come you guys do it?"

Mother had been looking out of her window so intently I thought she wasn't listening. That was a mistake. She spun around and she looked mad. "Buster, don't you dare tell anyone we drink liquor. Do you hear me?"

I couldn't ever remember catching my mother in a mistake, but I had her and I wasn't about to let her off easy, even if I got the belt for it. "But if someone asked me right to my face and I said no, that would be lying, and lying's a sin, isn't it?"

At first she just looked upset. But then I saw a startled look on her face. A moment later her expression changed to an angry-looking frown. "Damn it, Billy, there's a stain on your shirt."

I pulled my shirt out so I could see it. The stain was a chocolate color about the size of a softball. I realized Donna had probably seen it, which was worse than having my mother mad at me.

I told her that's why she shouldn't make me dress up or go to stupid parties.

With her lower lip quivering as though she was about to cry, Mother said, "I'll be up half the night cleaning that shirt so you can wear it to church tomorrow."

I'd forgotten about church because we didn't go very often back home. The idea of going ruined the good feeling I'd gotten from escaping the party.

I guess Dad was still worried I'd say something about them drinking because he changed the subject back to that. "Buster, if anyone asks you if we drink alcohol, you tell them we don't, is that clear?"

I said, "Yes sir," but if I hadn't been in trouble already, I would've asked him why it was okay for me to tell a lie for them but not for myself. That definitely wasn't fair.

Later, as Dad was pulling the car into the driveway at home, Mother said to him, "According to Mrs. Madison, an old man who lives up the hill from us was bitten by a rattlesnake right in front of his house and died from it."

41

Mother said, "Let's take a drive past his place tomorrow." That was okay. But then she said, "We can do it after church."

I knew complaining would try her patience but I couldn't help myself. "Aw, Mom. Do we have to go to church?"

"You're going, young man, and I don't want to hear any more about it."

Without thinking I said, "But Mom, I can't breathe in these clothes."

Mom spun around in her seat and glared at me. "You're getting up early tomorrow for church, so get right to bed when we get home. And don't throw your suit on the floor. Hang it up carefully so it doesn't get wrinkled. And leave your shirt in the bathroom so I can work on that stain."

Later, after we'd gone to bed, I heard Lisa's voice from out of the dark. "Did you really see a wild dog?"

"You believe me, that it was real?"

"No, stupid, of course not. But I wish it was and that it ate you."

I ignored her giggling and rolled over to think about Donna, replaying the moment when she touched my hand and when she leaned so close to me that I smelled a faint, sweet scent on her that must have been perfume. I fell asleep thinking about her.

SINNERS

Our mother woke us up early the next morning by singing, "Get up; get a wiggle on. Get up and put a giggle on."

After years of Mother waking me up for school by singing that, just the sound of her footsteps in the hallway was usually enough to get me out of bed. But that morning I suffered through the whole thing because we were going to church. Mother won, of course. She knew I'd get up if she kept repeating it.

"Okay, okay," I said, rolling out of bed, sleepy and annoyed, "I'm up."

She hung my dress shirt on the doorknob. The stain was gone. "Damn it, Billy," she said, bending down to pick my suit up off the floor where I'd dropped it the night before. "I told you to hang this up."

She shook her head as she laid it out on my bed. "Take your clothes to the bathroom and get dressed, right this minute."

Sis still had her covers up over her head. When saying her name didn't get a response, Mother went over and yanked her covers off. I stayed to watch the fun. Sis groaned and sat up with a scowl.

"Get dressed, both of you" Mother said, as she turned around to leave, "and you'd better hurry if you want breakfast."

After she left I asked Sis, "Don't you hate it when she sings that stupid song?"

Sis groaned and flopped back down on her bed. "Not as much as I hate sharing a room with you."

I told her she was mean.

After saying, "Gee, sorry," sarcastically, she said, "Now get out so I can get dressed."

I took my clothes to the bathroom and threw them on the floor. While I dressed I thought about what I'd do when we got home from church. I decided on starting a fire by rubbing two sticks together. I'd wanted to try it ever since I'd seen someone in a TV western do it.

All through getting dressed and eating breakfast Mother nagged me to hurry. When I'd finished eating I found Dad in the living room reading the paper. He actually got my tie right on the first try. When we got to the kitchen Mother and Lisa were dressed and waiting for us by the door. All of a sudden, my stomach didn't feel good.

When I told Mom she yelled, "Don't you dare make us late, " at me while I ran for the bathroom.

When I came out Mother ambushed me with a wet finger, wiping something off my face. And if that wasn't bad enough, my shirt was scratching my neck, my suit jacket was cutting off the circulation in my arms, and my stomach was still churning, I felt awful and I wouldn't get home from church for hours, which was just about forever.

On the way, Mother told Sis and me we'd be going to church-school on Sundays. After lots of nagging she gave in and told us we could sit with them that day instead. I was afraid the Bible school teachers in Tuscumbia would expect me to actually know something about the Bible, which I didn't. Back home in Ithaca bible school had been like daycare. If I learned anything there it was an accident.

I planned to daydream about exploring the woods around our house during the sermon. I hadn't expected to hear a real "hellfire and brimstone" sermon, as my parents called it. I don't remember the preacher's actual words, but I remember how angry he sounded, practically yelling at us.

44

I sometimes heard people sitting near us murmur, "Amen," and even heard someone shout, "Praise the Lord," one time when the preacher sounded especially angry about something. For a while he raved about the evils of alcohol, accusing everyone of being what he called, "peddlers and consumers of the devil's brew." And although he never mentioned them by name I noticed he often glanced at the Madisons.

He paused and looked around the room. I got excited – I thought he was done. But then he said anyone who had ever fornicated, whatever that was, or anyone who had been tempted to fornicate, was under the spell of the devil. And once again he glanced at the Madisons, who along with a lot of the people sitting around us, looked away to avoid his gaze. He took his time looking around the room silently while most of the audience fidgeted like little kids who'd been caught doing something bad. Then he told us that God would forgive our sins. That didn't make me feel much better, because I'd been taught that sinners went to hell. Did that mean that God would forgive us then send us to hell anyway if we did something bad?

He started his sermon up again by telling us, "Each and every one of you can make a difference."

But since he never told us how, I figured he wanted us to go on sinning so we'd keep coming to church and he could keep his job.

The good kids who hadn't skipped bible class joined their parents for the rest of his sermon. He didn't sound angry or talk about grown up stuff after that. But he went on talking, just about forever.

When we finally got outside I said to Mom, "Sermons back home were shorter."

"People here take their faith very seriously."

"How come?"

She said, "It's the culture," which did not answer my question.

"Does that mean the sermons will always be this long?"

45

"Yes, and it's followed by a dish-to-pass lunch which they hold outdoors when the weather's nice. That's followed by an afternoon sermon. Everyone stays after that to visit with friends."

The thought of being at church all day filled me with dread. "Are we really gonna stay for all of that?"

"The afternoon sermon is a part of the service. So yes, we will be staying for it. And even though the dish-to-pass isn't part of the official service, leaving early is frowned upon."

So God was going to ruin all of my Sundays for the rest of the year. Why would he ruin them in Tuscumbia if he didn't in Ithaca? How was that fair? By the time I got home on Sunday I'd have to rush to get my chores done before dinner. Lucky for me that day, Dad had brought work home that he wanted to finish that afternoon, so we left after the morning sermon.

Someone asked why we were leaving. Mom told her we weren't settled from the trip. I could tell from the way people looked at us that we'd done something wrong. So Mom was right about leaving early, and that settled it – we wouldn't leave early again, not as long as we lived in Tuscumbia.

Walking out to the car everything seemed better; the sun felt warmer, the sky looked bluer, and the grass had that fresh-cut smell. Best of all I got to loosen my tie, unbutton my collar, and take off my shoes as soon as I got in the car.

Passing the Madisons' house reminded me of what the preacher said when he was looking at them in church. "What's a 'fornitator'?"

That got a snicker from my sister. "The word's 'fornicator,' stupid."

If I'd noticed Mother turning around I wouldn't have elbowed Lisa.

Boy was Mom ever red-faced. "Don't ever do that again, Buster. Do you understand me?"

Then she told Sis, "And as for you, young lady, don't call your brother 'stupid'."

After Mother turned around, I stuck my tongue out at Sis

46

then tried my question again. "So what's a 'forrni...,' what Lisa said?"

Mom turned around in her seat again. Blushing, and with a fake-looking smile, she told us, "That's nothing either of you need to worry about," which meant it was definitely something I wanted to know about.

When Dad didn't slow down for our driveway I remembered what Mother had told us on the way home the night before, about the old man who lived up the road. I asked Mom if we had rattlesnakes around our house.

"You stay out of the woods, young man."

Sis moaned and rolled her eyes. "Oh, great," she said, "now I have to worry about snakes."

I thought about the two eyes I'd seen in the field behind our house. There were things a lot scarier than snakes out there.

A few seconds after we passed our house Dad slowed the car as we passed a shack in a weedy patch of field. It was as small and rundown as the ones in Valdosta, and so close to the road I could see brown spots in the siding where the nails had rusted. Under its rusty tin roof, a limp piece of dirty shredded fabric hung in the one front window. The cartoonish-looking warped siding stopped about a foot above the ground.

I saw bare feet moving below the siding, but when I told my parents that they didn't answer me. So I told them again, but louder.

Mother said, "Yes, dear, we heard you the first time."

"But Mom, they don't have a floor."

Just as Dad gave the car some gas the rag in the front window was pulled back by a little girl with big round eyes like a doe, and dark hair cut short like a boy's. She was so close I could see she had an overbite so bad she appeared to be biting her lip.

She looked like the dirty-faced little kid I'd seen in a picture of a bombed-out city in my Dad's WWII history book. But this little girl didn't live in some faraway place a long time ago; she lived right next door.

As we rounded a curve leaving the place behind, I

remembered Mr. Ford telling us that a bootlegger lived a little ways down the road from us. "Dad?"

"Yes, Billy."

"Was that the bootlegger's place?"

It was Mom who answered. "You stay away from there, Buster. Do you hear me?"

I knew from taking the dog out at night to do her business that nights can be cold, even in Alabama. "Those poor people must get cold."

"Yes, I suppose they must."

"Then how come they live there?"

"I'm afraid that's complicated, Billy."

I felt like asking her why she was afraid. I knew she wasn't. It was just one of the stupid things my parents said when they didn't want to explain something to me.

We drove on for a while but I'd already lost interest in the guy who'd died from the snakebite because I couldn't stop thinking about the little girl I'd seen and wondering what it was like for her living in such a junky place.

We got home early in the afternoon. For the next few hours, Monday morning and my first day of school still seemed to be a long way off. After I did my chores I snuck off behind the house to start a fire by rubbing two sticks together. I soon decided it was some kind of trick because all I got was a sore arm. I climbed a tree and looked at the hills around our house and thought about going exploring in the woods.

Good thing I didn't because Mother called me in early. She wanted me to try on my school clothes to be sure they still fit me. My school clothes were only slightly more comfortable than my dress suit. My mother insisted that I try on all of my school shirts and pants, which took almost forever. And she stayed with me to make sure I didn't lie to her about how they fit, which she knew I'd do to get out of trying them on. And she made me put all of them back on hangers instead of throwing them on the floor in my closet.

But the worst thing was trying on the clothes with her in

the room. And more than once Sis came in without knocking. Each time she gave us a lame excuse then made a face at me before Mother sent her away. I knew she was doing it on purpose. I could her trying to hide a smirk.

Then, just when I thought Mother would let me go back outside to play, and nothing else bad would happen, she handed me my baseball cap.

I was saying, "I wondered what had happened to that," when I saw she'd written my name on the inside of the hat rim.

I was so upset I almost couldn't talk. "Ah, Mom, why'd you write my name in it?"

"You'll thank me for it if you lose it."

I told her that only little kids had their names in their hats.

"If you lose that hat, I'm not buying you another one."

If the kids at school saw my name printed in my cap they'd laugh at me. Going to school was bad enough without having that to worry about too.

Then Mom trimmed my hair and made me clean under my fingernails. And of course she didn't think I did a good enough job, so she did them again, digging up under them until it hurt. With all of the fussing I couldn't get my mind off of school and that kept me depressed and nervous all afternoon.

That night Mother made popcorn chowder for Sis and me, my all-time favorite dinner. She made it by melting a stick of butter in a pan of hot salted milk. She poured that over soup bowls piled high with popcorn, which shriveled into salty, chewy, little chunks.

My parents had pork chops with rice and that slimy okra stuff. After dinner, Mom and Sis and I moved into the living room to watch "Walt Disney's Wonderful World of Color," which showed a cartoon of Goofy going on vacation, pulling a little travel trailer on a super highway so fast it bounced off the road every time he went around a curve.

Dad joined us when "The Ed Sullivan Show" came on. By then it was so close to the end of my last day of freedom that

49

nothing could relieve my feeling of dread, not even a funny ventriloquist act. Mother sent Lisa and me to bed when "The Dinah Shore Show" came on.

After I got settled I daydreamed about Donna until my mind reminded me of the two eyes I'd seen in our back yard. Then I remembered the bootleggers down the road and wondered if their little girl had a nice place to sleep. But no matter how hard I tried not to think about school, it kept rearing its ugly head and that kept me awake for a long time.

Of course, after all my worrying about my first day at school, it happened anyway, and as bad as I'd imagined my first day at school would be, the real thing turned out to be worse.

MY FIRST DAY OF SCHOOL

The next morning was my first day at Cave Street Central School. Mother took Dad to work then came back to take Sis and me to school. Because Lisa was a year older she went to a different school. Mom stopped at mine first, leaving Sis in the car while she took me in.

The school was a big, old, rundown looking three-story building in a rundown-looking neighborhood. The school grounds were big, bare, brown yards where dust devils appeared on windy days because only crabgrass grew there, and that only in places where it was protected from countless little feet.

There were no shrubs to break up the barren school grounds, and no trees to shade us from the blazing sun during recess. The only thing in the whole schoolyard besides the flagpole out front was a set of swings rusted to a uniform reddish-brown color.

Mother parked in front of the school then turned around in her seat and looked me over. Her gaze settled on my head. She licked her hand and reached for it.

I brushed her hand away. "Geez, Mom, someone might see you."

"What are we going to do about that cowlick?"

I told her she should've let me wear my hat.

As she was getting out of the car she said, "Not on your first day."

I followed her in, glad all of the other kids were in class so they wouldn't see her bringing me to school. I felt super, extra nervous. Then I saw the sign over the doorway that read "School Office," and I got lightheaded.

An older lady who looked like a librarian greeted Mom then opened the door to an inner office and said something to someone inside. Then she told us we could go in.

A little man sitting behind a big desk stood up and reached across it to shake my mother's hand, introducing himself as Mr. Stephens, the school principal. We sat in two chairs opposite his desk.

I think, he was older than my parents and shorter, with a face the shape of a "V," narrow at the chin with a wide forehead, topped with short brown hair. He kept his chin down, looking at us over the top of his glasses which kept sliding down his nose. He had on a rumpled white shirt that looked much too long in the sleeves.

I didn't think he looked scary enough to keep several hundred kids under control. But then, as if he'd read my mind, he pointed at a canoe paddle hanging on the wall behind him desk and said, "We've never had a discipline problem here."

Glancing at my mother he added, "Of course, I don't expect to have a problem with, ah...."

He looked down at one of the papers on his desk then looked me in the eye. "We won't be having any problems, will we, Billy?"

He told my mother it was important that I got to school on time so I wouldn't be late for the morning assembly in the auditorium. And he assured her that I would do well and be happy there, but I wasn't having any of that nonsense. Then he told her she could leave, that he'd take me to my classroom.

I followed him upstairs to one of the many doors in a long hallway. The room became so quiet when we entered I could hear my heart pounding. As the kids eyed me warily a tall woman standing near the blackboard came over and told me her name was Miss Martin. She didn't look young enough to be a miss. She smiled then asked me my name.

I said, "Billy," and was glad I'd been able to say that much without my voice cracking.

"Do you have a last name, Billy?"

That got a few snickers from the kids. She snapped her fingers in their general direction and said, "That's enough, class."

I managed to choke out my last name, but I mustn't have said it loud enough, because she asked me to repeat it, which got a few more snickers.

She had one of the boys in the front row move to a desk in the back and she put me there in his place. While she looked in a bookcase for text books for me, she asked me a bunch of questions, like, "Where did you live before you came to Tuscumbia?"

I answered that question okay, but her next one, "How old are you?" set me up to be laughed at again.

I suppose it seems like a pretty easy question. But I didn't know people in Tuscumbia pronounced the word "ten" as 'tay-yan,' so when I said the word with a flat New York accent, I got a much louder round of giggling from the class.

Then Miss Martin practically invited the kids to take another shot at me by asking them, "Class, is there anything you want to ask Billy?"

She called on a kid in the back of the room with his hand up. "Okay, Brian."

His question, "How come you talk funny?" got the kids laughing out loud until she silenced them with an angry look.

At lunchtime, Miss Martin took me to the cafeteria to show me how the lunch lines worked. The cafeteria was a big open room filled with a hundred or more noisy kids, so it was hard to hear what she said. As soon as she left I got into the line for ham and asparagus. I hated asparagus, but it was the closest food line and I didn't want to stand around deciding on a food line with a hundred kids staring at me.

After I got through the line with my tray, I sat at an empty table in the back of the room, as far away from the other kids as possible. I couldn't imagine the day getting any worse, but it did. Donna Madison came into the cafeteria. I watched her go through the salad line, looking away when she looked in my direction, pretending I hadn't seen her. I picked at my ham and hoped she hadn't noticed me. Next thing I knew she was setting her tray down across the table from me.

She smiled at me, asked me, "Why'd you sit over here all by yourself?"

I couldn't very well tell her the truth; that I wanted to get away from Tuscumbia and everyone in it except for her, so I shrugged my shoulders and said, "Hi."

I thought she must like me because she sat with me even though all of the kids in the cafeteria could see us. I liked sitting with her and I didn't. I liked looking at her but I knew I'd say something stupid and then she wouldn't like me anymore.

She asked me a question I was not expecting. "You went to see those awful bootlegger people, didn't you?"

I didn't ask Donna why she thought the bootleggers were awful. That felt like trouble. I asked her how she knew we drove past their place.

"Your mother called my mother and told her all about it."

"They don't have a floor in their house. I saw the kids' bare feet below the siding."

Her right hand, holding a fork with a small bite of lettuce on it, stopped halfway to her mouth. Looking at me warily, she put her fork back down on her plate. "You don't feel sorry for them, don't you?"

I said, "They must get cold."

She said, "Those people are nothing but poor white trash, and if you know what's good for you you'll stay away from them."

It was a mean thing to say and I wished she hadn't said it. I had assumed that Donna was nice. I don't know why I thought that, probably because I liked her. I wanted to ask her

54

what they had done to her to make her say something like that, but couldn't put the question into words before Donna started droning on about some romantic nonsense. I half-listened to it.

After a while she stopped in the middle of a sentence to say, "Hey, I saw you at church yesterday but you weren't at bible school."

I felt another scolding coming and froze, while I tried to think of an answer.

She frowned. "And I saw you leave early."

I'd known from the moment she sat down it would go horribly wrong. I didn't see how she could possibly like me anymore. I told her my parents had to leave. She told me I could have stayed without them, which I couldn't even imagine doing. I shrugged my shoulders.

After announcing that we should get back to class, she stood up with her tray, saying, "I hope sitting with you wasn't a mistake," before walking away.

I was miffed at Donna for being mean and unfair, but I still liked her and that made my head ache. It didn't help that the kids sitting nearby were looking at me as though I was a two-headed, six-eyed Martian. I added lunch to the day's growing list of disappointments.

The last entry on the list was added by Miss Martin when she gave us a spelling list to take home and memorize. I could spell my name and a short list of easy words. None of them were among the twenty words she gave us. She told us we'd have a quiz on them Friday morning. My teachers back in New York had never given me homework. I'd never memorized anything, ever, and I didn't want to waste my afternoons and evenings doing that. I decided to put it off until Thursday night. Thinking about all the reasons I didn't like living in Tuscumbia kept me awake that night.

I could tell from Lisa's breathing that she was still awake. That made her fair game for a question. "Hey, Sis?"

I heard an exasperated "What" from the darkness across the room.

"Were the kids at school mean to you?"

She told me to go to sleep. I told her the kids at my school were mean to me.

She told me to go to sleep a second time.

"Do you think they'll always be mean?"

"They'll stop when it isn't fun anymore."

I asked her when that would be.

"Never, if you don't stop pestering me."

I wanted to say, "You're as mean as they are," but she'd probably call Mom if I did.

Things had gone horribly wrong with Donna at lunch, but I knew how to fix that - I imagined her asking me questions. But since I made them up, they were easy for me to answer, and naturally, all of my answers were so clever she couldn't help but like me. I played that game in my head until I fell asleep.

Tuesday morning, Mom dropped me off for school so early I had to wait outside until they opened the doors. By then there were a lot of kids milling about in small groups and glancing at me as they talked, like I was some kind of freak.

When the doors finally opened all the kids tried to get inside at the same time, bunching up at the doors then bursting out into the hallway. Walking fast to keep up so I wouldn't get trampled, I followed them into a big room with a high ceiling and puke-green walls filled with a hundred rows and rows of folding metal chairs.

Kids quickly filled the seats, except for the front row which was mostly empty. I took a seat there so I wouldn't have to sit next to anyone. There was a raised stage across the front of the room with a woman sitting at a piano near the back of it.

When Principal Stephens walked out on the stage, the whole room went quiet, as though someone had found a volume control and turned the sound off. I didn't hear any of the little noises you normally hear from hundreds of fidgeting kids.

Walking over to a microphone at the center of the stage, Stephens announced, "Mary Lou Dean will lead us in prayer today."

A girl about my age sitting near me in the front row stood up and walked over to the stairs and up onto the stage. I noticed the other kids bowing their heads so I did too, but just enough so I could still watch Mary. I don't remember anything she said after, "Let us pray," but she recited a prayer that seemed to go on forever. I expected something to happen when she finished it, some clapping at least, but it was followed by a spooky silence as Mary stepped aside and Principal Stephens took her place at the microphone.

They both put their right hands over their hearts then he started the Pledge of Allegiance. When the kids in my class back in New York recited it, it sounded as though they were talking in their sleep, and it always sounded sloppy because a few kids always lagged behind the rest of the class. But not at Cave Street Central; the hundreds of kids in that auditorium sounded as though they were one loud voice.

Then the woman sitting at the piano began playing "America the Beautiful," an impossible song for kids to sing, it sounded pretty bad, but they all seemed to know the words, which was more than you could say for me. I started faking the words when I noticed Principal Stephens staring at me. I tried to mouth the words as I heard them, but that never works.

When the song ended Principal Stephens made some announcements, including the name of the student who'd be leading the prayer the next morning. When he dismissed us, mobs of kids poured out of every door, racing through the halls as though their lives depended on getting to class first.

On the way upstairs one of the boys from my class elbowed me. He was taller than me and looked older. His hair was a little shaggy and his clothes weren't very nice, and his mouth turned down at the sides so I couldn't tell if he was frowning or not. He asked if I wanted to lead the school prayer. Dread barely describes what I felt because I thought he was going to tell me I'd have to do that someday. I shook my head.

"Then don't sit up front. Stephens only picks kids who sit up front to do the prayer."

I thanked him. It was the first nice thing anyone had done for me since I'd arrived in Tuscumbia.

He told me his name was Dalton.

"That's not the name Miss Martin uses when she calls on you."

"Dalton's my last name, but it's what all the kids call me."

"How come?"

"'Cause they don't like me."

It was obvious from his eyes that he was part Asian. I wondered if that was why the other kids didn't like him. I didn't care if he had three eyes; I was glad to have a friend. I found out later that all of the other boys, even the sixth graders, were afraid of Dalton. So as long as he and I were friends the bullies would leave me alone. But I could tell by the way they looked at me they were waiting for their chance.

Later that day, I heard the principal use his paddle for the first time. Crackling sounds and feedback come from the little speaker on the wall over the blackboard while Miss Martin was trying to explain to us when we should use the different spellings of 'to', 'too', and 'two.' She stopped the lesson to look at the speaker. We all looked at it.

Principal Stephens said some kid's name and that he had misbehaved. I heard a loud smack then the kid started whimpering. Stephens hit the kid with his paddle four more times, each whack followed by whimpering. I wondered what the kid had done. I did not want to make the same mistake.

We all stared at the speaker after it went silent, until the teacher said, "Alright class, let's get back to work."

So after my second day at school I had a new friend and something new to worry about – getting paddled by Principal Stephens. Miss Martin gave us a spelling quiz Friday. I had guessed at most of the spellings and thought I'd done pretty good job of it. And that ended my first week of school.

When Mother came to get me Saturday morning to go still smashing, I woke up in a panic thinking it was another school day. After she reminded me of our plans, I jumped out of bed

58

and dressed in a rush, buttoning my shirt as I ran out to the kitchen then pestering Mother to get ready as I wolfed down my breakfast, because I didn't want to be late and miss out on the adventure.

The plan was for everyone to meet along the road near the bootlegger's place, which was near enough to our house for Mother and me to walk. It was a clear, cool morning with a bright sun that felt warm on my face. By the time we got there, half a dozen cars were parked along the side of the road.

We joined several women who were waiting there for Mrs. Madison. Mother and the other women were talking and laughing like old friends by the time Mrs. Madison showed up a few minutes later. She had Donna and Peter and a man I didn't recognize with her. The women all started talking again. I thought they'd never stop. I didn't wear a watch; Mother wouldn't get me one; she said I'd just lose it, but I bet they were still talking an hour later. Given half a chance, my mother would talk the whole day away.

Unlike me Peter Madison wasn't afraid to interrupt them. "Are we going to look for the still or not?"

Mrs. Madison glared at Peter. He glared right back at her. Then she smiled at the man who came with her, the only man there that day, an unfriendly-looking man about my dad's age she had introduced to my mother as their foreman, Joe Quinn. "Go ahead, Joe," she told him, "you lead the way."

With the rest of us following single file, he set out on what once might have been a dirt road, but was now too rutted and overgrown for a car. The road took into the forest where the tree branches got so thick overhead they blocked out the sun, which made it cool and dark.

Mr. Quinn might have looked about my dad's age, but he was dark around the mouth and chin, the way my dad looked when he didn't shave for several days. He had messy-looking, curly, brownish hair and a nose that looked like it had been broken. When he caught me staring at the pistol he carried in a holster on his belt he gave me a look I didn't like.

Mrs. Madison walked behind Mr. Quinn. Her outfit looked brand new; the shirt, pants, and vest all made of tan-colored material, like the outfits in the Tarzan movies they showed on Saturday morning television. Peter followed his mother. Donna walked behind him and in front of me. Both she and Peter had on new safari clothes like their mother, but somehow the clothes looked a lot better on Donna.

My mother was behind me and the rest of the people were behind her. It's one of the few times I can remember my mother wearing long pants. She also had her hair tied up in a clump on her head, probably so it wouldn't get caught on a low-hanging branch. My sister didn't come with us. She gladly stayed home with Dad to read a book while he did stuff for work.

The road became less like a road and more like a path as we followed it deeper into the woods. Mrs. Madison began beating the bushes along the path with a stick. I was afraid the bootleggers would hear her, but I'd been punished for being disrespectful enough times to know better than to say anything to her. I stepped aside until my mother was close enough to hear me whisper, "You should tell Mrs. Madison to be quiet. The bootleggers will hear us coming."

"Oh, Billy, we don't want to catch them. We're just looking for their still. Besides, Mrs. Madison is doing that to warn the rattlesnakes."

"But, won't that make them mad?"

"You'd think so," she said. "But if a rattlesnake hears you coming it'll shake the rattle in its tail to warn you off. It's when you surprise one that you get bit."

Although I didn't know what a still looked like, I assumed I'd know it when I saw it, and each time we rounded a curve I expected to see one, but after every curve there was just more trees and path. I was tiring of the whole thing when Mr. Quinn stopped and knelt down. He brushed a spot of dirt lightly with his hand. Mrs. Madison asked him what he'd found.

"Dog tracks."

She asked him why he'd stopped for dog tracks.

I thought I saw him grin but it was gone so quickly I wasn't sure. "Never seen 'em so big."

I thought about the thing I'd seen behind my house. Then I was glad Mr. Quinn was with us and that he had a gun. He headed down the path and everyone fell in behind him again. As I walked past the spot where he'd seen the tracks I took a close look because I wanted to look for tracks like them behind our house when I got home. If I found some my parents would have to believe me.

Later when we came to a spot where the path was wide enough for us to walk two-by-two I caught up with Donna. I wondered if she'd let me catch up because she liked me. The thought made me so nervous I couldn't think of anything clever to say. Not Donna; she droned on about her dad and how important he was.

Walking around a tight curve in the path a few feet behind her mother, Donna and I came into a small clearing just as her mother let out a shriek. She was looking up at a body hanging from a tree limb over her head.

A DEAD BODY

I thought it was a dummy dressed to look like a man but the women were so upset I figured it had to be a real person. The mask covering its head had a long, narrow, furry snout, with glassy yellow eyes and little tufts of hair on its ears. The lips were curled back in a permanent sneer exposing a huge set of teeth. The skin around the edges of the mask was chewed up and gross-looking. The body smelled worse than our garbage did after sitting out in the hot sun for a day. I looked away and tried really hard not to lose my breakfast in front of Donna.

Everyone was upset except for Mr. Quinn, who didn't seem bothered at all. So once again I was glad he was with us. He took out a folding knife that had a blade as long as a new pencil and cut the body down then dragged it into the bushes.

While he was doing that Mrs. Madison headed back to the cars at a fast walk with the rest of us following her. No one said a word and everyone stayed close together, except for Mr. Quinn who walked about a car length behind us. When we got back to the road where the cars were parked, Mrs. Madison told us she'd call the sheriff as soon as she got home.

On our way home, Mom told me to let her tell Dad what happened. When we got there I sat with my parents in the kitchen while Mom told Dad about the man hanging in the tree. The more she talked the more upset she got about it. If it upset Dad I couldn't tell.

Mother told Dad some things more than once, like the

awful way the dead man smelled, and how his face looked as though something had been chewing on it. I suppose those things had upset her the most. Mother did stop talking eventually and that's when she looked at me.

She got all teary-eyed and dramatic-sounding. "Oh, Billy, I'm sorry you had to see that."

Sis appeared in the living room doorway holding a book. "What'd he see?"

Mother told her, "Never you mind," then told me, "Go to your room and take off your clothes. I need to check you for ticks."

I hated getting naked in front of my mother but Dad made me do it. It had to be as embarrassing as crying over the school intercom, especially when she checked my private places.

And as if things weren't already bad enough she told me I needed a bath. "And be sure to scrub your neck. I swear I don't know how you get so dirty."

I told her it was easy.

She told me to put my dirty clothes in the hamper. "And when you're done with your bath put your toys away in the closet."

I hated it when she called my things toys – little kids had toys and I wasn't a little kid anymore. After my bath, while I was putting my stuff away, the sheriff came to talk to my mother. I rushed into the kitchen to hear what they were saying. Dad told me to go back to my room, which I did, but instead of staying there I closed my door hard enough for him to hear it, then snuck into the living room.

I heard the sheriff tell my mother, "Bootleggers can be dangerous, ma'am. Busting stills might seem like fun, but that's their livelihood."

I was really sorry when Mother assured him that we wouldn't ever do that again. He told her that the bootlegger's name was Clayton Damon, and that he would ask Clayton about the body because he'd heard rumors that Clayton had a still near where we'd found the body.

"Oh my," Mother said, "Do you think he killed that man?"

He told her he didn't know. "But I don't think you need to worry about him." Before he left he warned her to stay out of the woods.

I couldn't wait to see Dalton on Monday so I could tell him I'd seen a dead man and that we had a killer living right next door. I decided to sneak off and spy on the bootlegger's place, but on my way through the kitchen Mother warned me to stay within earshot. I wondered if she could read my mind. So I looked for the dog tracks instead. I kept up the search until I was so hot and scratched up from walking through the tall field grass I couldn't stand it then went to look for Mr. Ford.

When I found him, he was sitting on an upturned pail next to a piece of farm machinery watching a dark liquid drip into a Mason jar.

"Hey, Mr. Ford. What're ya doing?"

He stood up and wiped his hands on a dirty rag then used the back of his sleeve to wipe his forehead. "Let's you and I go up to the house, Billy. We'll see what Thelma's got cooking and you can tell me what the sheriff was doing at your house."

He stuffed the rag in the back pocket of his coveralls which had so many dark stains on them only a few patches of the cloth were the original blue-gray color. I followed him to their back door and up three wooden steps into the kitchen where Mrs. Ford was mixing something in a glass bowl on the counter.

The full-length green apron she had on over her dress was covered with about a million tiny flowers in all kinds of colors. Her gray hair was tied up in a little round bun on her head. When she moved the overhead light glinted off the hairpins holding it in place. The skin on her face sagged a little, especially around her mouth, and when she laughed, her tummy jiggled up and down. That afternoon she had something baking in the oven that smelled of bacon and corn. Mitch took off his cap and sat down at the table. I sat across from him.

He said to Thelma, "I told Billy you might have a treat for him."

Thelma smiled at me, a big friendly smile. "Well then I'd better have a look-see."

She took a round tin containing what looked like a thin layer of yellow cake out of the oven and put it in the center of the table on a hot pad.

"That's real hot," she said, looking at me, "so don't you go touching it, ya hear?"

It sure smelled good, even if it didn't smell like any cake I'd ever had. Thelma got a pitcher with ice cubes floating in it out of the refrigerator and set it on the table. Water drops appeared on it immediately, running down the sides of the pitcher, making a puddle around it on the table.

Mitch poured us each a glass from it. When I made a face at the bitterness Thelma put a bowl of sugar in front of me. Mitch frowned. The more sugar I put in my glass, the darker Mitch's frown got and the better it tasted.

Thelma sat down at the table with us to stir whatever it was she had in her mixing bowl. She and Mitch listened patiently while I told them about the dead man I'd seen.

When I finished, Mitch said, "That's a mighty big story for a little man."

I didn't like him saying "little man" but knew better than to complain about it. I asked him why the dead man looked like a wolf.

Mitch used his sleeve to wipe the sweat off his forehead again then took a sip of tea. "Things aren't always what they seem, if you get my drift."

Thelma told him, "Billy doesn't have any idea what you mean. He's just a boy."

I told her I'd be eleven years old in a few months but they acted as though they hadn't heard me.

"Look here, Billy," Mitch said, "some people, like the Madisons, aren't what they seem. That Mr. Madison might be a judge, but I hear he's doing things that aren't right. And that wife of his would be the first one to tell you she's a devout Christian, but I've got my doubts about her too. You see what I'm saying?"

65

I didn't see what any of that had to do with a dead man wearing a wolf's mask.

I think Thelma saw my confusion because she told Mitch, "He's too young for that kind of talk. You gotta say things straight out for him."

"Okay Billy," he said, "what about this? You stay away from that Joe Quinn fella. There's something wrong with him. You can understand that, can't ya?"

Even though I thought Joe Quinn was pretty cool because he wore a gun and he knew about animal tracks and he wasn't afraid of a dead body, I didn't tell Mitch that. Instead, I told him that I didn't like Mr. Quinn much, which was sort of true because he didn't seem very friendly.

"Well then I reckon you're pretty smart for a kid. And as for the Madisons, I think there's some kind of poison festering there, so don't you believe everything they tell you."

"Yes, sir," I said. "But what's 'festering' mean?"

He blinked then for a moment he just stared at me. Then he said, "Never mind that. Just don't believe everything they tell you. How's that?"

"Can I ask you about something else, Mr. Ford?"

"Sure, Billy."

"I saw a huge dog out behind our house, but today when I looked for tracks I couldn't find any."

"Then you must've seen this dog before last night."

"How'd you know?"

"The rain we had last night was the first rain we've had in a week, and without rain the ground gets too hard for animals to leave tracks."

His answer meant I couldn't prove I'd seen a dog, and while I thought that over Mitch slid the pan of yellow cake-like stuff between us and said, "Let's see if this is any good, shall we?"

Thelma got up and put her mixing bowl in the refrigerator then took out a plate of butter which she put on the table along with a butter knife. Mitch flipped the stuff out of the baking pan onto a plate and cut out two pie-shaped pieces. The same color

66

as the butter he spread on it, the stuff glistened when the butter melted. He put one piece in front of me and took a bite of the other one.

My arm had stuck to their plastic table cloth because of the humidity, so my tea almost spilled when I reached for my piece of the cake. I had expected it to be soft and sweet like a birthday cake without icing, but it was gritty and salty and tasted of corn and bacon. I looked at it and made a face.

Mitch looked amused by the face I made. "I reckon you never had cornbread."

After the next bite I decided I liked it. I ended up eating four slices of it and would've had more if Thelma had let me. She said if I had any more I wouldn't eat my dinner, but it was too late for that. I didn't tell my mother why I wasn't hungry for dinner. She would've been mad at me for ruining my appetite.

That night, lying in bed, I wondered why seeing a dead man hadn't bothered me much, or maybe it had. After all, I did wake up in the middle of the night in a sweat.

In my nightmare I saw bodies hanging from trees in the woods, and even though none of them had faces I knew they were people. A crow had landed on one of the bodies and started pecking at it, making it bleed. A few more crows came; then a few more. Soon there were so many the sky was black with them, and the people were covered with bloody wounds, and the bodies were all twitching, as though the people were still alive and could feel the crows tearing at their skin.

I awoke to the gory image of a crow pecking on a man's head. The image went away when I opened my eyes, but I still heard the tick, tick, tick of the crow's beak on his skull. When I saw that our bedroom window was open wide enough for a crow to get inside I searched the room for it.

Then I remembered the window had a screen on it. Moments later a wind gust blew the curtains into the room. Their flapping sounded like the beating of a bird's wings, and the little plastic ring on the end of the string used to pull the rollup shade down ticked against the glass it sounded the same as the crow pecking on the man's head in my nightmare.

Even though I knew what had caused my nightmare, the gory images of the crows pecking at the people haunted me and kept me awake. I thought about the dead man I'd seen; about going to a new school with spelling tests and kids who were mean to me and a principle who punished kids with a paddle; about being stuck in church all day every Sunday; about new rules and having to talk funny. I wished I could go back home to New York.

Dalton was standing off by himself outside the school when I got there Monday morning. I'd been waiting all weekend to tell him what had happened. "We went through the woods looking for a bootlegger's still so we could smash it, but instead we found a dead man hanging from a tree, and the sheriff came to our house to talk to us about it."

You'd think he'd just seen a flying saucer the way his face lit up. "Gosh, I wish something like that would happen to me."

I spotted Principal Stephens opening the doors to the school which meant we'd have to go in soon, so I told him the rest of it in a rush. "And the guy had on a mask like a wolf's head, and the skin around the mask was all chewed up."

Dalton asked me what it was like seeing a dead guy. I was about to tell him when the school bell rang. We joined the crush of kids pushing through the doors of the school and hurried along to the auditorium with them because neither of us wanted to get stuck sitting near the front.

As we were swept along with the crowd toward the auditorium Dalton asked, "He was hanging from a tree and he looked like a wolf?"

"Yeah, big teeth and all."

"Oh my God," he said. "That must've been the 'Wolf's-Head Man'."

"That's just some silly legend.'

"No it's not. I know some older kids who went out in the woods to neck and found a guy with a head like a wolf hanging in a tree just like you did. They thought it was a dead guy, but on their way back to the car they heard something behind them. When they looked back they saw the thing that had been hanging in the tree coming after them, and it almost got 'em."

"I wish the one we saw had come after us. I bet Mr. Quinn would've shot it."

"Who's that?"

"The Madison's foreman. He had a gun."

"Cool. Who else was there?"

I told him about Mrs. Madison; that she was a rich lady and that her husband was a judge.

"How do you know they're rich?"

"Because we went to their house for a big party, and us kids ate by ourselves in a room as big as our whole house, and a bunch of servants brought us kids our dinners, and everybody there except us had an expensive car."

When I stopped to catch my breath, Dalton asked, "If it was a party for rich people, how come you were there?"

I didn't have an answer for that, and I didn't get to tell him about the Madison's Ford Thunderbird convertible before we were pressed into the auditorium by the crowd.

Even though there was a scramble for seats at the back of the room, none of the other kids got in Dalton's way, or mine either, I guess that's because I was with him.

As we waited for the assembly to start, Dalton leaned over and whispered, "Did you touch it?"

"Touch what?"

"The dead body."

I made a face and shook my head.

Just as Principal Stevens stepped to the microphone, Dalton grinned and said, "I would've."

At recess that morning a bunch of boys decided to play softball. Dalton said he didn't want to play. But I played Kiwanis back home and liked it, so I got in with the kids waiting to be picked. Dalton, who was standing in the shade leaning on the school building to watch, looked kind of like that guy James Dean. My sister had a poster of him on the wall over her bed.

The same two kids always got to be the captains and pick the teams because they were extra good ball players. Pretty soon there was only one other kid left besides me; a big kid named Jimmy that the mean kids called fatso.

Because he never wore new clothes, and the ones he did wear never fit right, I figured either they were hand-me-downs, or his folks were poor and his mom got his clothes at the used clothing sales the church was always having.

Jimmy was at least a head taller than anyone else in our grade, and I bet he weighted as much as any two other kids put together. I didn't exactly know him, but he was never mean to me, and that was saying something at Cave Street School.

As big as he was, you'd think the ball would go all the way to the next county when Jimmy hit it. But I only ever saw him hit it once. The ball rolled down the first base line and Jimmy ran after it. It didn't look as though either of them would make it to first base.

The catcher, a mean kid named Butch, yelled, "Jimmy's hit another bullet." Then he yelled, "You'd better hustle, Brian," to the kid playing first base. Everyone laughed, me included.

You know how, when you run too fast, you stumble, then to avoid falling you take longer and longer strides then you fall anyway? That's what Jimmy did when he got about halfway to first. There was more laughter then. I didn't laugh at poor Jimmy that time.

Brian walked down the first base line toward Jimmy, taking his time, scooping up the ball, which had stopped about two feet past Jimmy. Brian tossed it in the air a few times, pretending to be bored. When Jimmy got up he was panting. Brian pretended to miss the tag.

I'm sure Jimmy knew that Brain had missed the tag on purpose, we all knew it. I don't know why Jimmy still tried to make it to first base, but he did, struggling to breathe the whole way. And all the while Brian was right behind him pretending that Jimmy was just out of reach. At the last possible instant Brian gave poor Jimmy the tag.

I had only laughed the one time, but I wished I hadn't because you can't un-laugh at somebody. Not that Jimmy had heard me, or that one less kid laughing would have made a difference. But I didn't like myself for it.

That afternoon as Dalton and I made our way through the crush of kids leaving the building at the close of school, I asked him why he didn't do something about Butch picking on Jimmy.

"Butch has a lot of friends."

"I bet they'd be nice to him if you told them to."

"You really think it would change anything?"

"They'd leave him alone."

He stopped and turned to face me, "You don't get it do you, Billy?"

We were disrupting the flow of kids. A few of them gave us dirty looks but didn't say anything. Dalton asked me if they had hurt Jimmy. I shook my head.

"Then what's the big deal?"

"It was mean."

"Why should I have to fix it? You're the one who laughed at him."

"Because I can't and you can. Besides you're not afraid of anything."

"You read too many comic books. Life ain't like that. Those kids leave me alone because I beat one of them up. What if I got in anther fight and lost? What then?"

I shrugged my shoulders. It hadn't occurred to me that Dalton could get beat up by one of the mean kids. I was sorry I'd brought the whole Jimmy thing up.

I knew from the way Dalton was still looking at me funny that he wasn't done giving me grief about it. "If I told those kids to leave Jimmy alone, and they did, their meanness would just get bottled up, and that would make them even meaner. Someday all that meanness would bust out and they'd really hurt Jimmy or some other kid. That would make it my fault, wouldn't it?"

I didn't like thinking about it because I thought Dalton

71

was a good guy. But if he wouldn't stand up for Jimmy then maybe good guys weren't always good. That was too upsetting to think about, so I didn't.

YOU CAN'T TELL FROM THE SHELL

I went to see Mitch when I got home. I found him sitting on his front porch in his rocking chair, with his feet up on the porch railing and pipe smoke curling out from between his lips. His cap was tipped back on his head so the brim pointed almost straight up.

I jumped up onto the porch, clearing all three steps. "Hi, Mr. Ford."

He pointed to the other rocker with his pipe. I got my rocking chair moving in sync with his by pushing against the railing with my feet, all the time hoping Thelma would hear us talking and bring us some cornbread.

I looked at Mitch, watching him for a reaction as I told him, "My friend Dalton thinks the dead guy I saw was the 'Wolf's-Head Man'."

Mitch talked with his pipe stem clinched between his teeth. "That ain't nothin' but an old wives' tale. Folks use it to scare their kids so they won't run off and get lost in the woods."

"But Dalton told me the 'Wolf's-Head Man' chased two of his friends."

Mitch smiled at me and shook his head. "Sometimes it's easier to believe something like that than it is to believe the truth about a matter. You see what I'm saying?"

"No, sir."

"When changes are a comin' people act different than they would when things are normal."

I asked him what kind of changes.

"A lot of people have to be poor so a few people can be rich. Take your friends the Madisons. They only get to live real fancy-like if other folks like them bootleggers, the Damons, live real poor."

That reminded me of a question I'd had ever since I'd seen the little girl at the bootlegger's house. "Mr. Ford?"

"Yes Billy."

Who decides who's gonna be rich and who's gonna be poor?"

He seemed to think really hard about my question. "Mr. Madison's great-granddaddy had a lot of slaves, and he made a lot of money off em'. The Madisons are still living off that same money, only they like to call it old money. Maybe they think the years have cleansed it of all the sins the old man committed while he was making it. Or maybe they just think people have forgotten what the old man did because it was so long ago. But either way they're wrong."

I wasn't sure what to make of that. "So their money's old and it's got sins on it, and that makes Donna's parents bad?"

He gave me a sideways glance. "Who's Donna?"

"The Madison's daughter. I see her at school."

I knew from his silent but intense gaze he thought there was more to the thing with me and Donna. Thank goodness he didn't ask me about her. He'd figure out that I liked her, and he surely didn't like her parents. "So," I said, "does that make Donna's parents bad people?"

His gaze returned to the tree next by the porch. "No," he said, "not directly it don't. But some day, when the world crashes down around them, they're gonna think life dealt them a bad hand. See, they think they deserve to be rich just because their family's been rich for a long time, and they don't understand why that's wrong."

74

"Why's the world gonna crash on them?"

He took his pipe out of his mouth and gazed at me silently for so long I thought he wasn't going to answer. Finally he said, "Things are a lot different where you come from, ain't they?"

"Yes, sir," I said, nodding my head, "they sure are."

"Then I reckon it'd take a heap of talking to explain why things are the way they are around here, so let's save that for another day, shall we?"

Thelma came out then carrying a brown paper bag, a bowl, and an empty coffee can. She asked me if I wanted some pecans.

I hesitated because I didn't want to get stuck having to eat something I didn't like. She gave Mitch a nut cracker and a long thin tool that looked like the thing my dentist used to pick at my teeth.

I watched Mitch squeeze a pecan with the nutcracker until the shell cracked, watched as he split the shell into two neat halves with his fingers then pried the two pecan pieces out with the pointed thingy. He gave me both pieces. They tasted surprisingly good. He handed me the nutcracker. I put a pecan in it and squeezed. It shattered into a million pieces, most of them falling on the porch floor.

I tried to give Mitch the nutcracker so he could crack more pecans open for us. He shook his head, told me I needed the practice. I tried to crack another one. I mashed that one into smithereens too.

Mitch took three nuts out of the bag and squeezed them together in his hand until the middle one cracked, then handed it to me. I gave him the remnants of mine. He told me I'd get the hang of it. I didn't believe him.

I ate dozens of pecans that day, most of them ones Mitch had given me because I never did get the hang of it. At first, Mitch picked the tiny pieces of nut meat from the ones I destroyed and let me have the nice pieces from the shells he opened. After I had destroyed a couple dozen more he handed me the bowl. He said I'd never learn how to crack them as long as he was doing all the

75

work for me.

Mitch hadn't warn me about checking the nuts, so I suppose it was only a matter of time before I ate a rotten one. I gagged on it.

"Got a bad one, did ya?" he said," as I jumped up and leaned over the railing to spit the awful tasting stuff into the yard.

I managed a feeble, "Yes sir," then spit some more and kept on spitting until I ran out of spit trying to get the taste out of my mouth.

When I sat down he handed me the pieces of shell from the rotten pecan and told me to take a good look at it.

"Looks okay to me."

He said, "It's the same with people."

I asked him what he meant.

"You can't tell if a person's bad from the way they look on the outside; you can't tell from the shell. See what I mean?"

"So people can't tell what the Madisons are like just by looking at them?"

"That's right, Billy, and the same goes for the Damons."

I thought about that for a minute. "The bootleggers are the same as the Madisons?"

He shook his head. "What I'm trying to say is; we can't any of us tell which people are good and which people are bad just by looking at 'em."

"I think I get it, Mr. Ford," and I thought I did.

"You're gonna hear all kinds of talk about the Madisons, Billy, and about that Damon feller too, and when you do, I want you to remember that pecan you spit out."

That's when Mom called me for dinner. Later, after some really persistent pestering, my mother gave in and let me sleep over at Dalton's house the following Friday night. I took a bag of clothes to school that day so I could walk home with him. The plan was for my mother to call me at Dalton's Saturday morning before she left to pick me up, and I would walk back to the school to meet her.

After school Friday, we ran most of the way to Dalton's

76

house just because running felt good. But it was far enough, and we ran fast enough, for me to get super thirsty. So I was glad when Dalton stopped for sodas at a rundown little store in a rundown neighborhood.

The place was plastered with sun-faded rusty signs advertising Orange Crush soda, Red Man chewing tobacco, Delco car batteries and a bunch of other names I'd never heard of back home. The siding that wasn't covered by signs wasn't covered by paint either, so the place looked like the buildings I'd seen in a show about the Depression I'd watched on TV with my dad. I didn't see a single building in the whole neighborhood with decent looking paint, not one house with grass in the yard or one porch that looked safe to walk on, although one house did have a flowerpot on the porch with one lonely lower in it.

I followed Dalton into the store, letting the screen door slam shut behind us, announcing our arrival to the store's owner as sure as if he'd had a guard dog. The narrow isles were so crammed with stuff we had to walk kind of sideways so we didn't knock anything off of the shelves.

Dalton went straight to the soda machine in the back, one of those chest type soda machines with rows of glass bottles hanging by their necks in icy cold water. After you put in your dime, you held one of the bottles by its neck as you slid it through the water to a spot where you could lift it out. But when I reached for the lid of the cooler Dalton held it down.

"Don't bother with them," he said. "We're gonna have us a couple of them sixteen ounce Coke-Colas."

He took two of them out of the upright refrigerator where they kept the cold beer, because the new Cokes were too big to fit in the old soda machine. They looked so big I wasn't sure I could finish one by myself, and so cold and wet I couldn't wait to try. I don't remember how much Dalton paid for them, but I know they cost more than ten cents apiece because he put a pile of coins on the counter that included two dimes and he didn't get any change back.

We took our sodas outside and sat in the dirt at the edge of the street to watch the people and cars going by. The store was in the part of Tuscumbia the locals called "Poor Town." The street surface was hard packed dirt, so when a car went by it blew dust in our faces and grit in our teeth which we washed down with soda. I felt uncomfortable sitting there, as though I didn't belong. I asked Dalton where we were.

"Poor Town."

"Why's it called Poor Town?"

"Because it's where all the poor folks live."

"How come?"

"Dad told me that when the railroad came to Tuscumbia a hundred years ago they laid the track right straight across the county, cutting Tuscumbia in half. One side of the town grew and got expensive. The poor people moved to the other side.

I was glad when we finished our sodas and headed for Dalton's house. On our way there we passed an old man staggering toward us carrying a paper bag, weaving and stumbling like he just got off of a tilt-a-whirl. He stopped and held the bag up toward us and mumbled something.

Dalton yelled, "Go sleep it off, you old drunk."

The guy shouted some four-letter words in our direction then stumbled along in the direction he happened to be leaning.

Dalton laughed at him, said, "Sometimes late at night I hear the old drunk walking by our house talking up a storm." It made me glad I didn't live near Dalton.

The same railroad tracks that ran behind the store ran behind Dalton's house. We passed some kind of farm store then a Ford dealer's lot. We looked in the showroom windows at the new cars. That was a disappointment. They didn't have any Thunderbirds, and the rest of their cars were no big deal. Someone came out and chased us off anyway.

When we turned onto Douglas Street, Dalton pointed out his house two blocks away on the corner where the pavement ended as it entered "Poor Town." When we were almost to his yard a car passed us, revving his engine to get traction in the sand. A big live oak tree shaded most of Dalton's front yard.

I didn't see grass growing anywhere under the tree, not even crabgrass, so their front yard was mostly sand and tree roots and anthills crawling with red ants.

The open porch with no railings that ran across the front of his house had three rocking chairs on it that the paint had abandoned long ago. Dalton's mother must have been expecting him because their screen door latch wasn't hooked. Not that it mattered - it was so flimsy-looking I doubted it would keep anyone from breaking in anyway. Their living room wasn't much bigger than the bedroom my sister and I shared. The couch against the far wall had a crooked leg. It had stains on it where had people spilled stuff, and low spots in it where the stuffing had bit the dust.

Dalton led me to the right through an arched doorway into the dining room. A china cabinet and a table with six chairs took up so much space there was barely enough room left for us to pass through to the kitchen. Lots of old black-and-white photographs hung on the walls, but most of them had yellowed and faded so badly the people were hard to see.

Dalton's mother was in the kitchen standing at the counter leaning over a cookbook, her eyes squinting as she traced the words on a page with her finger. Only a little taller than me, and skinnier than my sister, she had a wide face, a flat nose, and shiny coal-black hair. Her dress was so damp with sweat it was stuck to her back.

At first she seemed surprised when she saw me. Then she frowned and asked Dalton, "Who's your friend?"

"I told you Billy was staying over tonight."

She made a face at him, said, "Yeah, okay, maybe so."

With a pot simmering on the stove and something baking in the oven it was terribly hot in the kitchen, even though their back door was in the kitchen and only the screen door was closed. A small oscillating fan on top of the refrigerator blew hot air at us.

When Dalton lifted the lid off of the pot on the stove his mother slapped his hand and told him. "Stay outta there."

She took a ceramic cookie jar that looked like Mickey Mouse out of a cupboard and put it on the counter. "You have these," she said. It sounded as though she'd said, "You have deeze."

Dalton got a pitcher of cold tea out of the refrigerator and filled two glasses. He told me to hold them while he took a handful of cookies out of the cookie jar. I followed him outside to the porch where we sat in rocking chairs to have the cookies and tea. Even though Dalton hadn't brought any sugar for the tea, I was so hot from being in the kitchen that I enjoyed it anyway.

Dalton told me that the cookies, which I'd never had before, were called Snicker Doodles. He grabbed six and gave me three. I could have eaten three hundred of them. My mother was going to hear about them when I got home.

I was listening to a cicada in the Live Oak tree and watching an old man walking past Dalton's house carrying a bamboo fishing pole. When Dalton asked him if he'd caught anything, the man held up a line with several fish hanging from it. The water dripping off of the fish, caught in the reddish glow of the afternoon sun, looked like a shower of red jewels.

"Caught me these here catfish," the man said with obvious pride.

Dalton asked him where.

The man pointed back over his shoulder with his thumb. "Yonder, in the creek behind the grocery store."

He stood there holding the fish up for a few awkward moments before going on his way, like a child who wasn't sure if he had been dismissed. A short time later a colored woman walked past carrying two full bags of groceries.

Even though she was dressed like the women in an old war movie I'd watched with my dad, her dress looked as nice and clean and as if she'd bought it that very day. I felt bad watching her carry two big bags of groceries on such a hot day. If she had any ice cream it'd melt for sure.

She had walked past us, was in front of the neighbor's house, when a car full of older kids came up behind her with

80

all of the windows rolled down. They shouted things at her that would get me grounded if my parents heard me say them. As the car passed the woman, a kid in the back seat leaned out of his window to spit at her. I didn't see whether or not his spit hit her but she kept walking as though nothing had happened.

Dalton stood up and said, "Those assholes did that to me once."

I expected his mother to come out and scold him for cussing, but she didn't. Maybe she hadn't heard him.

When the car was out of sight Dalton said, "We oughta teach them a lesson."

"What can we do?" I asked, hoping he'd forget about them, because they were older and bigger and looked as though they'd enjoy beating up a Yankee kid.

He was still looking off in the direction they'd gone. "I'll think of something," he said, "and I know right where to find 'em."

After that we sat in the rocking chairs and waited for dinner. I tried to swat a pesky mosquito that wouldn't leave me alone while Dalton told me which of the kids at school to watch out for. Dalton was telling me about a bully named Craig when a car Dalton said was his dad's pulled into the yard and parked under the big live oak tree.

I think the only thing his dad had in common with my dad was his age. Instead of a suit his dad had on a blue uniform like the ones the gas station attendants wear. His dad was a lot thinner than my dad. My dad's hair was a lot thinner than his dad's hair.

Mr. Dalton came and stood at the bottom of the porch steps with a rolled up newspaper tucked under his arm and a scratched-up, tin lunch pail in his hand. He asked Dalton who I was.

"That's Billy; he's staying overnight."

His dad didn't say another word as he walked past us into the house. When the screen door closed behind him Dalton leaned over and whispered to me. "Don't mind him, he doesn't

81

say much."

A little while later his mother served dinner, putting more food on the table than we could possibly eat; more food than my mother put on the table at Thanksgiving. Dalton told me they always had lots of food because his mother served leftovers every day until they were gone.

I tried most of the food and even liked some of it, and ate the stuff I didn't like because I didn't want to get in trouble with Dalton's dad, who looked a lot scarier than my dad. His mom had left the oscillating fan in the kitchen going and I could feel the hot air on me when it pointed in my direction. It's no fun eating hot food on a hot day with hot air blowing on you.

His dad was the last one to finish eating, but no one got up from the table until he was done. Then, squeezing Dalton's shoulder hard enough to make him flinch, he told Dalton, "You help your mother clean up the dishes before you go anywhere."

Even though Dalton said, "Yes, sir," his mother did most of the work. All we did was carry the dishes into the kitchen. When we were done Dalton told me to go outside and wait for him on the porch.

Outside, everything was tinted gold by the late evening sun, and the air felt wet, the way it does after a rainstorm, even though it hadn't rained. Besides an occasional car out on the main road, I heard a dog barking somewhere in the distance and faint rumbling of far-off thunder. Dalton brought out a pile of comic books. We sat on the porch floor with our legs dangling over the side, reading about Superman, Spiderman, and Dick Tracy.

A few minutes after the sounds of his mother washing dishes had died away, his parents came out on the porch. At the foot of the steps his dad turned around and gave Dalton a stern look. "We've got some errands to run. I expect you two to be here when I get back."

Dalton said, "Yes, sir," without looking up from his comic.

His dad came over and stood in front of us so Dalton had to look at him. "I don't want you boys getting into trouble

82

because I don't want to have to explain anything to his parents. You understand?"

This time when Dalton said, "Yes, sir," it sounded convincing.

Their car turned left at Main Street. As soon as it disappeared behind the corner drug store Dalton jumped up and said, "Come on. I've got something to show you."

I followed him inside, through the living room then through an open doorway between the living and dining rooms, into a bedroom smaller than the one Sis and I shared. There were clothes on the bed and some underwear draped over a chair, which had to be his mom's. Dalton dragged a chair over to the wardrobe and took a cigar box down from on top of it.

After he set the box down on the bed and opened it, he stepped back so I could look inside. It contained a pistol sitting on an oil-soaked rag and two boxes of bullets. The gun's metal was almost black with a blue tint and smelled of oil. The honey-colored, cross-hatch patterned handle grip had been worn almost smooth where a hand would hold it.

Dalton said, "Sometimes Dad goes out in the woods to practice. He took me with him once."

"He let you shoot it?" I asked, amazed and envious.

"Well, sure," he said, "why else would he take me?"

"What's it like shooting a gun?" I asked, thinking Dalton had to be just about the luckiest kid alive.

He grabbed my hand when I reached for the gun. "We gotta get outta here before they get back."

After he put the box back up on top of the wardrobe and slid it out of sight we went outside to wait for his parents. Instead of reading comics we watched bats swoop in and out of the light from the streetlamp at the corner catching insects. I asked Dalton why his dad had a gun.

"He was in the Korean war. That's where my mom's from. They got married over there."

"But how come he's got a gun?"

"My dad worries about what people might do because my

mom's a foreigner. Hell, you see how the kids at school make fun of you just because you sound different. It's a lot worse if you look different."

I didn't know what to say to that. I was still trying to think of something when Dalton spotted his parents' car turning off the main road. Two long cones of light projected from the car's headlights through air so humid it looked as though a fog had set in. The beams swung toward us in a long slow arc as his parents' car pulled in under the live oak.

After his parents had gone inside Dalton whispered to me. "Pretty soon he'll fall asleep in his chair. Then we can go."

I asked him where we were going.

I've got a friend who knows everything that's happened around here since just about forever, so I figure he'll know about the 'Wolfs-Head Man'."

TROUBLEMAKERS

As we waited for his dad to fall asleep, I watched the last remnant of the big red ball that was the sun until it was gone and there was nothing left but shades of darkness and an almost continuous display of heat lightning flickering at the horizon. Most of the birds had already found places to hide for the night and the grating sounds of the cicadas had ceased; so, except for the crickets and an occasional car out on the main road, it was quiet.

I would have been happy just sitting on the porch until bedtime, but Dalton had other ideas. After a while he got up and went inside being careful the screen door didn't slam and wake up his dad. When he came back outside he put a finger to his lips signaling me to be quiet, then hopped off the porch.

I followed him around to the other side of the live oak where he handed me a crumpled paper bag. It contained a small cardboard box labeled "cigarette loads," and a partial pack of Chesterfield cigarettes. I'd heard about loads but had never actually seen one. I asked him where he got them.

"Ordered them from an ad I saw in the back of a comic book. But don't say anything in front of my folks."

"How come?"

"When I got the stamp from Mom she asked me why I wanted it. I told her it was for one of those dumb mail-order magic tricks."

"Where'd you get the cigarettes?"

"Bought 'em from a kid at school."

"What's that stuff for?"

I didn't like the way he looked at me when he said, "You'll see."

He took the bag from me then headed toward downtown. We'd gone six or seven blocks when Dalton stopped by some trees at the edge of a big gravel parking lot. Girls on roller skates wearing short frilly skirts, like the ones girls wear on the ice-skating shows my mom watched, carried trays of food from a diner called "Walt's Malts" out to the cars in the parking lot. Sometimes the girls flirted with the boys in the cars.

The cars were parked across the lot from us, next to posts with speaker boxes like the ones at drive-in theaters. We had a place like it back home. You pressed a button on the post then talked into the box to place your food order. A girl would bring your order out on a tray that she hooked on the driver's window. You pressed a different button when you were done eating and wanted one of the girls to come pick up your tray.

I pointed at a car across the lot. "That Chevy over there, that's them, isn't it, the ones who spit at the colored lady?"

"Yep."

I had a really bad feeling about it. "That's why we're here, isn't it?"

"Yep."

When I asked him what he planned to do he handed me the paper bag. "You're gonna do it."

I felt queasier than I had after riding the tilt-a-whirl at the county fair. "Why me?"

"They all know me, so you gotta do it."

He asked me if was scared. I had to lie, tell him I wasn't. After that it didn't matter what he had planned, I had to do it. If I chickened out I'd lose my only friend, and if he told anybody that I chickened out, it'd be all over school and the bullies would have a field day with me.

Dalton pushed loads into the ends of all but one of the cigarettes then handed me that one. He put the rest of them back

86

in the crinkled cigarette pack which he put in my shirt pocket. He took a matchbook out of the bag then took the cigarette I was holding. He asked me if I was ready. I told him I was; another lie. He lit the cigarette without the load, his face glowing in the light from the match.

As he handed me the cigarette he said, "Take in some smoke just before you get to their car. Make sure they see you blow it out, but whatever you do, don't breathe the smoke in 'cause it'll make you cough and you'll get sick as a dog."

"Then what?" I asked.

"I'm betting they'll take the pack of cigarettes from you."

"That's when I scram, right?"

"No, you gotta walk back here like nothin' happened. If they see you running they'll know something's up."

He grabbed my arm when I started to leave. "When you hear those loads going off, get your ass back here, and fast, 'cause they'll come after you."

Afraid I might chicken out if I had time to think about it, I started walking toward the Chevy, which looked as though it was a mile away. I made it across the lot by thinking about Donna and how impressed she'd be if she knew what I was doing. I planned to tell her all about it first chance I got.

Looking down and thinking about Donna and watching my feet instead of watching where I was going, I almost bumped into the back of the Chevy. I took a drag on the cigarette then blew the smoke toward the open back window of the Chevy.

A guy in the back seat leaned out of his window and yelled, "Hey, kid," at the same time the driver opened his car door, blocking my way. Towering over me when he got out of the car, I knew he was at least five years older than me because he was old enough to drive.

He poked me in the chest then said, "Kinda young to be smoking, aren't ya?"

If I said anything they'd know I was a Yankee. No telling what they'd do to me then, so I just shrugged my shoulders.

The kid told me to hand over the cigarettes, and even

87

though I gave him the pack, he shoved me anyway, so hard I bounced against the next car over. A string of swear words came from that that car.

The driver said, "Go on, git" then lunged at me.

He laughed when I flinched, but I felt pretty good when I started the long walk back across the parking lot because I wasn't as scared as I thought I'd be. I was about halfway back to where Dalton was waiting for me when I heard the first pop. I heard another one a split-second later and took off running.

Just before I got to Dalton he took off at a dead run, cutting through people's yards to avoid the streets where the kids in the Chevy would be looking for us. I had to push to keep up with him. We ran hard until the pain in my side got so bad I had to stop. I bent over and put my hands on my knees and gasped for breath. Dalton came back. He walked in circles breathing hard, but not as hard as me.

"In a way, I wish they knew it was me," he said.

I was the one they'd seen, so it was me they'd be looking for, not Dalton. The thought left me feeling as though I'd been punched in the stomach. It was another reason to hate living in Tuscumbia.

Before he took off at a jog Dalton told me, "I knew you could do it," which definitely made it worth doing, as long as those kids never caught me.

When we finally got to the sandy streets of "Poor Town," where streetlights were rare and rarely worked, we slowed to a walk. At one point an old black sedan roared past us. It reminded me of something I'd seen the drive to Tuscumbia.

"Hey Dalton, I bet you can't guess what I saw."

Dalton stopped to pick up a stick and threw it over the trees. While we watched it sail high into the darkness I told him I'd seen a chain gang, but he seemed more interested in what happened to the stick.

He shrugged his shoulders, said, "So?"

"So there was a guy sitting on the hood of a black sedan holding a shotgun, and there was a whole bunch of men in the ditch chopping weeds with those big things with the long curved blades, and they were chanting something, and all of them were chained together with leg irons."

"That ain't nothin," Dalton said. "We see 'em all the time around here."

I felt silly for telling him about it, but after seeing that chain gang I'd had a nightmare where I was chained up with some men in a ditch and they were singing a song I didn't know, and they were going to do something bad to me when they caught me faking the words, like Principal Stephens had seen me doing.

At the train crossing Dalton followed the tracks, holding his arms out as he walked on one of the rails pretending it was a tightrope. The steel gleamed dully in the faint light, the two lines of it so straight and long I could barely see where they met, so far away it might as well have been past forever.

A mile or so farther, the tracks, and the same creek that ran all the way to town from out near my house, and the road Mom drove every day to take me to school, all came together near the bridge into Tuscumbia, with the tracks on our side of the creek and the road on the other.

Dalton stopped and knelt down in the grass behind a small house. "There's somethin' you gotta see."

The back yard was bordered by a one-car garage on the right, a fenced dog-run on the left, and the railroad tracks along the back edge of it. I knew the owner didn't have a dog anymore because the sagging fence was holding up the dog run posts, instead of the other way around. A pile of cement blocks under each corner of the house raised it up so I could see under it all the way to the street out front. Wooden steps led up to the back door of the house, which had a screen door hanging crooked on sagging hinges.

A broken window in the back wall of the garage a few feet away had long thin pieces of broken glass sticking out of the top and bottom of the sash, like jagged teeth in a big square mouth.

When I asked Dalton why we were there, he went to the

broken window and signaled for me to follow him. In spite of the dim light inside the garage, I could tell that the car parked in it was a Ford Thunderbird convertible just like the Madisons'.

"And it's white," he said, "so I bet it's the same one you told me about. There can't be two of them in Tuscumbia."

I asked him how he found it.

"When some kids I know told me they saw one, I made them show me where. I've been watching the place ever since then, and I see it parked here a lot."

"I don't get it," I said, "only rich people have cars like that."

Dalton pointed at the house with his thumb. "The guy who lives here parks his car out front on the lawn. This car belongs to a woman who comes to see him real regular like. I think she puts her car in the garage so no one will see it."

Saying, "Come on," he started to walk around the garage but stopped and turned around to face me. "We gotta be really quiet," he whispered, "and if he comes after us, we gotta run in different directions. I know the streets around here better than you so I'll run out to the street and go that way. You follow these tracks back to my house, but don't stop there if he's chasing you."

"Why not?"

"'Cause if you do he'll know where I live. So if he's chasing you, keep running until you come to a bridge. Hide under there and wait for me. If you're not at my house when I get there, that's where I'll look for you."

I followed him to the side door of the garage. Before he opened it he whispered, "There's junk all over the place, so watch out or you'll make one hell of a racket."

Inside the garage, Dalton pointed to the driver's side of the car. I walked around the car, opened the door and slipped into the soft white leather of the driver's seat. I couldn't think of the words to describe the feelings I had sitting behind the wheel of that Thunderbird. I imagined the world becoming a blur and the pavement disappearing beneath me as I raced down a winding country road. I wished I could reach the gas pedal and see over the dashboard.

Pretty soon Dalton tugged on my sleeve and whispered, "We can't stay here." I figured he probably wanted a turn, so I switched places with him.

He sat staring straight ahead with both hands gripping the wheel, probably speeding down a road winding through his imagination like I had done.

After a while he whispered, "I'm gonna have me one of these someday."

I told him I wanted one of the atomic powered cars from the future I'd read about in Popular Science magazine.

He slid out of the driver's seat. "Come on, we gotta go. If that guy comes out here we'll be trapped. But you've gotta be extra quiet from now on. Don't even whisper."

Back outside, Dalton started off across the yard toward the house, stooped over as though he was running behind a low wall. We were out in the open so it was a silly thing to do, but I did it anyway because I'd seen it done in a movie. He stopped under a window with his back and arms against the side of the house and I did the same. We probably saw the same movie.

As I listened for a sound that would mean someone had seen or heard us, he reached under the house and pulled out two wooden crates and set them below a window. Standing on a crate he was tall enough to see over the window sill. I had to pull myself up and stand on my tiptoes to see in.

Through a crack under the window curtains I saw a man and a woman on a bed across the room, both of them naked and moving as though they were swimming under water together. I recognized the man as Joe Quinn, the Madisons' foreman.

I'd never seen people having sex before, but I'd learned enough about it from the boys in my Scout pack to know what they were doing. I started to climb down because spying on them didn't feel right, but Dalton grabbed my arm and shook his head. So I stayed at the window even though my legs ached from standing on my tiptoes.

The woman was on top of Quinn, leaning forward over him with her naked back toward us. Through the closed window

I heard her moan as she threw her head back. I thought she was going to scream. I figured Quinn was hurting her.

I heard him grunt, as though he'd lifted something too heavy, then his body jerked under the woman. For another minute or so her hair, so long it almost reached her waist, swayed with the motion of her hips. Then she fell forward on top of him. They were silent after that; Quinn lying as still as a dead man, the woman still moving, but just barely.

I had just lowered myself off my tiptoes to give my legs a rest when Dalton poked my arm and pointed at the window. I raised myself up again and looked in, and that's when I got a good look at the woman's face. She had turned her head toward us as she rested it on Quinn's chest. It was Mrs. Madison alright, and I'd seen her naked. Luckily for us she had her eyes closed.

Ashamed as I was for staring at Mrs. Madison lying there naked, I couldn't look away. I wondered if the preacher knew about Mrs. Madison and Quinn, wondered if that's why he seemed to be talking to the Madisons during his sermon.

With the room light on, I knew the glass in the window would look like a mirror to them, but all of sudden Quinn looked right at us. He pushed Mrs. Madison aside and got out of bed. Walking toward the window, he tipped his head sideways, as though he was trying to read something written on the glass.

Dalton and I ducked below the window. I would have jumped down off the crate if Dalton hadn't put his arm out and held me against the house. Quinn stood at the window above us. I could tell because the ceiling light behind him created a blurred outline of him on the grass. I heard the window slide open.

Mrs. Madison's voice was faint and slurred, as though she'd just awakened from a dream. "What is it, Joe?"

"I thought I saw something."

She rolled over and pulled the sheet up.

"You know," Quinn said, "it's just a matter of time until we get caught, and what I've got going here working for your husband is worth a lot more than a few minutes in the sack with you."

92

Quinn's shadow on the grass disappeared. Right after that he told Mrs. Madison, "Get your clothes on and get out." Then I heard the window close.

First she said, "You're a real bastard, Joe," then, "I should've quit coming here a long time ago."

Dalton got down off his crate and put it under the house. I did the same with mine then followed him out behind the garage where he knelt down in the grass near the railroad tracks.

"Pretty cool, huh?" he said, grinning.

I shrugged my shoulders and told him I thought it was kind of weird.

Snapping off a long blade of grass he chewed on it like a TV cowboy. "You never heard your parents doing that?"

I shook my head.

"You know that they all do that, don't ya?"

Thinking about my parents doing that made my stomach queasy.

Dalton said, "Women make noises if they like it. Some of them even say stuff. My mom does, but I can't understand what she saying because she always talks in Korean when she gets excited."

"How come you showed me that?" I asked, trying to get rid of the image I had in my head of my parents doing that.

"Because it's cool," he said, "and because I wanted to know if she was the rich woman you told me about, the one with the big house where you had dinner."

"That's Mrs. Madison alright."

"Well she sure looks nice."

I thought about her being Donna's mother, and wondered if Donna looked the same with her clothes off.

Dalton said, "I wish I knew who that guy is."

"That's Joe Quinn, the Madisons' foreman."

"Well I'd like to see Mr. Madison's face when he finds out what she's been doing."

"How's he gonna find out?"

"Are you kidding?" he said. "You can't drive a car like that and not get noticed. Somebody's gonna see her coming here regularly and rat on them."

Then even from way out there behind the garage I heard Mrs. Madison shouting something at Quinn inside the house. I couldn't make out the words but moments later the screen door at the back of the house slammed shut.

That's when I saw the match and the M80 firecracker Dalton was holding. He whispered, "Get ready to run," as he struck the match on the garage siding and lit the fuse.

He counted to three then lobbed the firecracker over the garage toward the house. We peeked around the corner of the garage. All hell broke loose when it exploded. Mrs. Madison screamed. Joe Quinn burst out of the back door.

We ducked back behind the garage, but he must have spotted us because he yelled, "I'll get you, you little bastards."

Dalton took off through the neighbor's yard toward the street. I took off down the railroad tracks as fast as I could. About a block from Quinn's place I stopped and looked back to see if Quinn was chasing me. I saw a dark figure in the distance standing on the tracks. Figuring he could see me as well as I could see him, I took off again to put some more distance between us.

Giving me one hell of a scare when he reappeared a few minutes later, Dalton said, "That Mrs. Madison's a real screamer."

The firecracker wasn't the sort of thing I would've have thought of, but it had been great fun. Hell, I'd had more fun and excitement in one night with Dalton than I'd had in years.

"HELL NO, I AIN'T SCARED"

At the next street crossing Dalton left the tracks to follow it. I knew we'd passed into "Poor Town" because there were no more working streetlights and the road was nothing but rutted sand. At what seemed to be a random spot Dalton turned into the woods. We walked past an old car squatting low to the ground because all four of its tires were flat. It didn't look as though it had been driven in a long time, or that it ever would be again.

I followed Dalton to the door of a shack almost hidden in the trees just beyond the car. It looked like something kids might build out of scrap wood in an afternoon; something that would collapse in a light breeze, but Dalton pounded on the door anyway.

Someone in the darkness beyond the shack yelled, "Who's there?"

Dalton yelled, "It's me, Sam" then headed through a thicket so dense and dark I had to stay close behind him so I wouldn't get lost.

His friend must have known from the noise we made coming through the brush there were two of us, because he asked, "And what might you boys want?" before we got to the clearing.

An old colored man sitting on a wooden crate holding a fishing pole was watching a red and white plastic bobber floating in coal-black water that didn't appear to be moving. The thought of eating something pulled out of that river made me queasy.

Low cloud cover set aglow from the city lights of Tuscumbia lit up the little clearing along the riverbank, enough for me to see willow trees along the banks, and little clusters of rotted posts, probably the remnants of old boat docks, poking up out of the water every so often. So maybe the water had been clean enough to swim in years ago, but fish floating on their sides, their bloated white bellies glowing eerily in the mucky shallow water lapping against the creek bank, were proof enough that I didn't want to drink it.

Slouched over and clad in baggy, limp clothes the old man looked like a scarecrow. His work boots were untied and pulled open at the laces, and in the weak light I could see a day or two of beard stubble that was the same gray color as his eyebrows and short wiry hair.

Dalton asked him, "How come you're always fishing, Sam?"

"I tire of eating my dinner out of a can. Sides, when a fish takes your hook..."

Leaving the thought unfinished, he lifted his line out of the water to check the worm on his hook then swung it back out over the river, letting it drop into the water mid river. Dalton sat down on a sun-bleached log as smooth and white as an old dog bone. I sat next to him.

Sam spit a wad of chewing tobacco into a can between his feet. "You boys want a pinch?"

Dalton didn't seem at all surprised that Sam had offered us chewing tobacco. As for me, I couldn't believe it. But instead of answering Sam, Dalton asked him about the "Wolf's-Head Man."

Sam spit another glob of dark juice at the can then told us, "There's poles enough in my place if you have a mind to do some fishing."

I was glad Dalton didn't take him up on the fishing. I like

to fish as much as the next kid, but not after seeing the dead fish floating in the shallows.

When Dalton repeated his demand, that Sam tell us about the "Wolf's-Head Man," Sam frowned at him and asked, "Why you wanna know 'bout that?"

Dalton nodded his head toward me. "Because he saw him, that's why."

Sam looked at me, as though deciding whether or not he should believe it, and while he was staring at me a mosquito bit my neck. I had almost forgotten about the mosquitoes. Once in a while a fish would break the surface of the river to eat one of them, and high overhead, bats feasted on them, but there were still clouds of the blood-thirsty little devils swarming around us.

I think Sam could tell from my expression that he'd made me uncomfortable because he grinned at me. "You look like you're waiting on the grade from a test you ain't studied for."

Then he turned away, sitting very still, silently watching his line.

After a while Dalton said to him, "Hey, you gonna tell us about the legend or not?" and he sounded angry.

If my dad heard me talk to a grownup that way he'd tan my hide.

Sam checked his worm again before he answered Dalton. "That legend ain't goin' nowhere, so I don't see why I gots to hurry about it."

"'Cause we ain't got all night," Dalton said, and he sounded angrier than before.

Sam glanced at Dalton then spit at his can again. "Legend says there's something out there that's part man and part wolf; everything about him like a man 'cept his face. It started because of a charcoal maker who lived in these parts a hundred years ago or more. You have to tend a burning mound of wood for weeks to make charcoal. They say his skin was always covered with soot. They say he looked as black in the sunlight as he did on a moonless night.

"But people were happy buying his whiskey and left him

alone, until someone found some bones in the woods near his still, people bones. Legend says he robbed people traveling through the woods at night. He killed 'em so they couldn't tell anyone about being robbed then fed 'em to his dogs so nobody would find the bodies. I reckon he didn't bury the bones deep enough."

Dalton interrupted Sam, asked him, "His dogs really ate the people?"

"If you believe what the legend says. And they weren't real dogs; they was half-breeds, part dog and part wolf. There were still wolves around in those days so something like that could've happened. A half-breed is bigger and meaner than a dog, meaner even than a wolf. Wolves can smell people more than a mile away, and they'll run from 'em if they can, but not a half-breed. They don't know enough to be afraid of humans. And if you believe the legend, the fur on them half-breeds was so black, that if it weren't for their eyes glowing yellow and bright as a lantern you wouldn't even know they were there."

I looked at the dark wall of woods around us and thought about the bright yellow eyes I'd seen and wondered if the big black dog behind my house could have been a half-breed wolf. And I thought about walking back to Dalton's house. And I wondered if I'd see that one at our house again. I noticed Dalton looking around too. I guess Sam saw us eyeing the woods because he asked us if we were scared.

"Hell, no," Dalton said, "I ain't scared," but I think he was.

And he sounded mad. I don't think he was mad at Sam. I think he was mad at himself for being scared. I think Sam knew it too because he shook his head and grinned at Dalton.

Dalton asked him, "So is that all there is to the legend?"

Sam shook his head. As he watched his bobber drifting slowly downriver, he told us. "Well the locals got suspicious when some travelers they was expecting never showed up. Then a farmer going home through the woods one night spotted the charcoal maker going somewhere with his half-breeds and he followed them. When he saw them sneak up and attack

98

a guy who was sleeping by the trail he went for help. He came back with some folks from the village. They tracked the charcoal maker and his dogs by torchlight and eventually got 'em cornered in a barn. They burned that barn down and those devils with it."

When Sam stopped to lean over and spit I told him I'd seen a half-breed wolf. He looked at me funny, said I sounded like a Yankee. I told him I was from New York.

"Well, I'll be damned," he said. "That makes you as much if an outcast as me and your friend Dalton and those half-breed dogs in the legend."

Dalton asked Sam what had happened to the bootlegger.

"Don't reckon anybody knows. But folks been claiming they seen him as far back as I can remember, and that's a fur piece. I asked Sam if he believed in the legend, but instead of answering me, he took his line out of the water to check it. Except for a little nub on the hook his worm was gone, which meant there was one less hungry fish to eat the mosquitos that were eating us.

Sam bent over a Maxwell House can on the ground beside him and fished around in it with his finger until he found a worm he liked, impaling it on the hook twice, so no matter how much it squirmed, it wasn't likely to get free. Then he swung the line back out over the river, the motion as smooth as a clock pendulum.

The three of us sat quietly for a while. I watched Sam's red and white bobber drifting downriver with his hook until the line went taut and his pole curved into a crescent the same shape as his back.

I figured Sam would answer me when he was good and ready, but in a loud, angry-sounding voice Dalton said, "Hey Sam, Billy asked you if you believe in the legend."

Dalton's outburst didn't seem to bother Sam. He just looked at Dalton. But Dalton was on his feet with his head tipped a little and glaring sideways at Sam. "You gonna answer him, or what?"

Sam spit a big glob of tobacco juice toward the river. It hit the water ten feet out with a splat. A fish broke the surface there immediately.

With his shoulders shaking from a silent laugh, Sam said, "Fish probably thought he got hisself a big fat bug. I bet that nasty ole tobacco juice surprised the hell out of him."

Dalton walked over to Sam. He looked so mad I thought for sure he was going to hit him. "Well, do you believe in the legend or don't you?"

I would've been mad, but Sam wasn't. "If that devil's out there, I don't wanna meet up with him. No sir, I don't. 'Cause I figure he ain't but one pitchfork shy of being the devil hisself."

Dalton kicked a stone loose with his shoe and tossed it into the creek near Sam's bobber.

When the stone hit the water Sam shouted, "Hey, boy, my dinner might've been swimmin' round that worm."

Dalton kicked at the dirt on the riverbank, sending a cloud of it into the river so it looked as though a hard rain was falling then said to me. "How do you like them apples?"

At the same time Sam said to Dalton, "Damn, boy, you're gonna scare all my fish away," I told Dalton, "Tell Sam you're sorry."

Dalton shoved me so hard I fell off the log and landed on my back in the mud. When I got up and rushed at Dalton he tried to push me aside, but I grabbed his shirt before I lost my balance. We fell to the ground together.

Then we were rolling back and forth in a confusing blur of swinging fists and kicking feet. I was getting madder with every poorly delivered blow. It didn't go on for long before my belt cut into my stomach taking my breath away.

I was being pulled up and off of Dalton. For a moment we were just the right distance apart to land a couple of solid blows that actually hurt. Then we were too far apart to do any more damage, but still angry as hell. I know I was. I stood up and rubbed my sore ribs. Dalton stood up and glared at me.

Sam held his arms out to keep us apart. "Don't you boys be

fighting over me, ya hear? It could mean serious trouble for me if you do, an' I don't want no trouble with your parents. No sir, I surely don't."

The three of us might have been there still if a fish hadn't jumped completely out of the river and landed flat on the surface, which sounded like someone getting their face slapped.

Sam rushed back to his crate to pick up his fishing pole. "I bet that fish was looking for my worm."

As he dropped his line back into in the river, he said, "You boys oughta get yourselves some poles. Ain't nothing like fishing to ease whatever's troubling ya."

I headed for Sam's shack to look for a pole. It was pitch black inside Sam's shack because the dim light outside couldn't get through the thick coating of grime on his windows. As I stood inside waiting for my eyes to adjust to the darkness, I heard something coming through the bushes. My mind went right to the half-breed wolves from the legend. I backed farther into the room and held my breath. When Dalton's silhouette appeared in the doorway I was almost glad to see him.

"Damn it's dark in here," he said, striking a match on the doorjamb.

Shadows played spookily around the room by the flickering light of his match. I felt bad for Sam living in such a crumby little shack, even if all he wanted was a place to keep dry when he wasn't outside fishing. All he had was a table with one chair, a small metal cot, and a bare light bulb hanging from the ceiling with a pull string. I pulled it just as the match burned Dalton's finger and he let out a curse.

I didn't see anything that looked like a kitchen, just an old board set across two fifty-five gallon drums. I figured the rusty metal basin on the planks was Sam's sink. For Sam, running water meant him running to the creek with a pail to get it.

Still standing in the doorway, Dalton said, "Sam's alright. I like him enough and all, but Sam and me, we gotta stay in our places, right where people put us, or there'll be hell to pay. And Sam and I are the ones who'll pay, not the likes of you.

101

I didn't have an answer. So I untangled the lines for two fishing poles and gave one to Dalton. Back at the clearing we got worms from Sam to bait our hooks. Dalton and I sat on opposite ends of the same log and lowered our lines into the river so the worms could dance for the fish.

Sam was right about fishing - staring at the little red and white bobber and willing it to signal a bite drained the anger out of me. But not Dalton; he pulled his hook out of the water to check the worm too often, scaring away any fish that might've taken an interest in it.

So I wasn't surprised when he stood up and announced he was leaving. After propping his pole on the log he hurried off down the path that led through the thicket past Sam's place and out toward the road.

Sam yelled after him. "It ain't friendly, you running off like that."

I thanked Sam and scrambled to catch up with Dalton because I didn't want to walk through 'Poor Town' alone after dark. I caught up with him just after he passed the broken-down old car. We walked back to where the road crossed the railroad tracks then followed the tracks. Even though we'd walked through the same woods before, this time they looked like the kind of place where the nasty things in my imagination lay in wait for unsuspecting kids. I kept a wary eye on the woods and so did Dalton.

We sat out on the porch when we got back to Dalton's house. When his parents went to bed a little after eleven, we went inside to look for a late night Monster Movie on television. We watched one about an evil doctor doing research on cadavers he bought from grave robbers. Of course, things went very badly for the doctor.

Dalton's mother had set up a cot for me in his bedroom. It was comfortable enough, and I would have slept well enough if it wasn't for the cars going by headed for "Poor Town." The drivers revved their engines because their tires spun in the sand when they came to the end of the pavement near Dalton's house.

And the headlights of the cars turning the corner by his house swept around the walls of his room. I could tell from Dalton's breathing that he had fallen asleep right away, which left me with nothing to do but think about the movie we'd seen.

Dalton's mother got us up early because, as she put it, "Your father has to work today. I already made him breakfast. You eat now if you want any."

After stuffing ourselves on scrambled eggs and biscuits with jam we went outside to wait for my mother to call. The air was still cool but the sun already felt hot by the time she called. It would be one of those days that road tar would melt and pop like bubble gum when I stepped on it, leaving sticky black spots on the soles of my sneakers.

My mother met Dalton for the first time that morning. I'm sure she knew from looking at him that he was older, and from the way he talked and dressed that he was from a tough neighborhood, but she didn't say anything to me about that. Even though she had always wanted to fit in with the high society types, I'd never known my mom to be mean to anyone just because they were poorer than us. Besides, she knew Donna and Dalton were the only friends I had in Tuscumbia.

In the car on the way home I asked Mother if there were any poor people back home.

She said, "Yes, but not as many as there are here."

I asked her why.

I knew from her sigh that I was doing what she called "trying her patience," but she answered me anyway. "Well, for one thing, Cornell University drives the economy back home."

Sometimes when grownups answer your questions you end up with more questions. "I sorta know what a conomy is," I told her, "but how do you drive one?"

She made a funny sound. I must have said something stupid. It made me glad Lisa wasn't around.

"The word is 'e-con-o-my,' Billy." She explained how Cornell paid my Dad, and how when we bought things in Ithaca, the money went to other people. She said there were lots more

103

people in Ithaca spending money than there were in Tuscumbia, and that's why there weren't as many poor people there.

I asked her why the poor people in Tuscumbia didn't move to Ithaca.

She made that sound again. "If too many poor people moved to Ithaca, there wouldn't be enough money there either. They'd just be poor there instead of here."

I gave up trying to figure it out and I bet my mother was glad.

Even though it wasn't quite summer yet, the next Friday afternoon was hot and muggy, and according to the radio we were in the path of a big thunderstorm. In all the excitement over the coming storm I forgot Mitch's warning about the bootleggers.

THELMA AND THE BOOTLEGGER'S WIFE

When Mother left to pick up Dad that afternoon she told Sis and me they'd be home in an hour and a half. After she left I sat outside on our front steps with the dog. Star wagged her tail and licked the side of my face while I scratched behind her ears. My face ended up slimy and smelling of dog food.

At the first clap of thunder Star began shaking, like she did the night we saw the big black dog in the field out back. Poor Star had always been terrified of storms, so I took her inside. After that, I sat outside by myself to watch the storm, following its progress by counting the seconds between the flashes and the thunder. Dark storm clouds had rolled in from the west changing the red-tinted, late-afternoon sunlight into an eerie yellow glow.

Pretty soon a refreshing gust of cool air blew past me, flipping the leaves in the trees over so their bellies showed. A minute or two later a stronger gust blew through which made the leaves flutter wildly, and sound as though the rain had already started, which it hadn't. But I could smell it. As the wind buffeted my hair, I watched few wispy, fast moving, low-hanging pieces of cloud blowing by.

I knew there'd be lightening soon when the hair on my

head stood up. And sure enough, a long, crooked, blindingly-white line flashed from the black cloud overhead down to the woods across the road. That was followed by a thunderclap so loud it made my ears ring.

Moments later I heard the first raindrops, big fat ones slamming into the earth, leaving little indentations in the dirt that looked like moon craters. Then I heard another noise in the distance. At first it sounded like a broom being dragged on a sidewalk, but as it came closer it sounded more and more like water gushing out of a bathtub faucet.

That's when Sis opened the door and yelled, "Get in here, Billy, before you get soaked."

She was right of course - I was about to get very wet. But I didn't like her telling me what to do, so I yelled back, "Who made you the boss?" If she wanted to be in charge I wasn't going to make it easy for her.

"Billy, if you don't get in here right this minute, I'm gonna tell on you."

I went inside because I knew she'd rat on me.

Lisa and I were going through the house closing windows to keep the rain out when the phone rang. After another threat from Sis I agreed to close the rest of the windows while she answered the phone. I ran through the house cranking windows as fast as I could then ran to the kitchen to find out who had called.

"That was Mom. She'll be late getting home. She got caught in the storm and took a wrong turn. She wants me to call Dad and tell him because she's out of quarters for the payphone."

When Sis got Dad on the phone I heard her tell him, "Mom just called. She got lost in the rain."

Dad must have asked Sis where Mom was.

"Somewhere in Tennessee."

I laughed out loud at the thought of Mom ending up in the wrong state. Of course, I found out later Tennessee was less than an hour from our house. Sis tried to poke me when I laughed, but she couldn't reach me because the phone cord was too short. I

106

stuck my tongue out at her.

With Mother in Tennessee, Dad would be stuck at work for a long time and that meant Lisa and I would be home alone for a long time. There was nothing to do but watch the storm raging outside, and the best view of the storm would be from our parents' bedroom window, so we flopped down on their bed to watch the lightening.

Star had followed us to our parents' bedroom with her ears laid back and her tail between her legs. Hoping we'd make the storm go away I suppose. Then to escape the thunder, she crawled under their bed, getting wedged under it so tightly she couldn't get out. The bed was too heavy for Sis and me to lift, which meant that Star would be stuck there until Dad got home.

Sis and I had left all of the house lights off so they wouldn't spoil the show outside. That turned out to be a mistake. By then it was raining so hard we had to yell to each other to be heard over the din, and there were so many lightning strikes it looked like that scene in "Godzilla" when the monster walked into a power line.

The wind whipped the bushes and field grass around like a woman's hair on a windy day. The rain came down so thick and hard it looked as though a thick fog had settled in. The lightening was so bright I could close my eyes and still see it, and it came so fast I couldn't match the flashes up with the thunder any more.

That's when I saw a woman frozen in mid-step outside our parents' window, lit up by an especially bright flash. When the lightening flashed again she was a lot closer. The phone rang then.

Lisa jumped up from the bed and yelled, "I'll get the phone; you lock the front door" then ran out of the room.

As I ran through the doorway from the hall into the living room I flipped the light switch on, but it didn't work. I tried the switch several more times before I gave up and rushed over to lock the door.

Sis came in to tell me that Thelma had called. "She's

bringing us a candle."

I saw a shape in the darkness near the driveway. It was too large to be. The next time lightening lit up the driveway I saw that it was actually two people. Their swaying and twisting looked like some kind of weird alien dance. But they were fighting. In the next bright flash I saw the Damon woman's face. Then she was running toward the field behind our house.

The other person slumped into a pile. Sis yelled, "No" then pushed me aside to open the door. She ran outside into the storm. I ran after her, getting soaked instantly. The pelting rain stung my face, making it hard to keep my eyes open. The body lying in the driveway was Thelma. Sis knelt down next to her. I knelt down on the other side of her.

I could barely hear Lisa over the roar of the storm when she yelled, "We have to get her in the house."

The two of us tried to pick Thelma up but couldn't. Sis yelled something about going inside to call for help. Then she was gone and I was alone in a frightening world, one where bad things happened to nice people.

After what seemed like an eternity, Sis came back out and bent down to yell in my ear. "Our phone doesn't work. I'm going to Thelma's to try theirs." Then she was gone and I was alone with Thelma and my fears again.

Headlights came up the driveway before Sis came back. I was so glad I wouldn't be alone anymore I didn't care who it was. But then the car slid toward us on the loose driveway gravel and I thought for sure it would run over us. When the bumper stopped just feet from us I recognized the Fords' car. Lisa joined us about the time Mitch knelt down next to me.

He yelled something. I missed some of the words because of the pounding rain and nearly continuous thunder, but when he pointed at Thelma then the car, I knew he wanted us to help him carry Thelma to it. When we had Thelma lying on the back seat he pushed us into the backseat with her.

He yelled for us to tear off a piece of her dress and press it down on the place where she was bleeding. I used my teeth to tear her dress. Sis took the scrap of cloth away from me and pressed it against Mrs. Ford's stomach, which was fine with me because I did not want to do that.

It seemed like a terribly long ride to the hospital, and then we had to wait in the car with Thelma while Mitch went inside to find help. He came out with two men in white uniforms who carried Thelma into the hospital on a stretcher. Sis and I sat in the waiting room with Mitch. He didn't say a thing when we told him what we'd seen.

I think an hour went by before a doctor came out to tell him Thelma would be okay. I'm sure Mitch wanted to stay there, but he drove us home and sat at our kitchen table with us while we waited for Mom or Dad to get home.

When we saw headlights in the carport Mitch ran out the door and left for the hospital. Dad had gotten a ride home from one of the men he worked with at TVA. We told him the same things we had told Mitch while we helped him get Star out from under the bed. Poor thing made a mad dash for her water bowl in the kitchen.

See her dog food bowl reminded me I was hungry and I let both Sis and Dad know it. Sis made a face at me, but then she and Dad helped me finish off the crackers and cheese she found. Mom got back much later, after Sis and I had gone to bed.

Mitch brought Thelma home the next day with stitches in her stomach. The doctor told her to stay in bed for a few days, so my mother made dinner for the Fords and had me take it to them. While I was waiting for Mitch to answer his door, the Sheriff's car came up the driveway and stopped near our house. After I set the Ford's dinners on their front porch and knocked on their door, I ran for home to see what he wanted.

I was already in flight when Mitch opened the door and yelled, "Thank you," at me.

I yelled, "Yes, sir" over my shoulder without missing a step. I got to our kitchen just as the Sheriff was sitting down at the table. Mother put a cup of coffee and a little pitcher of cream in front of him. He took his hat off and set it down on the table very carefully, as though it had to be placed just so. Then he sat there stern-faced, the way my dad usually did.

He didn't put any cream or sugar in his coffee, but he stirred it anyway, and as he stirred it he told Mom, "Mrs. Ford said it was the Damon woman who stabbed her. I stopped by to tell y'all that we picked her up last night. I'll stop next door to let the Fords know."

He didn't have to tell me it was the Damon woman who stabbed Thelma, or that she lived down the road, or that she was married to the guy who made bootleg whiskey and left stolen cars in our driveway.

My mother asked the sheriff why Mrs. Damon would want to hurt Thelma.

He picked up his hat, turning it slowly, studying it as he answered her. "Mrs. Damon told me she came here looking for something to steal. Said she thought no one was home because all the lights were off."

Mother was over at the sink and had gone back to washing dishes. I think she needed to keep busy. After the sheriff put his hat back down on the table he sipped his coffee then told Mom, "I don't think she meant to hurt anybody. She said Mrs. Ford surprised her and she panicked."

He tipped his coffee cup slightly and glanced inside, as though he didn't know what else to say and hoped to find the answer in there. Then he made the mistake of saying, "I think things just got out of hand after that."

When Mother heard that she slammed a pot down on the counter so hard the noise made me jump. Then she spun around to face the sheriff. I think he'd made her as mad as I ever had, so mad her voice quivered a little. "What if it had been one of my kids instead of Thelma?"

When he said, "But it wasn't," Mom yanked off her apron and threw it on the counter, telling him, "That's not good enough, Sheriff."

I saw the red in her eyes before she spun around to face out the window again, and I knew she was about cry.

110

The sheriff's next question was for me. "You weren't scared, were ya, young fella?"

"Oh, yes, sir," I said, "I sure was."

I suppose it was the wrong answer because he stirred his coffee and ignored me after that. Standing with her back to us staring out the window, as though there was something terribly interesting out there, Mother used her sleeve to wipe something from her face, tears most likely.

The sheriff stood up and put his hat on then adjusted the brim. All he said before he left was, "Ma'am."

While I waited for sleep that night I wondered how the Damon kids ended up with a Mom who could do what she did to Thelma. I asked Lisa because I figured all those books she read would've made her really smart.

I heard a moan across the room in the dark, then, "Why do you always bother me just when I'm falling asleep?"

"Don't know the answer, do ya, Miss Smarty-pants?"

She told me it was a stupid question and threatened to call Mom. I rolled over and tried to sleep but couldn't. All of the things I'd seen and didn't like and couldn't change since I'd arrived in Tuscumbia came to me in a mixed up, out-of-order jumble, and they came back over and over until I was so tired that nothing, not even seeing the big monster dog next to my bed could've kept me awake.

"THE BOOTLEGGER'S HOUSE IS ON FIRE."

The next evening as it was getting dark, I sat outdoors with Star, listening to a cicada calling for a mate while I slapped at the mosquitoes trying to make a meal out of me. When Star sat up suddenly and looked toward the Damon place with her eyes and ears on full alert, I knew she'd heard or smelled something that wasn't right. Then I heard a pop and glass breaking. And I saw light flickering off the clouds and knew something was wrong. So I tied Star's rope to the doorknob then ran into the field toward the Damon place, while Star barked up a storm.

When I got to the Damons' clearing I saw flames climbing up the siding on the front of their house. I heard talking and turned to see two men standing on the side of the road next to a pickup truck with a Confederate flag painted on the door. One of them pointed at me and said something. The other one ran toward me. I didn't wait around to see what he wanted. Ducking back into the field grass. I ran flat-out all the way home. I couldn't have run any faster even if that black half-breed wolf had been chasing me.

Running past Star, ignoring her crazed barking, I jumped the front steps and burst into the house yelling, "Mom, Dad, the bootlegger's house is on fire."

While running through the house yelling for my parents I crashed into Dad in the kitchen. He put his hands on my shoulders to stop me then scolded me for running in the house.

"But Dad," I said, "the bootlegger's house is on fire."

After stepping out into the carport to see for himself, Dad told me to go tell Mother, then he called the fire department. I found her in our bedroom helping Lisa with her math homework. When she had finished scolded me for interrupting, I told her about the fire.

After muttering, "Oh, dear Lord" she told me, "Stay in the house, Buster, or your bottom will be so sore you won't be able to sit for a week."

Sis and I went outside and stood by the carport swatting mosquitoes while we watched towering yellow flames in a column of swirling black smoke rise up to join the black cloud hovering over the valley. Sis asked me how the fire had started. I shrugged my shoulders but her question made me wonder about the two men I'd seen and the strange noises I'd heard.

I was wondering about them as I watched my parents' car speed down the driveway. Missing out on all the excitement was such a big disappointment, I didn't care how much trouble I'd be in for going to the Damon place.

After yelling, "You're really gonna get it this time, Billy," Lisa followed me into the tall grass.

The first thing I noticed when we stepped into the clearing around the burning house was the heat from the fire. Then I noticed Mom and Dad standing with the two Damon girls. I didn't think they'd seen me because Sis and I had come out of the field behind them. But one of the firemen saw us and looked our way. Dad must have seen the look of surprise on the fireman's face because he turned around. I guess Mom saw Dad turning around because she turned around too. I was sure my goose was cooked, but as long as I was in trouble anyway, I joined them to get a better view of the fire.

Mom had her arm around the older Damon girl. The younger girl had a wad of her sister's dress in one hand and her

113

teddy bear dangling by his tail from the other. I stood next to her. Sis stood behind us. My dad stood a little off to the side with his arms folded across his chest, cool and calm in spite of the commotion all around him. I wondered where the Damon girls' parents were. If we hadn't been there the girls would've been alone. A crowd of people had gathered but they had all stayed out near the road to watch.

The siding and roof of the house had burned away or fallen in, leaving a skeleton of blackened timbers standing over a pile of charred rubble that gave off a nasty-smelling dark smoke. The flames I'd seen high in the night sky had died down to an occasional flame that would burst to life on one of the timbers, scurry along it for a few feet then flicker out and reappear somewhere else.

The timber frame collapsed suddenly sending a blast of sparks skyward that looked like a thousand fireflies gone mad. The little Damon girl shrieked and backed away from the fire, letting go of her sister's dress when that happened. When she grabbed my hand I figured that the burst of flames had frightened her and she'd let go it in a moment, but she squeezed my hand and held on. Mother must have heard the girl's scream because she looked our way. She smiled at me. She could be a real mystery.

The people watching from the road began to leave then because there was nothing left of the fire but a foul-smelling smoke billowing out of the ashes that made my eyes sting. I heard a siren in the distance and looked for the sheriff's car. I saw his flashing light reflected in the tree limbs above the road coming our way. While I waited for him I watched the four firemen scrambling through the fields around the clearing to put out brush fires started by embers that rose into the sky then drifted back down into the dry field grass.

A flashing red light announced the arrival of the sheriff. He left his car by the road with the light flashing and walked over to us. He asked my parents what had happened. Mother told him that I was the one who had alerted them to the fire. He stared at me so long I began to wonder if he thought the fire was my doing.

Then he told my parents that he'd take the girls to a shelter. "They'll look after the girls until we locate their folks."

When the little Damon girl heard him say that she put her arms around my waist. Her sister pried her arms loose and picked her up. In spite of her big sister's promises that everything would be okay, she cried, the tears leaving lines through the soot on her cheeks. The sheriff led the girls to his car, the older girl carrying her sister, the little one looking back over her sister's shoulder, with her teddy bear dangling from her hand.

On the short ride home in the car, I asked my mother if she knew the little girl's name. I had to ask her twice because she was in one of her dreamy distracted states.

"Nettie, I think."

I told her it was a funny name. She told me it was an old country name, one she hadn't heard since she was a little girl.

Sis asked Dad why the firemen didn't try to save the Damons' house.

"By the time they got there it was too late to save the house. They did the right thing preventing a grass fire."

She asked why.

"Grass fires spread quickly in dry fields like the ones around our house. One ember caught on the wind could've started a wildfire that burned everything in the valley, including our house and the Ford's."

As we were getting out of the car I told my parents about the two men I'd seen. Mother told me to go brush my teeth and get ready for bed.

"But Mom," I said, "one of them chased me."

Dad ruffled my hair before I could duck away. "You do as your mother says. And get that imagination of yours under control before it gets you in trouble."

I took Star out so she could do her business, then got ready for bed. Lying in bed I wondered how I could get my parents

115

to believe me about the two guys I'd seen at the Damon place. It wasn't the last time I would see that truck, and it wasn't my imagination that would get me in trouble.

But that night I had something else to worry about; Mrs. Madison had invited my mother to her house for a visit the next day, and the two of them had arranged for me to ride home with Donna after school. And Lisa was going to her friend's house in Tuscumbia after school. That way Mother could spend the whole afternoon with Mrs. Madison and pick Sis up on the way to get Dad. And I'd have all day to look forward to seeing Donna, and all day to worry about what I'd say to her.

The thought of seeing Donna kept me distracted all through school the next day. I wanted to tell her I liked her but was afraid to say the words. And I wanted to be with her but could never be comfortable around such a pretty girl.

When school ended I got dragged outside by the usual mob of kids pushing and shoving their way out of the building. Somehow Donna beat me outside. I found her leaning against her parents' big black Chrysler New Yorker. One of the Madisons' hired men, dressed in a fancy black uniform with gray trim, stood next to the car as stiff and poker-faced as the sheriff had been.

When Donna saw me she cleared her throat the way people do when they expect someone to do something for them and they're getting impatient. The man in the uniform opened the back door of the car for her. She stood to the side to let me get in first. I slid all the way across the seat to the door on the other side. She slid across the seat, sitting so close to me our legs were touching. With the smell of her perfume filling the car and her leg pressed against mine I wanted the ride to last forever. But trapped in a car with a girl I knew would expect things of me, and knowing I would disappoint her, I wished I was down at the creek looking for salamanders.

A few minutes later, standing in the Madisons' huge entryway, I saw our mothers sitting on the couch in the south parlor, so excited about something they were both talking at the same time. I couldn't understand how anyone could do that, but they weren't even breaking a sweat.

Mr. Madison sat across the room as stiff as a statue watching them. He reminded me of the way the emperor guy sits on his throne in that movie, "The King and I," one of Mom's favorites. The night they showed that on the Saturday night TV movie I went to bed early.

Donna took my hand and led me into the parlor opposite the one where our mothers were. We sat together on a couch with fancy carvings that looked as though it came out of an old movie, except that it wasn't old at all. Donna didn't sit as close to me as we'd been in the back of the Chrysler. I listened to her ramble on about dances and parties.

Then she told me who was "respected" in Tuscumbia and who was not, and why. That people cared about stuff like that made no sense to me whatsoever. And Donna knew gossipy stuff about some of them. Then she leaned toward me until our bodies touched and I felt her hot breath on my ear, and she'd whisper their secrets to me.

She told me about some silly garden party next. I tried to act interested but she went on about it for so long I got bored. When she caught me daydreaming she asked me who Trevor Hamilton was. I shrugged my shoulders. I had no idea.

"I just told you." She sounded mad.

The only thing between us after that was an awkward silence. I didn't think I could be more uncomfortable until her brother, Peter, strutted into the room all puffed up like a bully looking for trouble and sat down across from us. Donna told him to go away. He sneered at her and shook his head.

Donna stood up, said, "You two deserve each other" then left the room.

I asked Peter when they were going still smashing again.

"You want to go again?"

I nodded my head.

"Maybe you're not so bad after all."

He walked to the parlor across the hall. I would've waited

117

quietly by the door until my mother asked me what I wanted, but Peter walked right in and interrupted his mother. "Billy wants to go still-smashing again."

I knew my mother would say, "No," right off because of the dead man we found the last time we went, but I hoped Mrs. Madison could change her mind. I walked to the doorway so I could hear them better.

Before Mrs. Madison had a chance to say anything Mr. Madison told his wife in a loud, angry-sounding voice, "I want a word with you in private."

When Mrs. Madison asked, "Can't it wait?" he said, "No."

I watched Mrs. Madison follow her husband through the entrance hall then up the big curved staircase. Soon I heard them arguing somewhere upstairs but couldn't hear what they were saying.

Peter went someplace and Donna hadn't come back and I needed a bathroom. In a house as big as the Madisons' there had to be one downstairs, but I only knew about the one upstairs; the one us kids were told to use the night of the dinner party. I didn't want to go upstairs where the Madisons were arguing, but was afraid I'd wet myself if I didn't get to a bathroom, and quick.

Mother asked me where I was going. I explained my predicament. She said to hurry. I rushed up the stairs then half-ran, half-walked toward the bathroom at the end of the hall. I tried to be as quiet as a mouse. But just as I passed the only room in the hallway with the door closed the floor squeaked. I panicked and froze, standing very still. I figured Mr. Madison would be angry if he found me there, would think I was spying on them.

From the room I heard an angry-sounding Mrs. Madison say, "You brought me all the way up here to tell me that?"

When I heard hard-soled shoes on a wood floor that seemed to go back and forth I figured it had to be Mr. Madison pacing. I heard him say, "Stay out of those woods."

"Why should I?"

"Because I told you to. That's all you need to know."

118

It was quiet for a moment. Mrs. Madison gasped then said, "My God, you're mixed up in the bootlegging, aren't you?"

I heard more pacing after that and I heard Mr. Madison tell his wife, "It has always amused me that people think you're a good little Christian soldier, when you're really just a drunk who finds amusement in destroying the source of her own whiskey."

Mrs. Madison's voice sounded feeble and shaky, the way my mother's did when she was about to cry. "Do you know why I drink?"

She answered her own question. "Because I hate my life. I drink to escape. As for the parties and the still smashing, that's just a façade I put on to fool people."

That's when the pacing stopped. "The way you reek of booze, you're not fooling anyone. Your so-called friends don't say anything to you about it because they're afraid they won't be invited to any more of your parties if they do."

She asked him about the dead man, accused him of knowing about it.

"Stay out of those woods or you'll regret it."

Someone grabbed my arm from behind. I nearly screamed, and would have if whoever it was hadn't clamped a hand over my mouth. A girl whispered the word, "Quiet," in my ear then turned me around to face her.

A young girl in a maid's uniform touched a finger to her lips to silence me then pulled me by the arm into a nearby room. She closed the door behind us and asked me what I was doing there. I told her I had to pee.

She rolled her eyes at me. "We'll be in a mountain of trouble if the Madisons find out we heard them arguing. So you gotta stay here with me until they go downstairs."

She had no idea how badly I needed to pee, and knowing I couldn't made me need pee to all the more. She opened the door a crack and listened. I did the "I-need-to-pee" dance. It didn't help.

Mrs. Madison said, "When you proposed to me you promised me we'd be in the governor's social circle in no time, like cream rising to the top of a milk bottle. Isn't that the way

119

you put it? Thought you were clever didn't you; you and your silly-ass metaphors? Well here I am, fifteen years later, stuck in this godforsaken little backwater."

I heard Mr. Madison pacing again, heard him tell his wife, "Have you got any idea what it's like being married to a drunk?"

"Do you have any idea what it's like being married to a failure?"

"I would've been elected to the senate, but word got around that I had a lush for a wife."

I heard Mrs. Madison's voice crack as she said, "I may have a drinking problem, but I come from good southern stock."

He laughed at that then said, "Yeah, and you were born with a name that gave you privileges you haven't earned."

He didn't laugh at what she said next. "Your mother thought that having your Daddy's kid would make her respectable. But it didn't, and nothing you do will ever change that."

He yelled, "You ungrateful bitch. You're living in the house my great grandfather built with hard work and sweat. Something you wouldn't know anything about."

"Well you're low-born scum just like your mother."

"And you don't do anything but spend my money and drink yourself stupid."

"I raised our kids and you never once lifted a finger to help."

"Tell me again what you did," he said, "because I seem to remember paying for their nanny, and for the maids who fed them and changed them and cleaned up after them.

I heard a noise that sounded like someone being slapped. I figured it was Mrs. Madison slapping her husband. Right after that I heard something shatter. It sounded like the time I knocked into one of mom's little porcelain statue things and it fell on the floor.

After that I heard Mr. Madison's boots on the hallway floor then on the stairs. He slammed the front door so soon after Mrs. Madison slammed the bedroom door it sounded like an echo.

The maid put her finger to her lips and checked the hallway then told me, "Stay here and count to a hundred before you leave."

I told her I couldn't hold it that long.

"You gotta, 'cause if they see us together it'll be really bad. And don't you dare tell anyone what you heard or that I talked to you."

She put her hands on my shoulders and bent down so her face was only a couple of inches from mine. "Promise you won't say a word about this to anyone."

I nodded my head.

"No, you gotta say it."

"Okay, okay, I promise I won't tell."

MORE TROUBLE WITH DONNA

The maid peeked into the hallway again then left. As soon as she was out of sight I rushed to the bathroom and relieved myself so I could think clearly. Then I counted most of the way to fifty before going downstairs.

My mother was waiting for me in the entrance hall and she looked mad. "What on earth took you so long?"

I told her I got lost but I could tell she didn't believe me.

She told me to say good bye to Donna. "And hurry or we'll be late to pick up your father."

I told her Donna had gone and I didn't know where.

Donna appeared in the doorway at the back of the entrance hall and said, "I'm right here, silly."

She walked over to me and gave me a kiss on the cheek right in front of my mother. I figured she must really like me. But instead of making me happy it embarrassed me. I hated being so shy, hated that I could never think of anything clever to say to a girl. And it seemed that the more I liked a girl the more trouble I had talking to her.

That night during supper Mother announced that, "Mrs. Madison arranged a luncheon for me so I can meet the rest of her friends."

She went on at great length about who would be there.

Dad sat there with a kind of blank stare the whole time. Mother didn't seem to care that he didn't care; she had that far-away look on her face again. I thought she was going to talk about her silly luncheon forever.

I interrupted her in spite of the danger because I needed to ask her a question. "Will I have to wear my suit again?"

Dad told me to apologize for interrupting.

"Sorry, Mom, but do I?"

"Oh, you kids won't be going this time. I do hope you aren't too disappointed."

You'd think my mother would know me better than that after ten years. I never, ever, wanted to go to a grownup party again. And I didn't think Dad wanted to go either. And if Sis was disappointed I couldn't tell by looking at her. But then Mother promised to make it up to us by doing something together on Saturday, which sounded only slightly better than going to a party at the Madisons'.

She asked Dad if he was working Saturday. He asked her why.

"A real stern-wheel riverboat called the Delta Queen will be in Florence on Saturday. I think the kids would enjoy seeing it."

We never did stuff like that. "Please, Dad, can we?"

That got a smile from Mom. "Sounds like Billy wants to go."

"You bet."

Dad said we were going. Sis groaned and rolled her eyes.

The next day at lunch in the cafeteria I saw Dalton going through the hot-food lunch line, which was always the slowest line. We always sat together for lunch. I would see Donna there most days but she usually sat across the room with the other rich kids. But that day she headed toward my table while Dalton was stuck in the slow line. She looked really cute wearing a blue dress, with her long wavy hair bouncing lightly on her shoulders. I wasn't the only kid who stopped eating to watch her. They looked away when she looked around the room. Then she

123

sat down next to me, which both scared and thrilled me.

The only thing on her tray was a small plate salad. I asked her why.

"I watch my figure."

She caught me looking at her figure. I blushed.

She smiled, said, "And that's why I watch my figure."

I hoped that meant she liked me, but it also made my face feel as warm as the macaroni and cheese on my plate. That was the day's hot lunch, one of my all-time favorites. But I couldn't eat it after Donna sat down because I was afraid of getting a stain on my shirt the way I had at her mom's dinner party.

After fussing with her hair she suddenly stared right at me, so fiercely and steadily I thought I'd done something wrong. "You know," she said, "if you ever skip afternoon church services again like you did last Sunday, I won't sit with you ever again. I simply can't be seen with someone of such low moral standards."

I looked at the macaroni and cheese on my plate. Making church a requirement to sit with me, and probably to like me too, made me so anxious my palms got sweaty. I wanted to tell her that I hated church. She'd find out eventually, and I wouldn't be comfortable living with the lie until she did. But first, I wanted to say something so clever she'd like me even after she found out I hated going to church.

I was still studying my food when I spotted Dalton coming our way. I'd forgotten about him. I should've been getting ready for trouble because I knew Donna didn't like him. But it still surprised me when she lit into him, so loudly that the kids at the next table stopped what they were doing to look at us,

He was standing there holding his tray when Donna told him, "They can make me go to school with white trash like you, but they can't make me sit with you."

Dalton asked me if I was going to sit with her. I struggled mightily to think of something to say, but nothing came to me before Donna said to him, "I guess you're too stupid to know you're not wanted."

He walked away.

"Good riddance," Donna said, adding, "To bad rubbish."

Mad at her for being mean, and disappointed in myself for not stopping her, I finally got up the courage to tell her, "That wasn't nice."

Making a big show of it by standing up then sticking her chin out, she said, "And I thought you were smarter than that."

"Well I'm not," I said, letting out my anger and frustration. Then I realized how stupid it must've sounded to the kids nearby, and I blushed big time.

"Well, Billy, you need to decide who you want as friends before it's too late." She stormed off after that.

That night, waiting to escape into sleep and hoping it would come soon, I tried to think of a way to get my friends back. Sure, Donna had been a real meanie to Dalton, but I wanted to see her again. I couldn't explain why. I just did, really did. And without Dalton I wouldn't have a friend to do things with or someone to keep the bullies away. I tried to think of a way to make them like each other. That was a huge waste of time.

The next Saturday morning, one of the last authentic stern-wheel riverboats in the country docked on the Tennessee River near where my dad worked in Florence. In spite of my sister's protests Mother got us all up and out the door early to go see it. It was a perfect day for an adventure; warm and sunny with a breeze blowing clouds that looked like big globs of shaving cream across the sky.

We stopped for breakfast at Morey's Diner, across the street from the town square in Tuscumbia. Mother chose a booth by the front window that had a view of the courthouse lawn across the street. There wasn't much to see outside, but across the room on the counter I spotted a large plate with doughnuts piled on it. My poor stomach growled at the sight.

I was about to beg for one when Mom pointed across the street and said, "They're flying a Confederate flag above the American flag at the Courthouse."

Dad looked at the flags but didn't say anything. Sis didn't

even look up. She was lost in the book she'd brought with her. I glanced at the flags. The Confederate flag looked just like the flag I'd seen on the door of the truck at the Damon place the night it burned down. I almost said something to Mom about it but didn't want to risk getting into an argument with her before I asked for a doughnut.

I checked out the rest of the place. Across the room I saw a hallway that went back to the kitchen. A sign that read, "Men," reminded me that I had to pee.

As I stood up, Mother reached across the table and grabbed my arm. "And just where do you think you're going?"

When I told her I needed to pee, she whispered, "Make sure you read the signs so you don't use the wrong bathroom."

I tried to leave but she had my arm in a vise grip. Eying me suspiciously she asked, "Did you hear me, Buster?"

I said, "Yes, ma'am."

She told Dad to go with me anyway. Unfortunately, she said it loud enough that the people at the next table heard her, and they saw me blush. Dad made sure I went in the door under the "whites only" sign on. He was back at the booth talking with Mother when I came out.

In a room at the far end of the hallway I heard a man talking who sounded a lot like Sam. So I checked to be sure my parents weren't looking then hurried to the end of the hallway to see if it was him. It wasn't. But now I was standing in a room that smelled from years of people cooking greasy food there. And judging from the dingy, grimy look of the walls and curtains the place hadn't had a good cleaning in years, especially the wall near the big exhaust fan.

The tables had mismatched silverware set out haphazardly on dingy tablecloths. The curtains on the back door window, the only window, were so faded the original colors were unrecognizable.

When I didn't hear anyone eating, just the sloshing and clunking sounds of someone washing dishes in the back, I realized I was the only white person in the room and that everyone in there had stopped eating to watch me, as though they expected me to say something. I left in a hurry.

"What'd I tell you?" Mother demanded when I got back to the booth.

Sis looked up from her book and chanted, "Billy is in trouble," until Dad gave her a warning look.

Mother didn't really expect an answer. Whenever she scolded me, she started by reminding me of the thing I'd done that she'd told me not to do. I might have gotten the complete lecture if the waitress hadn't come to our booth then. She took our orders from oldest to youngest, which meant she asked me what I wanted last.

When it was my turn the waitress smiled at me and said, "And what'll you have, darlin'?"

The way she said the word "darling," it sounded like "marlin," but it didn't matter because she seemed really nice – some lucky kid's grandmother. I didn't think Mom would embarrass me in front of the nice waitress so I asked for a doughnut. I was wrong. Mom told the waitress I'd have the breakfast special. Disappointed as I was for not getting a doughnut, we'd be leaving for the riverboat soon, which almost made up for it.

On our way back to the car after breakfast Dad stopped to read a flyer nailed to a telephone pole. We all crowded around him to look at it. The first line read, "Join us for the Civil War Centennial as we celebrate the defeat of the Union Army by Stonewall Jackson and Joe Johnston at the First Battle of Bull Run."

The next two lines were, "Grow a beard to show your support for the South," and, "Any male over the age of eighteen caught on the commons without a beard will be fined ten dollars."

I asked Dad what it meant.

"A centennial represents one hundred years. It's like having a one-hundredth birthday. The battle of Bull Run was fought one hundred years ago this summer and it was a big

127

victory for the South.

Lisa said, "It's just some stupid history stuff," before she went on ahead to the car with Mom.

"But, Dad, I thought the North won the war."

"They did, but for the first couple of years the South was winning."

When Dad and I got in the car Mom grinned at him. Then she nudged him with her elbow and asked, "Are you going to grow a beard?"

He shook his head. "I think I'll avoid the commons for a while."

We drove through Muscle Shoals on the way to Florence, the same way Mom took Dad to work. Before we even got near the docks, I saw the smokestacks of the riverboat towering above the buildings along the riverfront. The biggest boat I'd ever seen, it looked like one I'd seen in a history book. It must have been three stories tall and almost a block long, with a paddle wheel on the back as big as our house.

Standing on the dock waiting to buy our tickets, with a flock of screeching seagulls flying in circles over the boat, I listened to and felt the low chugging of the boat's engines. I told Lisa the engines must be huge, and. "I hope we get to see them."

She rolled her eyes, said, "I hope we don't" then asked Dad if we could go home soon.

Dad told her to be patient. I called her a spoilsport. Dad told us to be quiet. During the tour he asked our guide questions about the boat while Mother talked with the other women and smiled a lot.

We did see the engine room. One look at the huge engines with all the shiny brass dials was all it took - I wanted to work on a riverboat when I grew up.

When we got home Mother told me to play outside. But it was much too hot to be out in the sun, so I looked for something else to do. I spotted Mitch rocking on his porch and went to join him, sitting in the rocker next to him. I put my feet up and pushed on the railing to get my chair rocking.

"And to what do I owe the pleasure of this visit?" he asked.

I shrugged my shoulders and lied – I told him I didn't know. I wanted to ask him what I should do about Donna and Dalton, but then I'd have to tell him I liked Donna, and I wasn't sure I wanted to do that. I'd never talked to anyone about a girl before.

"Well, Billy, you do look like you have a question."

Ashamed to admit that I'd let Dalton down, I looked at my feet and nodded my head.

"Well, out with it," he said.

"Donna Madison said some mean things to my friend Dalton and now he's not my friend anymore."

"So you were there?"

"Yes, sir, I was."

Mitch lifted his cap by the brim and scratched his head. "And you let it happen, is that the problem?"

"Yes, sir."

After a short silence he asked, "And if he did that to you, how would you feel?"

"Pretty bad, I guess."

"What do you think you should do about it?"

I knew I was supposed to say, "Tell him I'm sorry," but I didn't think it would solve my problem because Dalton and Donna would still hate each other. I told him I still liked Donna even though she was mean to Dalton."

He stood up slowly, stretching out to his full height, making a face as though doing that hurt. "I reckon we're gonna need Thelma's help for that," he said then went inside.

When Mitch came back out Thelma came with him, wiping her hands on her apron. She tucked a loose strand of hair behind her ear. Mitch told me to sit on the stairs so Thelma could have the other rocker.

When she was settled he told her, "Billy here likes that Madison girl, but she was mean to his friend, and he doesn't know what to do about her. Is that about right, Billy?"

I nodded my head. "Yes, sir, that's about it."

"Oh my," she said, as she pressed the wrinkles out of the apron on her lap with her hands, "you do have a problem."

I asked her if I should stop liking Donna.

Her answer didn't help. "You can't just decide not to like somebody, Billy; that's not how it works. But I have a feeling that after a while you won't like her as much, and one day you'll wonder why you ever liked her at all."

Mitch told her just what I was thinking. "I don't reckon that's much help to the boy right now."

"Well, I'm sorry, Billy," she said, standing up, "but this is something we can't fix for you."

She went inside and came back out a few minutes later with iced teas for Mitch and me. The tea was cold enough but not nearly sweet enough, so I sipped it while I thought about what she'd said.

This time when Thelma sat in the rocker she let her head fall back against the top of the chair back and closed her eyes. The slow, rhythmic creaking of their rockers was all I heard until a cardinal, as red as fresh blood, landed on a branch in the trees next to the porch and began to chirp.

A question popped into my head from the last time I talked to Mitch. "Is Donna mean 'cause she's rich?"

He shook his head. "I reckon the Madisons are troubled because they know what's coming and it scares them."

I asked him what was coming.

"Did you hear about the dam that broke last year?"

I shook my head "no."

"It was the Wilson Dam on the Tennessee River, near where your dad works. We had a lot of rain last year and all that water was too much for that old dam, so it broke."

I asked him what that had to do with Donna and Dalton.

He got up and stood next to the railing. Before he answered me he took out a small jackknife. Then, holding the pipe out over the railing, he scraped the burnt ashes out of the pipe bowl. "Nothin', not directly anyway. It's about the water, see? As the water builds up, it pushes on every part of the dam all at once, and it doesn't stop pushing until it finds a weak spot. You can't predict when it's gonna break, but you know it's only a matter of time."

I started to say something but he held his hand up. "There's changes coming Billy, and people like the Madisons are trying to hold them back, just like that dam trying to hold back all that water. Someday those changes are gonna find a weak spot, and when that happens, folks like the Madisons are gonna have a hard time of it."

As Mitch put his jackknife away Thelma told him, "I think that's enough for him to think about." She was right; it was plenty for me to think about, so I went home and left them to their rocking.

I did some chores and still had plenty of time left to be lazy. And plenty of time to think about Donna and Dalton, but I didn't. I spent the rest of the day playing with the dog and chasing butterflies without a net then lying in the grass looking for things in the clouds.

Late that night, lying in bed in the dark, I thought about the Damons and how poor they were. I asked Lisa how they got that way.

"How would I know?"

"Do you think they did something wrong?" I wanted to know so we wouldn't do the same thing and end up like them.

"Forget about them."

"Why?"

"Because they're bad people."

That did it. Now I was mad. "Are not."

"Oh yeah, then why'd their mother stab Thelma?"

"The kids are okay."

"They're so bad their own mother ran away and left them behind when she got out of jail. What about that, Mr. Smarty-pants?"

I chanted, "Liar, liar, pants on fire," to make her shut up because I didn't want it to be true.

When I stopped she said, "Ask Mom if you don't believe

131

me. I heard her telling Dad about it."

I told her it didn't matter.

"Does too, because they'll put your girlfriend in an orphanage if she doesn't have a Mom."

"Nettie's not my girlfriend."

Lisa made kissing sounds.

When she stopped, I asked her, "So what if they do put her in an orphanage?"

"You never even heard of Charles Dickens, did you?"

"Who?"

THE BULLY

She was right of course - I'd never heard of Charles Dickens, and she couldn't wait to tell me all about him. "He wrote a famous book about a kid named 'Oliver Twist' who was put in an orphanage."

I told her I didn't care, but she told me about the book anyway.

"All they gave the kids to eat was a bowl of gruel, which is kind of like oatmeal only really watery, so Oliver kept getting skinnier because he was starving. Then one day when some other orphans tricked him into asking for a second helping, the nasty men running the place beat him with a cane and locked him away in a scary dark room for a week."

I told her the book was stupid.

She told me I was stupid.

When I said, "Not as dumb as you," Lisa yelled, "Mom, Billy's being mean."

From our parents' bedroom down the hall Dad yelled, "If you're not asleep in five minutes, I'm coming in there," which didn't make sense because he wouldn't know if we were asleep without coming to our room to check, but I wasn't stupid enough to tell him that.

I rolled over and thought about the school year ending soon, which should have cheered me up, but with Dalton mad at me I'd be on my own at school and the bullies would make trouble for me as soon as they realized it.

At lunch the next day I took my tray to the far end of the cafeteria looking for an empty table near the windows. It was raining so hard raindrops bounced off the sidewalk along Cave Street, which meant the cafeteria was more crowded than usual.

I saw Nettie sitting by herself at the end of a mostly-empty table, swinging her little legs under her chair while she watched something in the school yard. I guessed that the rain had driven her inside, because I'd never seen her in the cafeteria before.

She smiled at me when I sat down next to her then went back to looking out the window. Her poor beat up teddy bear, which lay on the table in front of her, was the color of milk chocolate, with big fuzzy ears, black button eyes, a pointy little black-leather nose, and a puffy round belly.

A paper bag as wrinkled as my great grandmother's face was lying on the table next to it. The peanut butter and jelly sandwich on it had two small bites missing. I didn't blame her for not eating the rest of it; the soggy-looking bread was flattened and had turned blue from the jelly. I still had a little money left over from my allowance, which I dug out of my pocket and put on the table in front of her.

She smiled at me again when she heard the coins drop on the table. Then she pointed outside and said, "Poor Mr. Birdie's getting wet."

I smiled. She went back to watching the robin.

Just after that I heard a boy say, "I bet you a quarter I can hit that white-trash from here," and turned around to see who it was.

The hot lunch that day was meatloaf with chocolate pudding so most of the kids ate their desert first. But two older boys sitting several tables away had found another use for the pudding; they were flinging it at unsuspecting kids with their spoons.

A mean kid named Craig, one of the bullies Dalton had told me about, flipped a spoonful of it at Nettie. When it hit her, she pulled her head down into her shirt collar and looked back over her shoulder, as though she expected to be hit again. A glob of it had landed in her hair. Another glob had landed on the back of her dress.

Nettie tried without much luck to get the pudding out of her hair with her fingers then wiped them on her dress. I told her to hold still while I wiped the pudding off the back of her dress with my napkin. I got a big gob of it off but smeared the rest into a big dark stain.

When I heard the same kid say, "Looks like white-trash has a boyfriend," I stood up and spun around and threw my napkin at him. Heavy with pudding, it was a good size and weight for throwing and my aim was dead on.

Craig saw it coming and pushed away from the table just before it landed on his tray with a splat. He glared at me. I turned around.

I felt good, like a comic book hero, but the feeling only lasted until I heard one of the other boys say, "You gonna let him get away with that?"

I looked down when I heard footsteps coming out way, hoping it wasn't Craig. It was. When I saw his two legs and feet next to my chair I looked at him. My world shrunk until the only things left in it were Craig's angry face and my queasy stomach. I'd been just about the world's biggest fool because Craig was a grade ahead of me and a lot bigger than me. And now that the other boy had said goaded Craig about it, he'd have to do something nasty to me to save face with his friends.

And he did. He slapped the back of my head so hard my chin hit my chest. The kids at the nearby tables heard it and stopped what they were doing just in time to hear him call me a punk and say, "You owe me for that lunch."

Unfortunately, I'd just given the only money I had to Nettie and I didn't want to take it back. So I told him I didn't have any, which was a stupid thing to do, because the money I gave her was still on the table in front of her. But that's the thing about trouble - getting into to it is a lot easier than getting out of it.

I expected Craig to be mad when I told him I'd bring him

135

his money the next day. I didn't expect him to say, "Then I'll beat it out of you," but he did, and it made me feel so sick I thought I'd throw up right there in front of the whole cafeteria. I hoped he'd go away and leave me alone. Instead of leaving, he slapped the back of my head again. "I'll be waiting out front after school. If you're not there I'll come find you."

He went away then, but the butterflies in my stomach didn't. They got worse when I heard him telling his friends he was going to beat me to a bloody pulp and heard them laughing. It was too wet to go outside and too early to go back to class so I stared at the food on my tray and tried to think of a way to escape the beating. I thought of playing hooky for the afternoon but Craig would just get me tomorrow or the next day, and unless I wanted to walk all the way home I'd have to come back to the school to meet my mom for a ride.

I had just decided things couldn't get any worse when Donna showed up. She didn't ask me about the trouble with Craig. I guessed she'd missed it, which was just as well, because I was embarrassed enough already.

Standing next to the table with her hands on her hips, she glared at me like an angry Mother. She pointed at Nettie and asked me why I was sitting with her.

"Nettie and I are friends."

"She's white trash, and you're a fool to be seen with her, Billy."

Nettie's clothes might have looked old and worn, but she seemed like a sweet kid, so I told Donna, "You can't tell from the shell," saying it so loudly that kids at the tables around us stopped eating to look at me.

"What the hell does that mean?" she asked.

I wanted to say something that would both teach her a lesson and make me look smart at the same time. So naturally my mind went blank, except for the realization that, if I insulted Donna in front of all these kids there'd be no turning back, ever. I had to decide between Donna and Nettie, and I had to do it right then.

136

Red-faced, with her fists on her hips, Donna obviously wasn't going to wait for me to recover. "Well?"

In a sudden burst of clarity, like when a cold wind blows away the morning fog, all of the confusion that liking Donna had caused me, vanished in an instant. Thelma had been right when she told me it would happen, and that when it did, I wouldn't understand why I'd ever liked her.

Freed from my crush on Donna, I wanted to protect Nettie from Donna's nastiness, the way an old brother might, and the words gushed out. "Nettie's not a bad person just because she doesn't have nice things to wear."

"You've got some nerve telling me about people."

"It's not her fault she's poor, and it's not your fault you're rich. If you can't be nice to her then leave her alone."

Nettie's older sister, Mary Anne, appeared then. She looked older and bigger than Donna. I'd heard that Mary Anne had been held back a year in school. She told Donna to leave Nettie alone.

Glaring at Mary Anne, Donna took a step closer. With their faces inches apart, Donna said, "Don't you dare get sassy with me."

Poor Mary Anne didn't look so tough after that. She took Nettie by the arm and led her away. Nettie's teddy bear banged against her leg as she ran to keep up with her big sister. Donna watched them until they were gone. She was smiling when she turned around. I told her to go away. She stormed off.

I felt good for telling Donna off, but then I saw Craig leaving the cafeteria. He stopped to point at me then made a motion with his hand as though he was cutting his throat. I didn't feel so good after that.

Then the teacher on cafeteria duty that day, a really big woman with a big puffy red face and chubby hands came to the table and demanded, "What's the problem here, young man."

Instead of giving me a hard time she should've said something to Craig when he hit me. Maybe she just wasn't looking then, but it didn't seem fair. I couldn't wait for the year to end when we'd move back to New York.

137

Class was a complete waste of time for me that afternoon. Each time the red hand on the big wall clock snapped forward I was another second closer to getting pounded by Craig's big meaty fists.

It reminded me of the time the rubbers had popped out of the hand brakes on my bicycle when I was going down a really big hill; I knew I was going to crash and I knew it was going to hurt, but the only thing I could do was wait for the pain, only that time I didn't have as long to wait.

When the bell rang at the end of the day I dragged my feet. I was the last kid out of my classroom, and one of the last kids out of the building. The rain had stopped. Now it was just gloomy and damp.

Word of my fight with Craig must have spread through the school like a bad cold because a big crowd was waiting outside the school entrance for me. You'd have thought I had two heads and six arms the way the kids stared at me. As I approached them they parted ahead of me and closed behind me, forcing me in toward the center of the mob where Craig was waiting for me with a big grin.

And they all knew how it would turn out. That made me feel lousy, because it meant all those kids wanted to see Craig beat me up. But no matter how much it hurt I couldn't back down. If I did the bullies would never leave me alone.

As he led us away from the safety of the school grounds and the excited crowd forced me to keep up with them, I heard kids saying things like, "Craig's gonna beat him to a pulp," and "The only good Yankee's a dead Yankee."

We crossed the street and walked through an alley between two rows of abandoned factory buildings, spilling out onto a large open field a block later. That's where Craig stopped. The crowd trampled the waist-deep, dead-looking yellow grass, into a small clearing as they shuffled around trying to get a good view, closing in and filling the gaps until they had formed a solid wall around us. By then the kids were calling for my blood, literally. When Craig had challenged me to a fight he'd set something in motion not even he could've stopped.

The moment I'd been dreading all afternoon finally came. The fight started with Craig moving to my left. I moved to my right and we circled each other the way wrestlers do while they look for a weak spot. For me, it was a chance to keep away from Craig and delay the inevitable beating without actually backing down.

I think Craig's name should have been Butch because of his chubby-looking, big-boned face. Too bad for me he didn't move like a fat kid. As keen to get the beating started as I was to avoid it, he took a few swings at me which I attempted to block without much success. They were quick little jabs that only hurt when he hit something tender like my face. I tried to land a few punches too, but they usually fell short because, with his long arms he'd be able to land some solid blows if I got too close.

I managed to evade his really big punches because of his slow windup, but the crowd was so anxious to see my blood spilled that the kids shoved me toward Craig whenever I backed away from one of his punches.

Didn't matter that all of the pressure to win was on Craig. If he couldn't beat me up they'd laugh at him tomorrow. The longer I stayed on my feet the worse it looked for him and the madder he got, and the worse it looked for me.

Then just as Craig wound up to throw another punch at me I heard a scuffle somewhere in the back of the mob, followed by a string of angry comments from the crowd. Craig looked to see what the commotion was about. When he looked, I did too, and that's when he landed the first solid punch. I staggered backwards with a sore lip just as Dalton burst through the crowd.

Some kid shouted, "Stay out of it," but when Dalton looked around to see who it was the all of the kids close to Dalton backed away. Then Dalton stepped between Craig and me.

Craig told him, "This isn't your fight."

Dalton shoved Craig so hard he staggered backwards into the crowd nearly knocking several kids down. That was enough for Craig; he turned around and disappeared in the crowd.

After asking the crowd, "Anyone else?" Dalton turned around slowly to see if there were any takers.

Melting away like ice cream on a hot day, most of the kids headed back toward the school. Dalton and I stayed back to let them get ahead of us. When we were a safe distance from the crowd Dalton stopped to warn me that, "Someone might've called the cops. So we gotta hurry, 'cause if they pick me up they'll call my dad. Then I'll get one hell of a beating."

Dalton took off at a trot. I followed him back down the alley, across the street, and through someone's yard. I stopped at the next street. When he realized I wasn't following him he stopped and walked back. I told him that I had to go back because my mother would be at the school waiting for me.

He said, "Okay, but if you see any cops take it slow, like you didn't know about the fight. And lick that blood off your lip."

I said, "Thanks."

Dalton said, "Forget it."

"Craig would've beaten me something terrible."

"He's bigger than you, and older. It wasn't a fair fight."

Craig was bigger and older than Dalton too.

Then Dalton said, "I guess it was nice, what you did for that little girl," but it wasn't very smart."

I didn't like living in Tuscumbia. It was just about the most unfair place in the whole world. I kicked a pebble as hard as I could. As it skipped down the sidewalk, I told Dalton, "She lives next door to us. She's poor because her dad's a bootlegger."

"So?"

"I saw two guys burn their house down."

He picked up a stone and threw it. It hit the stop sign at the next corner with a loud bang. "Too bad for them, but it's not our worry."

I might have argued with him but he had just saved me from a real beating. Besides, I still owed him an apology for not standing up for him against Donna like he did for me against Craig. I felt lousy about it, but even if I'd known the right words

140

for an apology, I probably wouldn't have been able to say them. So, "I'm sorry Donna was mean," was all the apology he got.

He shrugged his shoulders as though it hadn't bothered him, but it had. I knew it had because he turned around and walked away. I asked him if he wanted to come over to my house for an overnight.

He shook his head. "You should come to my house. There's more to do in town."

He caught me looking around nervously. "Don't worry, those kids won't bother you anymore, but I gotta go 'cause the cops are gonna be here soon and they know me."

On the way back to the school to meet my mother I got stares from some of the kids who'd been at the fight. But Dalton was right - none of them bothered me, and I didn't see Craig.

Dalton had been right about someone calling the police too. A patrol car slowed and drove alongside me. The policeman in the passenger seat took a long hard look at me before they drove on.

Mother was waiting for me at the school. When I got into the car she said, "Where have you been? I've been waiting here for twenty minutes."

Then she asked me what had happened to my lip. I didn't want a lecture, and I definitely didn't want her telling Dad I'd been in a fight, which would earn me the belt, so I told her I fell down. She gave me a look that said she wasn't fooled. But I knew that as long as I stuck to my story she'd never find out what really happened.

"LIFE AIN'T ALWAYS FAIR."

I got out of school in May because in the old days kids helped their parents plant the spring crops. That's what our teacher told us. I didn't like the sound of planting crops, but I did like getting out of school a month earlier than I would have back in New York.

The next Wednesday was my last day of school in Tuscumbia for almost three months. There wouldn't be any kids making fun of the way I talked, but best of all there wouldn't be any more homework or quizzes to study for. I'd have a few chores to do over the summer, but that was it.

So even though the weather my first day of freedom was the same as it had been the day before, it seemed infinitely better because I didn't have to read anything, or learn anything, or memorize anything. Even the grass felt softer, soft enough to lie down in while I watched the clouds float by and thought about three months without school, and when you're ten years old three months is forever.

I got out of bed so early that morning that Mom was just fixing breakfast for Dad when I got to the kitchen. She told me she was going to wake Sis before taking Dad to work. I told her that wasn't necessary. She looked at me as though I'd told her a really lame joke then went to wake up Lisa.

Since my house and Dalton's were almost five miles apart

I wouldn't have much to do for the summer besides visit the Fords, which is what I did as soon as Mom left to take Dad to work. I found them sitting on their porch drinking coffee. There wasn't a chair for me so I sat on their top step which meant they were behind me and I had to twist around to the left or right depending on who I wanted to talk to. I started by asking Thelma why the kids at school had been mean to me.

"Are all of them mean?"

"No, only a few of them are mean, but the rest of them weren't exactly nice?"

"And is it just you that they're mean to?"

"There mean to my friend Dalton too, but that's because he's a foreigner."

"Well, Billy, to them, you being a northerner is probably as bad as your friend being a foreigner."

"But my mom said Dalton's not a foreigner because he was born here."

She smiled. "Your Mon's right. But Dalton looks like a foreigner."

"Why don't they like foreigners?"

"I imagine they learned that from their parents."

"Why don't their parents like foreigners?"

"Kids have a simple way of looking at things, Billy. To some of them, anyone who's different is a foreigner. "

"That's not fair."

I turned around when I heard Mitch tapping his pipe on the railing to knock the old ashes out. He took a little tin can with a picture of Sir Walter Raleigh on it out of his shirt pocket and shook some tobacco into the bowl of his pipe. He tapped it down with his finger then struck a match on the seat of his pants. The flame, as long as my longest finger, curled into the bowl of his pipe each time he puffed on it. Soon smoke was billowing out of it like a steam engine. "Life ain't always fair, Billy,"

I asked him why.

Talking through the clenched teeth holding his pipe, he

143

said, "That's a tough question."

He seemed to think about it for a while then asked me, "Have you seen all the news on the television about civil rights?"

My parents had watched Walter Cronkite for as long as I could remember, and they made Lisa and me us watch too unless we had too much homework. I told him I had.

"All those marches and demonstrations mean that big changes are coming, Billy, and it's making some of the folks in Tuscumbia real uncomfortable."

I asked him what that had to do with me.

"These are difficult times, Billy. People here are being told by outsiders that what they've believed in for years is wrong, and that what they've been doing for years is bad, and that they have to change. Some are so angry they look for ways to get even. But civil rights isn't something you can see or touch, or hurt, or hate. So they look for people to hate, and it's easier to hate people who are easy to spot."

"Well it's not fair."

"No, but it's the way things have always been, with people everywhere."

"So the kids at school are mad at me for something other people are telling them?

Mitch frowned. "Let me put it another way. It's easier for folks to blame an outsider for their troubles than it is for them to admit that their troubles are their own doing."

Thelma stopped rocking and looked at Mitch. "You're making it too complicated; he's just a boy."

As much as I didn't like her saying I was just a boy, she was right – I only kind of got it.

Mitch explained it another way. "If you make a dog mad it might bite you, but if you make a dog mad and back it into a corner, it'll bite you for sure." Then he asked me if I understood.

"The kids at school don't like me because I backed them into a corner?"

He frowned. "What I'm trying to say is; folks here think people from up north are to blame for the civil rights stuff they see on the television. They feel like they're getting backed into a corner and they're mad about it."

"But they know it's not me doing that stuff."

"Doesn't matter, Billy. Some of them are so mad about it they hate everybody who lives up north.

"Then why doesn't somebody do something?"

"Because sometimes things have to get really bad before they get fixed."

Thelma told me I could do something about it.

I twisted around to face her. "But, I'm just a kid. You said so yourself. "

"You know the difference between right and wrong, don't you, Billy?"

I said, "Yes, ma'am," even though I knew she was going to say something I wouldn't like.

"Then decide for yourself what's right, and do it even if other folks don't like it."

I figured that was what got me into the fight with Craig, so I didn't think it was very good advice, but I said, "Yes ma'am," because I knew better than to argue with an adult. And I wouldn't have argued with Thelma anyway because I liked the Fords.

I twisted back around to ask Mitch a question. "Is that why Mr. Quinn is mean? Because he's backed into a corner?"

He pointed the stem of his pipe at the big Elm tree next to their porch. "You got more questions than that tree's got leaves. I tell you what; I'll answer this one question then we're done for the day. Is that okay with you?"

I told him it was.

Before he answered me he puffed on his pipe a few times, creating a cloud of smoke that rose up and flattened out against the porch ceiling. "That Mr. Quinn is a horse of a different color, and a dangerous one at that, so you stay away from him, ya hear?"

"Yes, sir," I said, and wondered what he would've said if I'd told him about Dalton and me sneaking around Quinn's house.

"I mean it, Billy. You stay away from that Quinn fella."

Even though he hadn't told me why Mr. Quinn was mean, I was tired of all the talk anyway.

Mitch stood up and stretched and told me, "You best run along now. I got me a passel of work to do before lunch."

He took his empty cup and saucer inside. Thelma followed him in, leaving me on the porch trying to make sense of civil rights and cornered dogs, but that soon gave me a headache. So I went home to see what Sis was doing. She was in the kitchen on the phone talking to her friend Susan. I got a deck of cards from our bedroom and sat down at the kitchen table.

I made as much noise as I could shuffling the cards, and kept shuffling them until Sis put her hand over the phone and demanded, "Do you have to do that?"

I nodded my head.

"I hate you," she said. She told her friend good-by and left the room.

I played solitaire until Mom got home from taking Dad to work. As soon as she came in she told me to clean up the dog droppings out front.

"When I finish my game."

"I'm going to make a pie. I need the table to roll out the dough."

I played another card.

"Don't make me tell you again, Buster."

I was picking up the cards when Lisa barged in and ambushed Mom with a question about the Civil War Centennial that Saturday in Tuscumbia. She asked Mom if she could go with her friend Susan. I took my time picking up the cards so I'd hear Mom's answer.

When she told Sis, "Yes, but only if you take Billy with you," Sis and I both said, "Aw Mom."

Mother said, "That's enough you two. "It won't kill you to spend some time together."

I said it would.

Mom said, "My sister and I did lots of things together."

146

Lisa said, "That's because you had a sister not a brother."

Mom gave Sis a warning look. "If you go you're taking Billy, and that's final."

"Susan's not going to like that."

Mom asked Lisa if Susan's parents would be there."

"It'll be at the town square. That's only three blocks from their house."

It would be worth going just to upset Lisa, but not if I had to stay with the girls, which is what I told Mom.

That made her mad. "If you go, you have to stay together. I don't want to hear another word about it."

Sis went away mad. That part was fun. And going to the parade would be too, as soon as I got away from the girls. On Saturday, Mother took Lisa and me to Susan's house a little before noon when the parade was supposed to start. Lisa and Susan left for the parade immediately, with me following about three feet behind them, which I considered to be a safe distance because they were talking about girl stuff. Once Sis whispered the word "cooties" so loud I could hear her. Then the two of them glanced back at me and giggled.

A huge crowd of people had showed up for the parade, filling the sidewalks and whisking us along with them like leaves in a stream. The parade was already passing by when we got to the commons in front of the courthouse, and people were packed about five deep along the street to watch it. I couldn't see a thing while we worked our way through the crowd so I followed close behind Lisa and Susan hoping they'd pick out a good place for me to watch the parade, one where people weren't blocking my view. They picked a spot behind some other girls their age that Susan knew, which was fine for them but I couldn't see a thing. So I told Sis I was going to stand in the street.

She grabbed my shirtsleeve. "Mom said you have to stay with us."

I twisted away from her and pushed through the crowd. From the edge of the sidewalk I could see three blocks in both directions - six blocks of parade including a high school

147

marching band, some old guys in uniforms carrying a big VFW banner, six women carrying a banner that read "Daughters of the American Revolution", and about a dozen guys dressed up in gray Civil War uniforms. Next came a young guy riding a big, shiny, red Massey Ferguson tractor followed by an old guy riding an ancient, green John Deere tractor, followed by two huge, farm machines pulled by pickup trucks. Behind them, firemen were throwing candy to the kids in the crowd from firetrucks.

Then I spotted a pickup truck in the parade just ahead of the fire trucks. It had a Confederate flag on the door just like the truck I'd seen at the Damon place the night it burned down. A banner strung up between two poles in the back of the truck read, "Keep America Pure. Support your local Klan."

When the truck got closer, I recognized the driver as one of the men I'd seen that night. I fought my way back through the crowd to Lisa and tugged on her dress to get her attention. She swatted my hand and told me to go away. I tugged on her dress again. She spun around and called me a pest.

I pointed to where I'd seen the truck. "See the pickup truck with the big flag thing in the back?"

Sis rolled her eyes at me without bothering to look where I had pointed. "What about it?"

I leaned closer to her so she could hear me over the noise of the parade and the crowds. "I saw them at the Damons' house the night it burned down."

"So?"

"So I think they started the fire."

Lisa said she'd tell on me if I didn't leave them alone.

I gave up and went back out to the street to watch for the firemen throwing candy. They weren't even close yet, but I did see a policeman standing on the corner at the next intersection. Stepping into the street, I ran along in front of the crowds, easily staying ahead of the slow moving pickup truck. The policeman saw me coming and yelled at me to get back on the sidewalk, but I stayed in the street until I got to him. He did not look happy about it.

I pointed at the truck. "Those two men burned down the Damon house."

He made a face at me and shook his head, as though he didn't get it.

"That one there," I said, pointing at the truck, "the one with the flag on the door."

It was almost even with us by then. I followed the policeman over to the truck. We walked alongside it next to the driver's open window. The driver had a black beard cut so short and thin it looked like he'd drawn a black line along his jaw with a magic marker. The hair on his head was black as night too, which made him look evil. But his nose and mouth and eyes were kind of dainty for his face, like he'd stolen them from a girl. His light-blue shirt looked brand spanking new.

The man in the passenger seat leaned forward. I guess he wanted to get a look at me, but that way I got a look at him too. Like the driver he had a beard, but his was long and bushy and looked like upholstery stuffing. It had grown together with his mustache, completely covering his mouth and chin like a dirty version of a Santa beard. Shaggy hair the same copper color as his beard curled out from under his old-timey cap, which had a little Confederate flag on it like the one on door of the truck.

The policeman pointed at me with his thumb. "Johnny, this kid says you burned someone's house down. Is that right?"

The way the driver grinned at me when he said, "Gee, I don't know where he got that idea," gave me the willies.

Then the driver yelled "Boo" which made me jump. The three of them got a big laugh out of that.

I backed away to watch them from the safety of the crowd. The policemen yelled at some kids to get out of the street. They didn't listen so he walked off in their direction, turning his back on me.

The next thing I knew the truck was gone but the man with the dirty beard, the one who had chased me at the Damons' place, was standing right across the street from me. I didn't like the way he was looking at me so I ducked into the crowd and

149

went part way down the block. When I stepped out into to the street to look for him, he was nowhere in sight.

Through the crowd I spotted the truck parked around the corner at the next intersection. The driver, standing at the curb looking up and down the street, froze when he spotted me. Then he started to run toward me, right through a high school marching band.

I ducked back into the crowd, dodging and weaving through the mass of people like a scared rabbit. I ran through a gap in the crowd, right into the man with the dirty beard. He grabbed the front of my shirt. I tried to pull away.

He pulled me back, so close that when he said, "You were at that bootlegger's place, weren't ya kid?" his hot, nasty-smelling breath almost made me throw up my breakfast.

He twisted my shirt with one hand, tightening the collar around my neck. I pried at his fingers but couldn't pull them loose. He grinned at me.

I told him I'd seen them start the fire at the Damon house, which was a lie; I hadn't seen them do anything, but I thought it might scare him into letting me go. It didn't.

A woman asked me, "Is that man hurting you?"

When the man holding me sneered at her and asked, "What the hell you looking at," she disappeared into the crowd.

The driver of the truck found us then. The man holding me turned away to say something to him. I spun around twisting out of tobacco-man's grip. He reached for me. I ducked. All he got was my baseball cap.

I had a few steps on them and could slip through little gaps in the crowd. And my lungs were young and clean and recovered fast, but the men had longer legs and easily forced their way through the crowds. When I looked back they weren't more than ten feet behind me.

Half a block later, still a few feet ahead of them but beginning to tire, I spotted the sign for Morey's Diner, the place where we'd had breakfast the day we went to see the riverboat. I waited until I was even with the door then made a hard left turn, breaking through the crowd, running right into the restaurant because someone had propped the door open.

The nice lady who had waited on us was standing at a booth taking someone's order. I hurried over to tell her about the two men chasing me. As I tried to get my breath back I noticed them standing on the sidewalk outside the diner looking in the window at me. I told her they'd been chasing me.

She pointed at them. "Those two?"

"Yes ma'am, that's them," I said, already starting to feel safer.

"Well," she said, "we can't have that, now can we?" Then she led me to an empty booth and told me to wait there for her. Relieved to have her looking out for me, I slid into the booth to see what she'd do about the two men. First thing she did was go to the doughnut display and bring me back a glazed doughnut wrapped in a napkin.

Then the nice lady went outside and talked to the men. I expected her to have trouble with them, but after a short talk the men disappeared into the crowd, leaving her standing there looking after them. I realized then I'd been holding my breath. I took a deep one and slumped back against the padded seat, feeling safe and very grateful.

When she came back in she filled a glass with milk and it brought to me. Standing next to the booth holding the milk in one hand and my hat in her other hand, she said, "I bet you'd like this back."

I'd forgotten all about my hat. I was lucky to get it back, especially since my mom wouldn't get me another one.

The nice lady said she'd call the police, that they'd come and take me home. "But we can't have you tying up a whole booth by yourself, not with the place so busy today because of the parade. You follow me. I'll take you someplace where you can have your milk and doughnut while you wait for them."

I followed her across the room and down the hallway, past the sign over the restroom that read, "Whites Only," into the "Coloreds'" dining room behind the kitchen. It was even

151

dirtier than I remembered, which was pretty dirty even by my standards, and it smelled grimy, like a mix of dirty socks and my grandma's jar of used cooking fat.

The windows on the back wall, which faced into an alley, were coated with something that made everything outside look fuzzy, like looking through an out-of-focus camera. The people in the room stared at me as the waitress led me to a table near the back door. My presence was obviously making them uncomfortable, which made me uncomfortable too.

The nice lady set my milk down on the table so I'd be facing them with my back to the door, then told me, "You wait right here, honey."

First thing I did was put my hat on so I wouldn't forget it when my parents showed up. Then I dug into the doughnut and milk, avoiding the stares of the people around me. I couldn't wait to get out of there. If I hadn't been so afraid of running into those two men again I would've snuck outside to go look for Sis.

A few minutes later I heard the door behind me open and close. The old man at the next table glanced behind me at the door then quickly looked away, like a kid who'd seen something he shouldn't have. I looked down at my empty milk glass and wished my parents would hurry.

A hand grabbed the back of my neck and squeezed it so hard I almost screamed, first from the pain then from the fright, especially when I recognized the nasty-smelling tobacco breath. Then the waitress appeared in the hall doorway. I felt relieved; then confused because she didn't come to help; then frightened because she turned around and walked away.

With one hand clamped on my neck and the other holding my arm like a vise, the man with the bad breath took me out the back door into the alley, lifting and pushing me into the pickup truck with the Confederate flag on the door, wedging me between them on the seat. Then the guy with the long, dirty-looking beard pushed my face against the dashboard. The unpadded dark metal had gotten so hot from being in the sun it burned my cheek.

Pressing my face against the hot dashboard he asked me, "What do you think we oughta do with you?"

Even with one cheek squashed against the dashboard, I managed to say, "I don't know."

He leaned over next to my face. "I'm gonna tell you something important, so you listen real careful. You hear?"

I held my breath so I wouldn't have to smell his and tried to nod my head.

"If you go around telling people you saw us the night the bootlegger's place burned you'll be mighty sorry. You got that?"

With my poor cheek squashed against the dashboard I couldn't help slurring my words. "I didn't see you the night of the fire."

After pulling me back away from the hot dashboard he asked his friend, "What should we do with him?"

"We gotta let him go unless you want to spend the next ten years on a chain gang chopping weeds."

The man with the smelly breath got out of the truck, then reached in and grabbed my arm and yanked me out so hard I landed face down in the alley. As I got up and brushed the grit off of my arms, I backed away from the bearded man.

He climbed into the truck then leaned out the window. "If you tell anyone about this, or that you saw us burn that house, you'll never see your mommy again."

I watched the truck until it disappeared then headed in the direction of Susan's house. A police car found me. Susan's parents had panicked and called the police when the girls showed up at their house without me.

I waited on a bench in the lobby of the police station while a policeman called my parents then Susan's parents. I told him I'd been kidnapped, and that the waitress had been in on it. After listening to my story without writing any of it down or asking any questions, he shook his head and told me to go back and sit on the bench. I wondered why grownups never believed me.

When we got home, my parents sent Sis to bed and told her to think about what she'd done wrong - they blamed her

153

for losing track of me. Of course, she didn't see it that way. She thought it was my fault for running away. She didn't speak to me for days, which was fine with me, because she didn't do any of the things she usually did to irritate me, like make faces at me, or stick her tongue out at me, or kick me, or try to tickle me.

Mom and Dad sat me down at the kitchen table with them. Dad cleared his throat several times, as though he was about to say something, but he didn't; he just sat there looking concerned. Mother started the questioning by asking me if I was okay.

Not knowing how much trouble I was in, I made a point of being extra respectful, saying, "Yes, ma'am," instead of just nodding my head.

Mother asked me if the two men had done anything to me.

I shook my head then quickly added, "No ma'am."

She asked me what they wanted.

"They said I'd never see you again if I told you."

Mom made a funny sound in her throat.

Dad said, "Told us what, Billy?"

"That I saw them at the Damon's house the night it burned down. They set it on fire. I know they did."

I couldn't believe how surprised they were.

"You don't remember me telling you that, do you?"

Mother shook her head. Dad said he'd remember it if I said something like that. I didn't dare tell him he was wrong. Instead of screaming, which is what I wanted to do, I asked them if they were going to tell the sheriff what had happened. Mother told me to go watch television. "Tales of Wells Fargo" was playing. It was a pretty good show, but I kept the volume low and sat near the door so I could hear what my parents were saying.

While a stage couch was being robbed on the TV I heard Mother say, "If we report this to the sheriff and he questions those men, they'll know Billy reported them. I'd worry about them coming after him."

Dad didn't say anything. Then even though she lowered her voice, I heard Mother ask Dad, "What if Billy's mistaken about seeing those men and we report it?"

When Dad said, "I wish one of us had seen that truck," I wanted to yell, "How come you guys never believe me?"

While Jim, the hero on the TV show, rode after the robbers I heard cooking noises in the kitchen. A few minutes later I smelled Toll House chocolate chip cookies baking. There's no mistaking that smell. It made my mouth water. I listened for the squeak of the oven door which would mean they were done.

Mother said, "I guess I'm gonna worry no matter what we do."

After Dad said, "I think we should assume Billy's telling us the truth," he called me into the kitchen.

I jumped up from the couch and stood in the doorway.

First Dad gave me one of his warning looks, meaning, "You'll tell us the truth if you know what's good for you. Then he said, "I want you to think very carefully, Billy."

"Yes, sir?"

"Did those men ask you for your name?"

I shook my head. He asked if I was sure. I nodded my head and told him I was.

"Did the waitress ask you for your name?"

I shook my head again and he told me to go back and watch my TV show. I sat on the couch and waited for the cookies and pretended to watch television while I listened to them.

Dad said to Mom, "That's it then. We'll let it go for now."

My dad was so cool when there was trouble, just having him around usually calmed my mother right down, like some kind of magic potion, but not this time. She started crying, quietly at first, but then she broke down and started weeping.

At one point between sobs, she shouted, "I wish we'd never come to this place."

I hoped Dad would say we could move back to New York, but he didn't. Mother burned the cookies. I tried eating one anyway but it tasted bitter and was hard as a rock. Dad sent me to bed when Mother started crying again.

Before I went to the bathroom to brush my teeth and

change into my pajamas, I hung my baseball cap on one of my bedposts, same as I did every night. But doing it that night reminded me of something, and the thought scared me so much I ran to the kitchen to tell my parents about it.

I found them in the living room watching "The Defenders," a boring courtroom show my parents liked. I slid into the room in my socks. Mother frowned then asked me why I wasn't in bed.

"Those men took my hat and the waitress gave it back to me."

Mother asked me what I was talking about, but she already looked as though she was going to cry. So I think she knew it was going to be bad news.

"You wrote my name in my hat, remember?"

She said "Oh my God," as the tears welled up in her eyes.

They sent me back to bed, but I stood at the bedroom doorway with the door open a crack so I could hear them. They turned off the TV and went into the kitchen. Dad called the sheriff and told him about the two men and about my baseball cap.

I hardly slept that night because of something Mother had said – that those men would figure out that I had ratted on them. I fell asleep wondering what the man with the nasty tobacco breath would do to me.

Next thing I knew, he was chasing me, closing on me as I ran out of breath, so close behind me I felt his hot breath blistering my skin like hot coffee, the smell of his breath so foul I fought back the urge to throw up. Johnny was there too, watching and laughing, a red-skinned devil with horns and a tail. Stinky-breath's hand wrapped around my leg. I woke up with my bedsheet tangled around my leg.

The sheriff, the same man who came to get our statement about the dead body, came back the next morning to talk to us. He sat at the kitchen table with Mother and me, writing a bunch of stuff down in a little notebook while I told him as much as I could remember about what the two men said and did to me.

156

He told Mother he knew a man named Johnny Vail who owned a truck with a Confederate flag on the door. I told him I'd heard the man with the bad breath call the other man Johnny.

"Well," he said, closing his notebook, "in that case I'll go pay them a visit." Then he pushed his chair back, and stood up to leave.

Before he left I blurted out, "It wasn't Mr. Damon."

He asked me what I was talking about.

"The dead body hanging in the tree. The one we saw the day we went still smashing with the Madisons. I don't think Mr. Damon killed him."

Mother smiled at the sheriff then reached over and patted my hand. "That's enough, Billy; we'll talk about that later."

And that was the end of that. I'd felt grown up talking to the sheriff until my mother patted my hand like I was a little kid.

The sheriff called later that day to tell Mother he had arrested Johnny and his friend, and that the waitress at the diner was Johnny's mother. My mom seemed a lot happier after that, not singing and dancing happy, but happy enough to make tomato soup and grilled cheese sandwiches for lunch instead of peanut butter and jelly. As for me, I was glad I'd never see those two men again. So we thought.

"WE'RE GONNA KILL US A LEGEND"

Two days later, Mother let me invite Dalton over for the night. We usually stayed at his house because his parents didn't care what we did as along as no one complained about us. But I'd told him about the creek I'd seen the day we went still-smashing and he wanted to see it.

Dad was at work. Lisa begged Mom to let her stay with her friend Susan in Tuscumbia because she didn't want to share the bedroom with Dalton and me. Mom agreed. She was going to see one of her friends in Tuscumbia, so she dropped Sis off on her way. The Fords had offered to keep an eye on me and Dalton while Mom was gone, so before she left she took us next door to introduce Dalton to the Fords.

After Mom left, Mitch told us to go wait for him out back at their picnic table. A few minutes later he came out the back door carrying a big watermelon. With the hot sun beating down on me, the thought of the sweet juicy melon made my mouth water and reminded me how long it had been since breakfast and how hungry I gotten.

Thelma came out with a stack of plates and a knife as big as a bayonet. She sliced the melon into pieces the size of platters then cut them in half and piled them onto three plates. She set one plate down in front of Mitch, one in front of Dalton, and one in front of me.

Then she smiled at us, not her usual grandmother-type smile, more like an "I've got a secret" smile. "Nobody can eat watermelon faster than Mitch." After counting down from three she yelled, "Go," and we dug in.

Dalton and I sat sideways on the benches, spitting the seeds out into the yard, leaning over the grass so when we dribbled the sticky sweet watermelon juice it wouldn't get on us or our clothes. It wasn't about staying clean. We didn't give a fig about that. It was about yellowjackets; the nasty little things won't leave you alone if you get watermelon juice on you.

No matter how hard I tried I couldn't keep up with Dalton who finished his pile first and raised his hands in victory. That's when I noticed Mitch had only eaten one slice. "But Mrs. Ford you said Mitch was the fastest."

"That's a young man's game," he said, grinning. He told us to throw the rinds into the field then he and Thelma took the plates and uneaten watermelon back into the house. Dalton and I walked over to my house to lie in the grass under a shade tree. I was too stuffed to do anything else. Dalton went inside to get something from his knapsack which he'd put in my bedroom.

He came back out carrying a small paper sack. When I asked him what he had, he held a finger to his lips, and knowing Dalton that meant it was something fun, and most likely something that could get us in trouble. Whatever it was, I didn't want Mitch to come over and catch us with it, so I told Dalton it was time for us to go.

To sneak off without being seen by the Fords we walked out to the road on a diagonal and cut through the fields behind my house. That kept my house between us and the Fords' place. We came out near the clearing where the Damons' house had been. Except for the house trailer Clayton had set up on cinder blocks near the charred remains of their old shack, the clearing looked like one of those places I'd seen on the country roads where people dumped and burned their garbage.

I'd seen the trailer one day when my folks had taken Lisa

and me out for a drive. It was a beat-up, rusty old thing but it had a floor and it looked as though it might do a better job of keeping the weather out than their old place. Dalton wanted to stay and poke around in the ruins but I didn't want Clayton to catch us. So I told Dalton that if we didn't hurry we wouldn't have time to get to the creek and back.

The old dirt road we'd followed Quinn down was harder to find than I'd expected, and farther down the main road than I remembered. And it was hot running along the road, with melting tar sticking to our shoes, making a sound like peeling masking tape. By the time we found the path and followed it into the woods sweat was running down my forehead into my eyes making them sting. I stopped in the shade to recuperate as soon as we were out of sight of the main road.

When Dalton got his breath back he held the bag up. "Guess what I've got in here."

Before I had a chance to guess he took a pistol out of the bag, a real one. I was surprised and excited and scared all at the same time. He held it down against his leg then pretended to draw and fire like a gunslinger in a TV western.

"Jeez," I said, getting more worried by the minute, because I'd be in really big trouble if my parents ever found out about it. I asked him if it was his dad's.

"Yep."

"What if he sees that it's missing?"

He asked me if I was scared. I told him I wasn't. No matter how scared I was, I couldn't let him know.

He pointed the gun at a tree and fired it. The smell of burnt powder hung in the air after the sound of the shot faded. I asked him if he brought the gun because of what Mitch had said – that something had killed one of our neighbor's dogs.

Even though he said, "Yeah, sure," he was grinning. That's when I realized why he wanted to come to my house. "You didn't want to see the creek. You wanted to shoot the gun and you couldn't do that in town."

If I was right he didn't admit to it, asking me a question

160

instead. "This is where you saw the 'Wolfs-Head Man,' isn't it?"

"Yeah, so?"

He pointed the gun into the woods. "We're gonna kill us a legend."

I asked him what he meant.

"We're gonna go look for him, and if we find him, he's dead."

I didn't see how Dalton could kill the "Wolf's-Head Man" if he was already dead.

Dalton held the gun out toward me. "You wanna try it?"

It felt surprisingly heavy as I held it out and aimed it at the same tree Dalton had shot at. It went off before I expected it to and jolted my shoulder a little when it did. But shooting the gun felt like a grown-up thing to do and I liked the feeling. I would have shot it more but Dalton told me to give it back, that we had to save the rest of the bullets in case we saw the "Wolf's-Head Man."

After a while we heard water gurgling and left the path to walk along the edge of the stream I'd told Dalton about, tipping up stones as we went so we could check under them for crayfish. Even though the water was only ankle deep the creek was wider than our driveway, much too wide to jump across. The water was moving fast enough to leave trails of gurgling whitewater below the big rocks in its path. Luckily, trees overhanging the creek shaded us from the harsh sun.

The stream was a lot like the ones we had back home in Ithaca, and I was having such a good time I couldn't imagine anything bad happening. I had no idea that the sound of the gun would carry all the way back to the Fords' house.

You have to be fast to catch a crayfish. You grab it right behind where its claws attach to its body. They'll squirm and try to get you with a pincer, and if they do it really hurts and they do not let go. You have to pull the pincer off. Lucky for them they can grow new ones.

Dalton found the biggest crayfish I'd ever seen. Holding it up to show me, its pincers opening and closing harmlessly in the

161

air, he said, "I bet this one's bigger 'n any in New York."

"Is not," I said, because I'd already lost the watermelon eating contest and didn't like the idea of losing another one.

We soon came to a sharp right turn in the creek where the water had scooped out the bank, leaving a deep spot where the current flowed much slower. Although it was too small for swimming, the water was deep enough for us to jump into off the bank. Dalton took his shirt and pants off, then without checking the water first, yelled, "Last one in is a monkey's uncle" and took a running leap off the bank.

From the way he gasped when he hit the water I knew it had to be cold. I might've jumped in anyway, just to cool off, but he dared me, so I had to do it. It took my breath away too. Then the horse flies found us. They like wet skin, so the only way to avoid them was to stay under the water, but it was much too cold for that. Dalton had bright blue lips and mine probably looked the same. To keep the horse flies from biting us we put our clothes back on while we were still wet.

I followed Dalton who followed the stream back to the path where he stopped and held up the pistol. "Let's get us a 'Wolf's-Head Man.'" Then, before I could react, he followed the path to the right, deeper into the woods.

The cold creek water having evaporated quickly in the heat, I soon felt trickles of warm sweat running down my sides under my shirt. Even without the sun beating on us it was a hot humid day for a fast walk.

When we came to the small clearing where a rotted, vine-covered fallen tree blocked the road we found two cars parked behind it, a new Chevrolet Belair and an older Pontiac Grand Prix. Dalton went over to the Chevy, dragging his finger along the driver's side from the front bumper to the taillight, where he stopped then spun around. "This is Quinn's car."

I shrugged my shoulders.

He pointed at a scratch on the fender. "I know it is. I remember this scratch. Gee, I wonder what he's doing here."

I wondered he same thing, but mostly I wished we

162

wouldn't run into the "Wolf's-Head-Man." Of course, I couldn't tell Dalton that 'cause I didn't want him to think I was chicken. So I shrugged my shoulders and kept my mouth shut and hoped for the best.

Dalton took off down the path again. After a while he slowed to let me catch up and asked me if I'd seen the new sci-fi movie *Atlantis, the Lost Continent*. I told him my parents would never go to a movie like that.

He said, "Then go by yourself," as if I hadn't thought of that.

My parents wouldn't let me do that either. Of course, I didn't tell him that. Instead I asked him if it was as good as *The Day the Earth Stood Still*.

He scrunched up his nose as though he'd smelled something bad. "That movie's okay when they show the robot, but there's too much talking, like when he's with that funny-looking old scientist guy or the woman at the boarding house. There's good stuff going on all the time in *Atlantis*, like when the guy fights a monster or when the town is destroyed by a volcano."

He was just saying that when we rounded the next turn and bumped our heads into a dead man with a wolf mask over his head that was hanging over the path.

Walking slowly around the body Dalton said, "I never seen a dead guy before," studying it as though it was something to be figured out, like the things in the freak shows at the county fairs, where if you looked real close you could see how they used mirrors to make a regular person look weird.

I told him it wasn't the same dead guy I'd seen before. "The other guy's face looked nasty, like something had chewed most of the meat off of the bones."

Dalton said, "Dang it" then pulled on one of the feet and let it go, which started the body swaying.

I asked him what was wrong.

"This isn't the 'Wolf's-Head Man,' just some dead guy with a mask over his head." He took the pistol out and he waved it at the body, saying, "I sure do hope we see him," before hurrying off down the path again. I followed, quick as a rabbit, so we wouldn't get separated.

When I heard a twig snap in the woods I wondered if whoever had killed the guy hanging in the tree was still around. Dalton pointed the gun in the direction where I'd heard the sound. He asked me if I was scared.

I lied, told him, "No," but imagined a vicious, knife-wielding killer out there waiting to slash me into little pieces.

Dalton said he wasn't afraid, said it was probably just a squirrel, but I noticed that he didn't put the gun away, and like me, he was watching the woods. I couldn't shake the feeling that I was being watched, which gave me a serious case of the willies.

I looked at the path ahead. That's when I saw him, the dead man we'd seen hanging in a tree, only now he was a stone's throw ahead of us, but his wolf face was looking right at me.

Several things happened then, in almost the same instant. I heard a noise behind us and spun around to look. Mitch came around the corner and Dalton fired his gun. I heard the shot echo in the woods behind me as I watched Mitch stagger. At first I thought he'd tripped on a root, but when I saw the red stain on his shirt I knew better. He fell.

I rushed over and knelt down beside him. He grabbed my sleeve, pulled my face close to his, and said between ragged breaths, "Get Thelma, Billy, hurry" then let go of my sleeve and went limp.

I ran for home as fast as I could, until the pain in my side forced me to stop. Dalton ran a few yards past me before he stopped. I walked in small circles, gasping for air until I heard someone or something crashing through the brush nearby. Forgetting about the pain in my side, I pushed on, past the parked cars, past the place where the path met the road, gasping for breath as my heart pounded in my head, trying to ignore the painful side ache.

Pushing on after we reached the road I soon saw Mrs. Ford sitting on her front porch. She stopped rocking and stood up when she saw us, watching us run across their yard. I didn't slow down for their steps, leaping over them onto the porch. My feet had hardly touched down on the porch floor when she asked me where Mitch was.

Gasping for breath, I told her that Mitch was hurt real bad.

Mrs. Ford bent down to my height and grabbed both of my arms and shook me. "Where is he, Billy?"

"He's on the path in the woods and so is the 'Wolf's-Head Man.'"

She shook me again and told me to make sense.

"We gotta hurry, Mrs. Ford. Someone shot him and he's bleeding real bad."

"Lord almighty," she said, "clutching her chest then running inside the house.

Dalton bent over, putting his hands on his knees to get his breath back. I paced in small circles to get mine back. He didn't talk and I didn't want to. I just wanted the time to hurry by, so Mitch would be back and healed up and everything could go back the way it had been when I woke up that morning.

I heard Thelma's voice inside, loud and anxious, telling someone that Mitch had been shot and giving them our address. She came out a few minutes later to ask us what Mitch said.

"He told me to get you."

"That's all?"

"He said to hurry."

"Are you're sure that's all he said?"

"Yes, ma'am."

She frowned and went inside. It seemed like forever before I heard the sirens. We waited for another forever until I saw red flashing lights through the breaks in the trees along the road. I yelled to Thelma through her screen door to tell her the sheriff had just turned into the driveway.

A moment later she burst out through the screen door, telling us to, "Get in the car and be quick about it," her purse slapping against her side as she ran.

After the sheriff turned his car around on the Ford's lawn,

we sped down the driveway with an ambulance behind us. On the way Thelma had me tell the sheriff how to get to the place where we left Mitch. I looked out the window at a world that no longer looked familiar or safe. The sheriff radioed his dispatcher to tell her where we were going.

A minute later he turned the cruiser onto the old dirt road that led to Clayton's still. He drove so fast, that even though he swerved to avoid the worst of the ruts, and I held onto the armrest with one hand and braced myself against the roof of the car with the other, I was still thrown around in the back seat. The car bottomed out on one rut so hard it made my teeth clatter. The whole time his car was breaking branches, large and small.

He slid the car to a stop and parked it when we got to the place where the old vine-covered tree blocked the road. The empty little clearing didn't look the same as when Dalton and I had walked through it less than an hour earlier, but then nothing looked the same anymore. Dalton hadn't said a word the whole way there; just stared out the window.

When Thelma opened her door to get out of the car the sheriff told her, "I think you should wait here with the boys, ma'am."

"No, sir, I won't," she said then hurried down the path.

The sheriff told Dalton and me to stay put and warned us not to touch anything while he was gone. Then he and two guys with a stretcher ran to catch up with Thelma.

As soon as they were out of sight Dalton said, "You can't tell a soul what happened."

I was about to remind Dalton that bringing the gun along had been his idea when I remembered he probably still had it. If the Sheriff caught Dalton with it he'd be in an awful lot of trouble. And even though it was Dalton who shot Mitch, I was there when it happened, and I had shot the gun too.

Poor Mitch would never forgive us for shooting him and neither would Thelma. Mom would give me a "talking to" I'd never forget, and I'd get the belt from Dad until I couldn't walk.

166

And we'd both be in trouble with the sheriff. I asked Dalton if he still had the gun.

Hearing him say, "I threw it in the woods," made me feel a little better.

"So then you're safe," I said.

"No, I'm not. I thought that my Dad wouldn't find out that I took it if the sheriff didn't catch me with it."

"So, what's the problem?"

"If Mitch saw me holding the gun he's gonna tell the sheriff."

"Maybe he didn't."

"Even if he didn't, next time Dad goes to get the gun, and it's not there, he's gonna figure I'm the one who took it. No one else but Mom knows about it."

"Maybe you can find it and put it back before that."

"You're right, unless the sheriff finds it first."

"So what if he does? He won't know whose it is."

"I saw a cop show once where they used the serial number on a gun to find the guy who owned it. That would lead them right to my Dad. So. I've gotta get it back, and soon."

I was imagining my Dad taking off his belt to whip me with it when Dalton said, "Jesus, Billy. When they figure out it was me, they'll send me away to reform school. And they'll send me to a real prison when I turn eighteen."

That was the last thing either of us said while we waited for Thelma and the sheriff. I couldn't get it out of my mind; the awful way Mitch's face looked after the gunshot, or the way he stumbled and fell, or the blood on his shirt. He was hurt bad and I knew it, and was afraid for him.

The two ambulance guys came back first, by themselves, carrying the stretcher between them, with something on it that was covered in a sheet. It had to be Mitch. It meant that he was dead. The world I'd known for ten years, the one where terrible things couldn't happen to me or the people I cared about, had been replaced by a frightening, new, nightmarish world where terrible things could and did happen to anyone, any time.

Forever had gone by when Thelma and the sheriff finally came out of the woods walking slowly; the sheriff with his arm around her.

IS IT STILL A LIE IF I DON'T SAY THE WORDS?

The sheriff helped a weepy Thelma get into the car. She looked out the window and didn't make a sound, but I knew she was still crying because I saw her shoulders shaking. While we rode back to her place I thought about never seeing Mitch again. It didn't make any sense. It had to be a mistake.

Then the sheriff stopped his car in front of the Fords' house and all my worries about getting into trouble came rushing back. Dalton wanted us to lie so we wouldn't get into trouble for killing Mitch. I didn't want to lie. I can't sleep or eat or have fun with a lie hanging over my head. I have to come clean about it. Besides, if I did lie about what had happened, before too long, Thelma, or the sheriff, or my parents would figure it out. I was sure of it.

Because of Dalton I'd lost my friend Mitch, and was in more trouble than I'd ever been in my whole life. He's the one who brought the gun and the one who shot Mitch, but I'd pay for it too and that didn't seem fair.

Thelma got out of the car and went into the house without saying a word. The sheriff told Dalton and me to go wait for him on the porch. From where we sat on the steps I could see him using his car radio. I tried to listen, but mostly what I heard was static.

When he finished talking on his radio he came over to the porch and stood next to me with his right foot on the top step. He took his hat off then leaned forward to rest his right arm on his knee. He spent a few moments looking at his hat, as though he was inspecting it. Then he looked me right in the eye without saying a thing. He did that just about forever.

He startled me when he finally said something. "Mrs. Ford gave me the phone number where we could reach your momma. I told the dispatcher to call her. She should be here soon."

I asked him if Mitch was dead. It was a dumb question; don't know why I asked it.

The sheriff nodded his head. He was still looking right at me when he asked me what I'd been dreading. "Why don't you tell me what happened?"

He said it casually, too casually, as though he was asking me if it had rained or what I had for lunch.

I blurted out as much as I could without telling a lie. "We went looking for the 'Wolf's-Head Man.' We found a dead guy hanging from a tree just like the one we found when I went still smashing with the Madisons. Only this time the 'Wolf's-Head Man' really was there."

Even though everything I told him was true, the Sheriff tipped his head sideways and squinted at me, as though he didn't believe me. And I think Dalton was afraid I'd spill the beans because he took over for me then. "We stopped when we saw the 'Wolf's-Head Man' on the path up ahead. Right after that we heard a noise behind us. When we turned around to look Mitch had blood on his shirt and was falling down."

The sheriff studied his hat again for a while. I think the sheriff suspected something wasn't right with our story. At least now he was staring at Dalton instead of me.

Finally he asked Dalton, "So Mitch came up the path behind you, and you heard a shot which came from where you saw this 'Wolf's-Head Man.' Have I got that right?"

By answering, "Yes, sir," Dalton added to the lies.

Then the sheriff looked at me. "Is that the way you remember it, Billy?"

My stomach felt like the time an elevator dropped when I wasn't expecting it. Even though it was disrespectful, I just nodded my head instead of saying, "Yes, sir," because I thought it might be less of a lie if I didn't actually say the words.

The sheriff studied his hat again for a while then stood up. "This'll be hard enough on Mrs. Ford without you boys telling tales, so I want you to think about telling me what really happened."

He slapped his hat against his leg then went inside. While I waited for Mom to get home and agonized over what I'd tell her, a robin pecked at the dirt near us, a cicada complained about being lonely, and a couple of cars sped by out on the road. Life was going on as though nothing had happened. But after the horrible thing we'd done, it wasn't the same world anymore, and it had no right to look and sound the way it had when Mitch was still alive.

I knew the call from the dispatcher would scare my mother and that she'd get home in record time. The first thing she did was try to give me a big hug, and I would've let her if Dalton hadn't been there. Then she went inside. Thelma must not have wanted company because my mother came right back out with the sheriff. That's when he left.

Mother told Dalton and me to wait for her in our car, that she was going to our house to call Dad, and that we'd pick him up early. The ride to Florence to get him was long and silent, and uncomfortable. The ride to Dalton's house after we picked up Dad seemed just as long, and just as silent, and just as uncomfortable. As we pulled into the driveway at Dalton's house Mother told me to wait in the car while she and Dad talked to his parents.

His father was sitting on his porch in a rocking chair reading a newspaper when we got there. He'd have known something was wrong as soon as our car pulled into his driveway because we were bringing Dalton home a day early. When my parents got out of the car he stood up and folded his newspaper then dropped it on the seat of the rocker. He put his hands in his pants pockets and watched my parents cross the yard and climb the porch steps.

Mom and Dad shook hands with him as they all met for the first time. Dalton, who had followed my parents, leaned against a post at the far end of the porch and picked off flakes of peeling paint. He had good reason to be scared. It was only a matter of time before his dad realized the gun was missing and that Dalton took it.

I suppose Dalton's mother heard them talking because she came outside. Instead of shaking hands with my parents she stood a little behind and to the side of Dalton's dad and did a funny little dip, not really a bow, just a hint of one.

My mom did all of the talking. When she stopped, the four of them stood there looking awkward until a breeze ruffled my mother's hair. After fussing with it she said something to Dalton's parents. Then Mom and Dad came back to the car, leaving the Daltons standing on their porch watching us.

On the way home Mother asked me what had happened. I told her the same thing we'd told the sheriff and nothing more. It wasn't something I had thought about and decided, but once Dalton had started the lie, I didn't think I had much choice. I didn't know the lie would own us after that, but it did, because from then on I had to think carefully about everything I said, working hard to keep my stories straight. It also kept me from facing my feelings about Mitch's death.

When we got home I told Mom I'd take Star outside to do her business, because while I was outdoors with the dog I'd be safe from dangerous questions. So, even though I was tired from the fright and worry, I stayed outside for a long time, sitting on the front steps petting Star. When I saw Mother walk over to Thelma's house I went inside because I knew Dad wouldn't make me talk about what had happened.

I was watching television when Mom came home. I wanted to forget what had happened, even for a little while. I thought watching television would help. It didn't. And Mother said it was disrespectful of me and told me to turn it off. I tried reading one of Sis' books, but after reading the first page three times I still couldn't remember what it said, so I went to bed early, long before dark. If I could just get to sleep I'd get a break from all the sadness, and guilt, and worry. I couldn't.

I could see from the bedroom window that it was after dark when I heard footsteps in the hallway. Mom opened my door and stood in the doorway. She didn't turn the bedroom light on, so she looked like a black cardboard cutout. I asked her what she wanted.

She came and sat on my bed, so I knew she was about to say something that would make me uncomfortable, and she did. "You understand that what happened to Mitch wasn't your fault, don't you, dear?"

I said, "Yes, ma'am," hoping it would make her happy and she'd leave without asking any more questions.

Instead she put her hand on my arm then talked extra softly, which made everything she said sound fake. That's the way she talked whenever she was trying to make me feel better. I wanted to tell her it made me feel worse.

In that half-whisper she told me, "You and Dalton being in those woods precipitated the events that led to Mitch's death, but that's not the same as being responsible for what happened."

"I thought 'preciperated' meant it was raining?"

She leaned over and stroked my forehead, petting me like a cat, while she said, "It means things happened just because you boys were there, not because you did anything wrong. It's alright for you to feel bad about losing Mitch, but you mustn't think his death was your fault."

I wanted to scream at her, wanted to get it out, tell her that it was our fault. And I hated it when she pet my head. I propped myself up on my elbow, making it harder for her to reach me. And I tried to change the subject. "I know all about the 'Wolf's-

173

Head Man'."

That made her frown. She took a deep breath, said, "We'll talk about that some other time" then she stood up to leave.

Maybe mentioning the "Wolf's-Head Man" had been disrespectful, but at least it had ended our talk. After she left I laid there in the dark for the longest time trying to think of a way out of the mess Dalton had gotten me into. I was still awake when Lisa came to bed.

After she put the light out, she whispered, "Hey, Billy."

I pretended to be asleep so I wouldn't have to talk to her about Mitch.

"Mom's right," she said, "it wasn't your fault."

The unexpected kindness made my eyes water. Unable to hold it in any longer, I rolled over and cried into my pillow so she wouldn't hear me. Letting go helped me get to sleep, but if I'd known about all of the terrible things Mitch's death would set in motion, and that I'd be caught in the middle of it all, I wouldn't have slept that night or any other night.

When I went outside after breakfast the next morning I saw the sheriff's car parked at Thelma's. I stood in the shade under a tree by the driveway, wondering why he was there. He spotted me when he came out. He waved me over then stood next to his car, staring at me as I walked toward him.

The thought of talking to him made me feel queasy. Just in case I said something stupid and he figured out that Dalton and I had lied to him, I didn't stand close enough for him to reach me.

He asked me if we could talk "man to man."

When my dad asked me that, he meant, "I'll know if you're lying."

I was afraid he'd hear the fear in my voice when I said, "Yes, sir,"

He asked me if I'd heard two gunshots a few minutes before Mitch was killed. Those were the shots Dalton and I fired at the tree. I didn't want him to know we were firing the gun, so I panicked and told him, "No, sir."

He squinted at me and frowned, and I knew I'd given him

174

the wrong answer. He probably knew that I lied, but he didn't call me on it. Instead, he asked me if I was sure about the gunshots.

Even as the words, "Yes sir," came out of my mouth I knew I was making a big mistake, knew I was digging myself in deeper. Each new lie was another thing I'd have to remember, and for every one I told, I'd have to tell another one later.

He took his hat off and tossed it on the seat of his car. I thought he was going to leave, that the danger had passed, but he didn't leave. "You know what bothers me, Billy?"

I shook my head.

"Mrs. Ford told me that Mitch went to look for you boys because they heard two gunshots. When Mitch couldn't find you at your house, he went looking for you where they'd heard the shots. Thing is, Mrs. Ford said those first two shots came from the same direction as the two she heard later, so you and your friend should've heard them."

His questions had been a trap and he'd caught me lying. I didn't know what to say. I shrugged my shoulders. Sometimes that worked with my mother. It didn't work with him. "You know what else bothers me, Billy?"

I played dumb, shrugged my shoulders again, but my stomach was in an awful knot. I didn't think things could get any worse. I was wrong.

"When you and Dalton were sitting in my car yesterday I smelled gunpowder. Can you explain that, Billy?"

I couldn't possibly think of an answer, not while he was staring at me waiting for one, and that lasted forever; well, until my mother came out to join us. Lucky for me, the sheriff didn't say anything to her about the first two gunshots the Fords had heard or about smelling the gunpowder. If he had, it would've made Mom suspicious, and she would've pestered me with questions in front of Dad until I spilled my guts.

Instead, he told her he was looking for Clayton Damon because Mitch had been killed near Clayton's still. Until then, Dalton and I had owned the lie. But if the sheriff was after Clayton for killing Mitch, the lie had gotten away from us. Now, like the monsters in those late-night movies I watch, the lie's tentacles had reached all the way to Nettie.

Mother asked the sheriff if he thought Clayton had killed Mitch.

"Your boy and his friend were the only witnesses, ma'am. I don't have much to go on but what they told me."

She made a face. I guess she didn't know what to make of his comment. I held my breath and worried about what she'd ask him next. He told her he'd let her know if there was any news. That seemed to satisfy her. She told me to stay in sight of the house then went back inside.

Before the sheriff got into his car he said to me, "You'd feel better if you told me what really happened yesterday."

I was glad my mother hadn't heard that. But I wouldn't be in the clear unless I thought of a way to explain why Dalton and I didn't hear the first two shots, the ones we fired at the tree.

While I watched him drive away I thought about something he'd said that didn't make sense; that Thelma told him the first two shots she heard come from the same direction as the two she heard later. I repeated it several times to myself, even said it out loud, wondering if I'd heard him wrong, or was just remembering it wrong.

I was on my way to Thelma's to ask her about it when I heard my mother knocking on the window over the kitchen sink. She waved her hand at me. I went inside expecting her to ask me a bunch of questions. Instead she told me to leave Thelma alone, and to stay away from the Damon place, which was silly because staying in sight of the house made going to the Damons' impossible.

Mother started taking cooking stuff out of the cupboards. I asked her what they'd do to Clayton.

"He'll go to prison."

I already felt bad enough about Mitch dying, and for lying about it. I didn't want Clayton going to jail because I lied to keep Dalton out of trouble. It wasn't fair that I had to choose between him and Clayton. I started for the bedroom then remembered something Sis had said about Nettie. I asked Mom how long Clayton would be in prison.

"A very long time, why?"

"Did Nettie's mom really run away?"

She was flipping through a cookbook with a faded picture of a pie on the cover and lots of paper scraps stuck inside it. She stopped what she was doing. "Did who what?"

"Mrs. Damon. Did she run away?"

I think she was only half listening to me because she bent down closer to the book and slid her finger down the list of ingredients for a recipe. "That's what I heard from Mrs. Madison."

I asked her what would happen to Nettie and her sister with their mom gone and their dad in prison.

She looked up from her book. "What, dear?"

It can be a real pain talking to my mom while she's cooking. "The Damon kids, Mom. What's gonna happen to them?"

"Why all the questions, Billy?"

I shrugged my shoulders.

"Well," she said, hesitating, as though she had to think about it before answering. "I suppose they'll be put in an orphanage."

As I watched her get three eggs and a stick of butter out of the refrigerator I thought about the kids at school and how they'd been mean to Nettie.

"Mom?"

I knew from the irritated way she said, "Yes, Billy?" that I was getting on her nerves. She went back to reading her recipe.

"Will the kids there be as mean to Nettie as they were to Oliver?"

"Oliver who?" she asked, without looking up from her book.

I gave up, told her, "Never mind" then left.

As I was going out the kitchen door Mom said she was sorry but she couldn't talk because she was in the

177

middle of making a pineapple upside-down cake. My mother loved pineapple upside-down cake. I thought it was yucky. Unfortunately, one of them would last for days and Mom wouldn't make any good desserts until it was all gone. It would've upset me if I wasn't in so much trouble.

I wanted some company, but not anyone asking me questions I couldn't answer, so I took the dog outside. We sat on the front steps and I told her the whole terrible truth about Mitch. When I finished my story and stopped petting her Star wagged her tail and licked my face. I felt a little better then, enough to play fetch. Foolishly assuming she would understand the game, I tossed a stick for her to fetch. She ran after it, even barked at it, but wouldn't bring it back. I soon tired of fetching it for her.

Star and I were lying in the grass under a tree when Mother called me back in. I expected to get a scolding but got a nice surprise instead. "Dalton's mother called. She invited you over to their house for the night. You can go there or you and Dalton can stay here. Either way, it's alright with me. But you have to let me know now so I can call her back."

If Mom and dad knew what Dalton and I had done, I'd never see him again. But I got lots of sympathy because I'd lied about it. And speaking of sympathy, Mothers have this thing about hanging around to help their kids when they're upset, so I tried not to sound too excited when I told her I'd rather go to Dalton's.

When I went back outside I saw Thelma kneeling in the garden along the side of their house. She saw me and waved me over. I didn't want to go, because I thought for sure she'd she see through my lies, or I'd say something stupid, 'cause it's what I do. But I couldn't very well avoid it after she waved me over there.

"THEY'LL PUT NETTIE IN AN ORPHANAGE"

I went over and asked Mrs. Ford what she was doing.

"I planted these pansies for Mitch. They were his favorite flowers."

The wrinkles around her eyes and mouth made Thelma look old and tired. I asked her if she was okay. Her chin quivered. I hoped she wouldn't cry.

"For forty years," she said, "I've hardly spent a day without Mitch. I don't want to be here if I have to live without him."

She blinked some wetness back from her eyes. Seeing Thelma upset like that made me feel so terribly uncomfortable I wanted to run away and die.

I guess she could see that she'd made me uncomfortable because she said, "I'm sorry, Billy, you've got enough sadness of your own. You don't need mine too."

Although I said, "That's okay," it really wasn't. I knew I should say something to comfort her, but didn't know what because nobody close to me had ever died. I didn't even understand what it meant to be dead.

Dalton once told me that you just disappear when you die, but that was too strange to believe. Once when I'd asked Mom about it, she told me you went to heaven when you died, but she couldn't tell me what it was like there, so I kinda doubted that story. But Mitch's death meant I'd be gone someday too, and so would everyone I knew, and no one could tell me where we'd go or what would happen to us when we got there.

Thelma was pulling out the crabgrass growing around the pansies. "I should've taken better care of these when Mitch was alive."

She asked me if I'd like to help. "We'd be doing it for Mitch."

I started pulling grass. How could I tell her no?

She told me that the yellow flowers were his favorites because they reminded him of the ones growing around his house when he was a kid. When we had all of the grass out of the flowerbed she asked me if I wanted a glass of iced tea. I was afraid she'd ask me questions I didn't want to answer. So I told her, "No thank you, ma'am," then went home to hide from her.

On my way through the kitchen Mother stopped what she was doing to tell me, "That was sweet of you to help Thelma."

To avoid seeing Thelma again I stayed indoors the rest of the day. To avoid Mom I stayed out of the kitchen. That only left my bedroom and Lisa was lying on her bed reading.

When I opened the door she looked up from her book to ask, "What are you doing in here?"

"I live here."

She warned me not to make any noise.

I was rummaging through the junk box I kept on the floor of our closet when she said my name.

"Yeah?"

"If you could have Mitch back for a day, what would you want to do with him?"

"Sit on their porch and talk and eat some of Thelma's cornbread."

She said, "I guess you're not such a bad little snot after all" then went back to her reading.

As long as she was being nice I figured it'd be safe to ask her a question. "Hey Sis."

"Yeah?"

"What happens to you when you die?"

She said she didn't know.

"Didn't you read about it in one of your books?"

She shook her head. "None of them come right out and tell you."

"What good is it if they don't tell you the answer?"

"The way they ask questions about things helps the reader understand them."

I told her that was dumb.

She shrugged her shoulders and went back to her reading.

The day dragged until dinner, which was pork chops and rice, one of my least favorite dinners, but way better than liver and onions. Dalton was sitting on their porch in a rocking chair when Mother dropped me off at his house after dinner. I saw his dad through the screen door, asleep in the easy chair in their living room. Dalton told me to wait outside for him while he took my overnight bag into the house, closing the screen door carefully so it wouldn't wake his dad.

Closing it carefully again when he came back out, he nodded his head toward "Poor Town" and jumped off the porch. We snuck away under a cloudy, threatening sky that made the early evening seem darker than it should have been. Spanish moss hanging from live oak trees so large their branches met over the street, blocked the meager light coming from the streetlights that worked.

When we were far enough away from his house that his parents couldn't hear us, I asked him where we were going.

"I gotta go see Sam."

"Why?"

"Because he stuck a note in our screen door. Lucky for me I found it before my folks did."

"How come?"

"Because they'd be pissed if they knew I go there to see him."

Half a block later Dalton stopped and grabbed me by the arm. "My dad still doesn't know the gun is missing. But when he finds out he's gonna figure out that we took it. Then he'll start

181

wondering what really happened to Mitch. So you gotta get it back for me."

I couldn't blame Dalton for being scared. His dad was a lot scarier than mine. But I didn't like him saying that we took the gun. That had been his idea. But he had helped me when I had the fight with Craig even though I hadn't helped him when he had the fight with Donna. So I figured the least I could do was get the gun back for him.

I told him I'd seen the sheriff at Thelma's house that morning. Dalton asked me what he wanted.

"He thinks the bootlegger who lives down the road from us killed Mitch."

Dalton picked up a stone and threw it so hard I heard him grunt from the effort. "Good," he said, as the stone sailed over the tree line.

I told him Clayton was Nettie's dad; that her mother left town, and that, "If Clayton goes to jail they'll put Nettie in an orphanage."

Dalton told me to forget about them. I hated having to choose between helping Dalton and helping Nettie.

"Is that it?" he asked.

"Is that what?"

"Did the sheriff say anything else?"

"He knows we were shooting a gun."

"Did he tell you that?"

"He said we smelled like gunpowder."

"Then you gotta find it so I can clean it and put it back, and you gotta do it soon."

He started to walk away. I grabbed him by the shirtsleeve and turned him around to face me. "Even if I do find it, your house is a long way from mine. What if I bring it all the way into town and you aren't home?"

After standing there for a while looking at his feet, Dalton said, "I know. Put it on the shelf under the window in Quinn's garage. He'll never see it there."

I asked Dalton how he'd know when it was there.

"I'll check his garage every night until I find it.

A mosquito landed on the back of my neck for a drink of blood. I swatted it so hard Dalton stopped and turned around. He looked at me for a moment, as though he expected me to say something, then shook his head and walked away.

The little bit of city light bouncing off the clouds from above was barely strong enough for us to see our way down the winding narrow path from Sam's cabin to the river. We found him sitting on his crate with a fishing pole in his hand and a bobber floating in the slow moving dirty river. It looked as though he hadn't moved since the last time we were there.

Without so much as a, "Hi, how are ya?" Dalton asked him, "What the hell were you thinking leaving me that note? You could've gotten me in a heap of trouble."

"The maid who works for the Madisons went missing."

Dalton looked so angry he could spit. "So what?"

Sam looked at me. "Who's that friend of yours, Billy; the one who got hisself killed?"

"You mean Mr. Ford?"

"Yes, sir, that's the one."

"What about him?"

"Well this girl Jessie heard Judge Madison and that foreman of his arguing about your friend. It was somethin' about how that Ford fella got hisself killed. It might've ended there, 'cept the judge's wife came in where Jessie was working. When she heard her husband and that Quinn fella arguing in the next room, she knew Jessie had heard them too. I find it a might peculiar that Jessie went missing right after that. That's why I done left you a note."

Dalton told Sam he should have called the police instead.

"Hell, you know they ain't gonna do nothin' to help a girl from Poor Town."

Dalton dug a pebble out of the riverbank and tossed it high and hard out over the river. "What'd you expect me to do?"

"I thought maybe the police would do something if you boys got your parents to call them."

Something bothered me about Sam's story. "If Jessie disappeared, how do you know what she heard?"

"I get a little work at the feed store now and again, and a guy who works there told me about it this morning."

"He heard it from Jessie?"

Sam shook his head. "Not directly, no. You see, Jessie knew Mrs. Madison would tell the Judge, and that he'd be angry as hell. But poor Jessie didn't have anyone to tell except the old woman who cooks for the Madisons.

"Well, the cook told her friends, and they told their friends. That's how it starts, and before you know it everybody in 'Poor Town' knows about it. They was talking about it this morning at the feed store. One of 'em said that Ford fella was friends with some Yankees that just moved here."

Sam who'd been watching his bobber while he talked to me, twisted sideways to look me in the eye. "Since you're the only Yankee I know of, I figured he might've been your friend and you'd want to know what Jessie heard. And I thought maybe you could help her."

"We're just kids," Dalton said, and there was an angry edge to his voice.

He walked away then, toward the cabin. I thanked Sam then hurried to catch up with Dalton. All the way back to Dalton's I wondered why Mr. Madison and Joe Quinn would argue about Mitch. Somebody needed to tell the sheriff. I'd never convince my parents to do it, so it had to be me.

When I told Dalton my idea he called me a fool, and asked me how I planned to tell the sheriff about it.

"When my mom goes to get my dad tomorrow I'll look his phone number up in the book."

He shook his head and walked away. When we got to his house we climbed into the big live oak and sat on a branch big enough to hold us both.

"You're just a kid," he said. "The sheriff's not gonna believe you."

Thelma and Mitch had always listened to me. If anyone

184

would help me, it was Thelma. I told Dalton I'd ask her to help.

"She's just an old lady."

"Yeah, but the sheriff will listen to her."

"And I bet she won't do it," Dalton said.

After his parents had gone to bed Dalton and I found a late-night horror movie about killer rabbits, something I would've liked if I hadn't had so many things worrying me. Sometime in the middle of the night I saw myself staring back at me from a mirror, and it scared the hell out of me because there was nothing but smooth skin where my mouth should've been. I felt my face to be sure my lips were there then fell back to asleep.

The breeze out of the south the next morning felt so warm it reminded me of sitting under a hair dryer, which I had tried once out of curiosity when my mom dragged me to one of those places where they fix women's hair.

Dalton and I sat on his porch reading comics and drinking iced tea while I waited for my mother to pick me up on her way home after taking Dad to work. Normally, I would've been happy just being lazy, but Dalton's dad was listening to the news on the radio, something about a guy convicted of murder who was sent to jail for life, a reminder that Clayton was going to prison because of me and Dalton. I felt lousy about it.

When I got home I went inside to get out of the hot sun. A few minutes later while I was rummaging through my junk box in the bedroom looking for something to do I heard the phone ring. Because we almost never got a phone call, I ran out to the kitchen to see who it was.

I heard Mother say, "I see," once or twice, but mostly she just listened, so I couldn't tell who had called. After she hung the phone back on the wall she stood there with her hand on it, just staring at it. I asked her who it was.

"I guess you won't be going anywhere for a while."

It was a fate worse than death. I asked her why.

Mother went on staring at the phone while she answered me, as though the answer was written on the wall next to it and she was reading it to me. "That was the Sheriff. He said that the

185

two men who kidnapped you are out on bail."

"They're not in jail anymore?"

"Which means you're not going anywhere."

"But that's not fair. I didn't do anything wrong."

When Mother turned around to look at me, I saw tears in her eyes. Rather than risk pushing her over the edge and getting the belt from Dad, I decided to argue about it some other time and went outside.

I picked stones from the driveway and threw them into the field behind the house. I threw them as hard as I could until my arm hurt. Then I wasted a few hours playing at nothing in particular while I worked up the courage to talk to Thelma about Jessie, because Thelma would get upset for sure when I mentioned Mitch.

The shadows were twice as long as the things that made them, and the temperature had dropped from sweltering to merely hot. On the way to Thelma's I imagined Mitch sitting on the porch smoking his pipe, imagined asking him what I should do about Dalton, and Nettie, and the lies I'd told. He would've told me what I needed to do.

I knew from the way Thelma smiled when she said, "Come in, Billy," that she was glad to see me, but sitting at her kitchen table without Mitch felt strange and awfully sad. And something besides Mitch was missing, but I couldn't figure out what.

Thelma asked me the same question Mitch used to ask me. "To what do I owe this pleasure?"

I shrugged my shoulders because I wasn't ready to tell her about Jessie.

She stood up and put on her cooking apron, the one covered with little red flowers. "I think I'll bake us some cookies."

Even though the thought of having cookies made my stomach growl, I told her, "'No thank you, ma'am," because I'd be much too nervous to enjoy the cookies until I told her about Jessie.

"Well," she said, sitting down and giving my hand a gentle pat, "I can see something's bothering you. Why don't you tell me what it is?"

I asked her if they had caught the "Wolf's-Head Man."

"Oh, Billy, there's no such thing as the 'Wolf's-Head Man.'"

"But we saw him, Mrs. Ford, we really did. He was standing right there in the path looking at us, and he looked just like the guy we saw hanging in the tree, only this time he came back to life."

Thelma patted my hand again, and said, "I wasn't there so I don't know what you saw, but I can tell you for sure there's no such thing as a 'Wolf's-Head Man,' and if anyone's going to come back to life, I hope it's my Mitch."

I realized then what was missing. Whenever I had visited the Fords, Thelma's kitchen had been filled with the mouth-watering smell of something cooking. She didn't have Mitch around to cook for anymore. It made me feel so guilty I almost ran away. I decided to tell Thelma about Jessie quickly so I could leave. I started with the time I heard Donna's mom and dad arguing.

"Folks argue all the time, Billy. You shouldn't worry yourself about that."

"I was with their maid when I heard them."

That made her smile. "Oh my," she said, "I'll bet there's a story in that."

I shook my head, told her there wasn't. "But Jessie, that's her name, she overheard some other stuff. That's what I came to talk to you about."

"I see. And what did she hear that's so important?"

"That guy Quinn, the one who works for Mr. Madison, the one Mitch told me to stay away from, Jessie heard him arguing with Mr. Madison."

I wished I'd taken the milk Thelma had offered me, because by then I was so nervous my mouth had gone dry.

"Don't keep me in suspense, Billy. What'd she hear?"

I blurted it out, to get it over with. "They were arguing about Mitch getting killed."

Thelma got up from the table and walked around

the kitchen, opening and closing cupboards without taking anything out, as though she needed to do something but couldn't remember what. It gave me the willies.

It was a big relief when she finally sat down and asked, "Jessie told you that?"

"No, ma'am. Sam told me. He's a friend of Dalton's. He heard about it."

Thelma frowned at me, the way my Mom did when she didn't one hundred percent believe me, so I didn't tell her Sam had heard about it at work. I did tell her that Jessie had gone missing.

Thelma stared at the table for a while. When she finally looked at me she said, "You're right, Billy, it sounds fishy. And I'd sure like to know what those two said about Mitch."

But even before she said, "I'm sorry, Billy, but I can't call the sheriff just because your friend's friend says it's so," I knew she wasn't going to call him. I knew it because she was frowning at me, and she was frowning because she knew she would disappoint me.

I suggested that we go find Jessie and ask her what she heard.

"What's Jessie's last name?"

I shrugged my shoulders and wished I'd thought to ask Sam that. Thelma asked me if I knew where Jessie lived.

"With her grandma."

Thelma smiled. "I see, and where does Jessie's grandma live?"

I told her I didn't know.

"What's her grandmother's name?"

I told her I didn't know that either.

"Well," Thelma said, laughing enough to make her tummy jiggle, "you're not much help, are you?"

She sat down. For a while we sat without talking, her looking at me, making me nervous, and me feeling guiltier by the minute. I thought she'd decided not to help, but when I started to say something, she put her hand up to stop me. "If I was the one that got killed, and you told Mitch this same story, he'd go find out if it was true, and what it meant."

Then she stood up so quickly she startled me. "We'll see if we can't find Jessie's grandmother." She told me to go ask my mother if I could go into town with her.

I had just jumped out of the door, clearing the back steps, when she yelled after me, "Tell your mother I'm going to town to run an errand. No need to tell her anything more."

I found my mother in the bathroom cleaning the tub, but I changed my mind about asking her if I could go to town with Thelma because she might say "no," and without Jessie, Nettie would end up in an orphanage because of me, and her dad would go to jail for a long time because of me. I made noise rummaging in the junk box in my closet pretending to look for a toy, so she wouldn't get suspicious then hurried back outside.

I ran across the driveway to Thelma's car. Even if Mother went to the kitchen and looked out the window over the kitchen sink, she wouldn't see me sitting in Thelma's car if I slouched down so my head was lower than the top of the seat. She might see me when Thelma turned the car around but then it would be too late.

Thelma's car had been sitting in the sun all day, so when I opened the door the blast of heart reminded me of standing near the Damon's burning house. To make things worse, the Fords had plastic covers on the car seats. I guess it made the seats easier to clean, but on a sunny day those covers get as hot and sticky as melted cheese. I rolled my window down to let in some not-quite-so-hot air.

I expected Mother to come out at any second and catch me while I waited for Thelma in the hot car. When Thelma did finally come out she walked to the car slowly, as though we had all the time in the world. I wanted to scream at her to hurry.

Mother would probably look for me before we got back. At first she'd be worried that those two guys had kidnapped me again. When she found out that I snuck out she'd ground me for about a million years. When Dad found out, I'd get an extra

189

helping of belt. So Thelma and I had to get everything fixed that afternoon in case I couldn't get away ever again.

With the car moving and both of our windows wide open the air inside the car cooled off a little. I leaned back on the sticky seat and asked Thelma where we were going.

"I've got a friend who does charity work in Poor Town. She might know where Jessie and her grandma live."

Her friend lived in such a crummy-looking little house I thought she needed some charity herself. Thelma told me to wait in the car. I saw her knock on the front door several times before a woman about Thelma's age came and talked to her through the screen door. The more they talked, the more I worried we might not find Jessie's grandma after all.

I was dying of thirst and dripping with sweat by the time we left her friend's place. As Thelma backed the car into the street she told me her friend knew where Jessie lived and that we were going there next. I was so happy we'd get to talk to Jessie's grandma that I forgot about how much trouble I'd be in when I got home.

As Thelma spun her tires trying to get the car moving faster than a walk on the sandy street, we passed a young couple walking. They stopped to watch us go by. When the man gave us a dirty look, I asked Thelma if she was scared. She reached for her purse, which was on the seat between us, and opened it just enough for me to see the checkered wooden pistol grip. My parents must've been the only grownups in Tuscumbia who didn't carry guns. At first the sight of it was reassuring. Then I realized that she wouldn't have brought it unless she thought we might need it.

"NO TELLING WHAT HE MIGHT DO"

Thelma pulled onto the hard-packed sand that passed for a front yard at our next stop, a tiny little house somewhere deep in "Poor Town." I followed her to the front porch which had posts that leaned to the left on a floor that sloped to the right, like a cartoon shack on the Deputy Dog show. The screen door rattled when she knocked on it. The clatter of it slapping against the doorjamb was louder than the sound her knuckles made rapping on the wood.

An old, old woman leaning on a cane answered the door. Barely taller than me, and older and skinnier than anybody I'd ever met, her dress looked lumpy where it hung on her shoulder bones. Under her skin, which was as see-through as the copy paper we used in art class, I saw the blue and red lines of her blood vessels and veins.

To look us over, which she did, the old woman had to turn her head sideways, because she was one of those old people who are permanently bent over looking down at their feet. I wondered if she was as worried about us as I was about being in "Poor Town."

When Thelma said, "We'd like to talk to you, Mrs. Miller," she didn't move or say anything for half a minute or more. I thought she wasn't going to let us in. But when Thelma told her we weren't selling anything, that we just wanted to talk to her about Jessie, Mrs. Miller took a step back and held the screen door open for us. We stepped into a room that looked as small as Dalton's living room and neat as a pin, except for the little girls' rag dolls she had on display just about everywhere.

Thelma didn't sit down but I did. After carefully lowering herself into a plain wooden chair Mrs. Miller sat with her legs tight together and her hands folded in her lap, like a good little girl. I couldn't help noticing how her left eye looked as clear and blue as the sky, but her clouded-over right eye looked as though it had filled up with milk.

I thought Mrs. Miller might offer us some iced tea, maybe even some cookies, but she didn't. Instead her bony fingers tightened on the arms of her chair and she asked Thelma, "Are you gonna make trouble for my Jessie?"

Thelma shook her head. "I promise, we just want to ask her a few questions."

The old woman grunted, as though she didn't believe it.

Thelma told her about Mitch and that someone had shot him, and, "I think Jessie might know something about it because she heard Mr. Madison arguing with his foreman about it."

The old woman wagged a bony little finger at Thelma. "I lost my husband too and both my children. Now, Jessie's all I got left and we got troubles enough of our own. We don't need you causing us any."

"Mrs. Miller," Thelma said, "if I don't talk to Jessie I may never find out what happened to my husband."

The old woman looked really tired all of a sudden. "I'll tell you what I know then you gots to leave. I recollect Jessie saying Mr. Madison and another fella were arguing about some old man who got hisself killed. Maybe it was your husband. Maybe it weren't."

"Did she tell you what the men said?"

Mrs. Miller shook her head. Thelma asked her when she'd seen Jessie last.

"My Jessie's a good girl. She always comes home after

192

work. When she came home two nights ago she told me about those men arguing. She didn't come home after work last night."

When Thelma told her she should call the police the old woman said, "They just be saying my Jessie's a bad girl, staying out late and doin' things she shouldn't be a doin'."

Thelma told Mrs. Miller that Jessie was probably in danger. As she pushed herself up out of her chair Mrs. Miller's skinny little arms shook like baby Bambi's legs.

Leaned on her cane, swaying a little, she pointed a tiny, boney finger at Thelma. "The judge might fire her if he finds out I been talking to you, and her job pays for everything we got." Mrs. Miller told Thelma she had nothing more to say and asked us to leave.

Back in the car I asked Thelma if we were going to the police station to get help.

"No Billy, I'm afraid not."

I asked her why.

"All we have is a second hand account of something a servant girl overheard Judge Madison say. But even if Jessie was here to tell them herself, they probably wouldn't take her word over his because he's one of the most respected men in Tuscumbia. I'm sorry, Billy, but I'm afraid there isn't anything else we can do."

"But you told Mrs. Miller that Jessie's in danger. Shouldn't we at least try to help her?"

"I'll tell you what I'll do, Billy. When we get home I'll call the sheriff. I'll tell him that Mrs. Miller hasn't seen Jessie for two days and ask him to keep an eye out for her."

So that was it. Thelma was ready to go home. But it might take a long time for the sheriff to find Jessie, if he even bothered to look for her. And without Jessie, Clayton and Nettie were doomed. I had to think of something, and quick, and for a change, I did. I told Thelma I had an idea.

"Yes, Billy."

"We could go talk to Mr. Quinn. He isn't respected like the judge is."

193

Thelma said it wasn't a good idea. I asked her why.

"We can't just go knock on his door and ask him where Jessie is."

"Why not?"

"If he was involved in her disappearance, he certainly isn't going to tell us about it, because that would land him in jail."

"You could use your gun to make him tell us."

She pulled the car off the pavement and stopped. After she put the gearshift in park she turned in her seat to face me. "Billy, Mitch was right about Joe Quinn. He's a dangerous man. Gun or no gun, there's no telling what he might do if we went to his house and confronted him. I told you I'd ask the sheriff to look for Jessie and I will. Now I want you to forget about all this and let him handle it. It's much too dangerous for us to do anything more."

I'd never been more discouraged in my whole life. Everything had gone wrong. If the adult world was that unfair I didn't ever want to grow up. And if things weren't bad enough already, by the time we got home Mother was hysterical. She must have been watching for us because she came running outside to meet us as soon as Thelma turned into the driveway.

I knew I was in big trouble, but when Mother yelled, "Where the hell have you two been?" as we were getting out of the car, it really took poor Thelma by surprise.

Thelma only managed to say, "We were," before Mother grabbed my arm and yanked me toward our house. I could always tell how mad my mother was by how fast she walked. I had to run to keep up with her that day. After she told me she'd been worried sick she sent me to my room. And she told me she'd be in later, and that I'd better have a damn good explanation for sneaking off the way I did.

I thought I'd gotten off easy until she told me, "Your father's going to hear about this."

If Dad was as mad as Mother he'd use his belt on me for sure. And on top of that I felt bad about Thelma. I knew Mother would be mad at me, but I hadn't expected her to be so mad at

194

Thelma. It was bad enough that Dalton and I got Mitch killed, now I'd gotten Thelma in trouble. I'd really made a mess of things again.

When Mother came to my room a little while later, I tried to tell her about Jessie and why we went to see Mrs. Miller, but she didn't want to hear about that. And telling her it was my idea to go into town didn't get Thelma out of trouble. It just got me in more trouble. Mother told me to stay in my room and think about what I'd done while I waited for Dad to get home.

As it turned out, I got a lecture from Dad instead of a beating. I think he felt sorry for me after what had happened to Mitch, because at one point during the lecture he said, "I know you've lost a friend and had to deal with some difficult things lately, so I'm going to let you off easy this one time."

Since Mom and Dad let me out of the bedroom for dinner I thought things would be okay if I could just stay out of trouble for a day or two, but it didn't work out that way. Right after we sat down for dinner Mother got weepy. She only got part way through Sis saying grace before the real crying started. When that happened she got up and stood at the counter with her back to us, sobbing and blowing her nose and slamming drawers.

All of sudden she yelled, "Damn it, Billy," and banged a pot down on the counter so hard the rest of us all flinched, even Dad.

She left the room then. I didn't hear so much as a peep out of Lisa or Dad for the rest of the meal. And I didn't dare make a sound. I even tried to eat quietly. Dad sent me to bed as soon as I finished eating and I went without the usual argument.

Lying in bed, unable to sleep, I tried to think of some way to help Nettie and her dad but all I got for my trouble was a headache. Then I fell asleep.

The racket Sis made rummaging through her dresser drawers looking for something woke me up early the next morning. I was still sleepy but I couldn't sleep, and if I stayed in bed I knew I'd start thinking about all the trouble I had caused and was in. I decided to ask Sis about my nightmare. "Hey, Sis."

She gave me a dirty look. "Yeah, what do you want?"

195

"I had a nightmare."

"Who cares?"

"It was weird."

"They're all weird. So are you."

"In my dream I didn't have a mouth."

She looked at me and frowned, said, "It means you have something you want to tell somebody but can't."

She had to be really smart to figure that out so fast. But I couldn't tell her that - if I did she might figure out that my nightmare was about Mitch's death and the lies I'd been telling. I told her she was crazy.

She shrugged her shoulders then went back to looking for whatever it was she couldn't find. Then I got a crazy idea. If she was so smart, and I was extra, extra careful, why couldn't I ask her what I should do about the lies?

"Hey, Sis?"

She closed the drawer and gave me a disgusted look. "Now what?"

"What if one of my friends did something bad."

"That doesn't surprise me."

"He asked me to lie about it?"

"Nothing good ever comes of lying."

"But it was an accident."

"Doesn't matter."

"And he's been a really good friend."

"It's Dalton, isn't it?"

"I can't tell you."

"Then it doesn't matter what I say."

"Thing is, two of my other friends will catch hell if I don't rat on him."

"How can one kid have so many problems?"

It was a good question, but for another time. "What do you think? Should I lie about it?"

"Did the other kids do bad things too?"

I shook my head.

"Then why would they get in trouble?"

196

"I can't tell you that either."

"Then I can't help you." She started to leave the room.

"Pretty please."

She stopped at the door, "Think about what I asked you."

She left. I thought about it. Clayton had done plenty of bad things like bootlegging and stealing cars. But I didn't know of a single bad thing Nettie had ever done. And she'd have a really bad time of it if she got sent to an orphanage. So I figured that the mess was least fair to Nettie.

I hated to admit it, and I would never tell Sis, but she really was a smart one. Just thinking about her question got me my answer, just like she said it would. If I'd been asking for advice from Sis all along, I might not have gotten into so much trouble. Next time I'd ask her for her help right from the start. But right now, I had to do what was best for Nettie.

Hungry as I was the next morning, I got up early and went out to the kitchen. I knew from Mother's puffy, red eyes that she was right on the verge of another crying fit. She didn't fix my eggs the way I like them and I didn't complain.

I did have a brainstorm while I was eating – Mom might let me go to Dalton's because she'd be happier with me out of her hair, but I waited until I was done eating to ask her, just in case it made her mad because I didn't want to miss out on breakfast. I asked her after I put my dirty plate and fork in the sink.

Her voice cracked when she said "No," so I knew arguing would be a bad idea.

I snuck over to Thelma's house later that morning. I thought she might be mad at me because Mom yelled at her. She was. She scolded me for sneaking out without telling my mom where we were going. When I apologized, she waved a hand, dismissing it, but she wasn't her usual friendly self.

Thelma told me her friend had called her early that morning, the one who told us where Mrs. Miller lived. Her friend said someone had burned down Mrs. Miller's place, that the old woman was okay, but there was nothing left of her house.

Thelma said to me in a dreamy sad voice, "I hope it wasn't

197

because of us being there."

I thought about the poor old woman whose back was so bent she was always looking at the floor, and how she'd been afraid of us. And now all her stuff was gone and she had no place to live. I told her I had to get home because I figured it was our fault and I didn't want to talk about it. I couldn't bear having something else to feel bad about.

When I walked into the kitchen Mom told me to go get in the car.

"Why?"

"Lisa's going to stay with her friend, Susan, for a few days."

On the way I thought about going to Quinn's house to look for Jessie, maybe even confronting him; asking him what happened to her. Then I remembered the demon-dog and wondered if I'd be brave enough to walk through the woods in the dark with that thing out there. And I'd be going right past where I'd seen the dead man and where Mitch was shot. And it was a long walk to Quinn's house through the woods. But I had to try. There wasn't anything else I could do to help Nettie. I'd made up my mind to sneak out after my parents went to bed. Having a plan felt good.

Mom and Dad had liver and rice for dinner that night. Mom had long since given up getting Sis and me to eat liver. So she made hamburgers for us. After we finished eating we moved into the living room to watch the news. A western called The Deputy came on next.

When that ended Perry Como's Kraft Music Hall came on. I asked if I could change the channel. Mother wanted to watch it so I took Star out to do her business. Then I laid down in the grass to wait until my parents went to sleep. As I listened to the crickets and gazed up at the Milky Way to watch for shooting stars I thought about sneaking off.

Being brave had been easy in the bright light of the afternoon, and my imagination had run wild, just like Dad was always saying. But now that it was almost time to leave, I started having doubts. The gun would be hard to find in the dark because I didn't know which direction or how far Dalton had thrown it.

Finding Quinn's garage would be easy. All I had to do was follow the railroad tracks into town. It would be a lot faster than taking the road. But the idea of walking through the woods in the dark was still scary. The thought of running into the half-breed wolf thing was downright frightening. So I was actually glad I'd have the gun.

In the light of day when it's a lot easier to be brave, I had decided to look for Jessie at Quinn's. I remembered thinking the gun would come in handy if Quinn caught me. But now, faced with shooting somebody, I didn't think I could do it, not even Quinn. It left me with a nagging worry: if Quinn caught me, and I couldn't shoot him, what would he do to me.

And that wasn't the only problem with my plan. Because I'd have the gun that killed Mitch, I'd have to come clean on all of the lies, or I'd be blamed for Mitch's death. Of course then my Dad would call Dalton's dad right away. Then Dalton would get the beating he'd been so worried about. I felt bad about that, and he'd probably never forgive me.

Then Mom would tell Dad and the sheriff and Thelma, and they would all know that Mitch's death was partly my fault. But at least Nettie wouldn't have to go to an orphanage and her dad wouldn't end up on a chain gang. Besides, I didn't think Dalton would go to reform school or prison because shooting Mitch had been an accident.

When the house lights finally went out I went in for bed. After Mom and Dad yelled, "Good night, Billy," to me from their bedroom, I counted to two thousand to give them time to fall sleep, all the time dreading what I had to do, and wishing Dalton and I hadn't made such a mess of things.

I had remembered to bring a flashlight, but didn't need it crossing our lawn or walking along the road to the turnoff for Clayton's still, because the moon was bright enough and my eyes were good enough to see my way. But I wouldn't have been able to follow the dirt road through the woods without it, and forget following the path without it.

Except for the bullfrog I heard when I passed near the stream, nothing sounded familiar. And nothing looked familiar, especially where moonlight pierced the thick canopy, creating long, spooky, crooked shadows. I was alone in a world that was pitch black beyond the reach of my flashlight.

I found the place where Dalton and I had been standing when Mitch was shot, but even with the flashlight I couldn't find the gun, and it was getting late. So I decided to go on without it in spite of the demon dog.

As if being alone in the dark where really bad things had happened wasn't frightening enough, it wasn't long before I heard something in the woods. I imagined all kinds of terrifying monsters out there waiting for a chance to do terrible things to me. I decided Dad was right about two things: I had an overactive imagination and I watched too many late-night monster movies. I swore that night that I'd never watch another one. The snap of a twig sent me running for home.

"WE WANNA SCARE 'EM, NOT KILL 'EM"

I'd run far enough to be winded and had stopped to catch my breath when I heard a branch snap and leaves rustling, and it wasn't my imagination either. Something big was moving in the woods on my left. I shined the flashlight in that direction, but whatever had made the noise was beyond its reach. I started running toward Quinn's again, because when you're "pee your pants scared" anything's better than standing still.

As I ran, the sound stayed off to my left but seemed to get ahead of me. I stopped again to look for it, willing my eyes to see something they couldn't. I watched and listened and waited, but the sounds stopped whenever I did. That sent a shiver down my spine because that's what predators do when they're stalking prey.

Then two small, bright-yellow circles just like the ones I'd seen behind my house appeared up ahead in the dark. The monster might have been a car length away; it might have been twice that far; I couldn't tell. Never show fear. That's what they tell you; that predators can sense fear and will attack you if they do. But how was I supposed to hide my fear? I was scared to death.

With my heart beating so hard I was sure the beast could

hear it, I waited for it to lunge at me out of the dark. Then it blinked and I held my breath. When I saw its eyes again the animal had come close enough for me to see its dark shape outlined in the beam of my flashlight.

I turned around and ran. Running on railroad ties meant I had to keep the flashlight pointed at my feet and my eyes looking down, because if I tripped on a tie at a full run I'd fall and break something for sure. I knew I couldn't outrun the thing, and I knew I couldn't hide from it.

I'd be safe if I climbed a tree, but then I'd have to stop running to find one with branches low enough to reach and strong enough to hold my weight. So I kept running. I hoped I could run all the way back to my house. I'd never run that far before, but I'd never been chased by a demon-dog either.

Watching my feet meant I wouldn't see the beast coming. Breathing hard meant I wouldn't hear it coming. I saw wolves run down a deer on a nature special, so I knew I'd feel its teeth dig into me right before it pulled me down. Try as I might, I couldn't run away from that image. My neck tingled at the thought. I was running slower but still running when I saw the main road up ahead. I'd be safe at home in a few minutes.

But as I made the turn onto the road toward my house I saw lights in the trees near the Damon place. I stopped and looked back expecting to see the beast behind me, but it was nowhere in sight. I looked at the Damon place again. Something was definitely wrong. The lights weren't moving the way the headlights on Clayton's car would move when he pulled into the driveway. I checked again to be sure the wolf thing wasn't following me then headed for the Damon place at a slow jog, looking back to check on the wolf more than once.

The pickup truck with the Confederate Flag on the door was parked in the Damon's driveway. After crossing the road I stepped into the field grass so I could get closer to the trailer without being seen.

At the edge of the clearing I knelt down in the grass. That's when I saw Johnny Vail and his friend. By walking in front of the headlights of Johnny's pickup truck the two men had caused the crazy-looking moving lights I'd seen on the trees. Why would they be at Nettie's? It had to be something bad.

I wondered if my parents would believe me if I went home and told them that the two men who kidnapped me and had burned down the Damon house were back. And even if they did believe me, could get home and wake them and get them to do something before it was too late?

While I struggled with whether or not I should run home I watched Johnny take a long drink from a bottle, tipping his head back until the bottom of the bottle pointed at the stars.

The man with the dirty beard and the chewing-tobacco breath pointed at the Damon's trailer. "Why'd we come back here? We already burned their place once."

Johnny pointed toward my house. "Because I heard that their momma tried to kill the white woman who lives two houses back that way."

Taking the bottle from Johnny then tipping the bottle back, swaying so badly he nearly fell down, Johnny's friend told him, "It's scum like them what's ruining the world, just as sure as a pond's got frogs." Then he took a bottle with a rag hanging from its neck out of Johnny's truck.

"Yeah," Johnny said, "let's finish this. We've got another stop to make tonight."

"Where at?"

"Judge Madison's house."

"Ain't he the one told you to do something about that old woman in Poor Town?"

"The very same one who said he'd let us go if we scared her off then reneged on his promise and told us we have to do jail time."

"Damned if we oughtn't teach that son-of-a-bitch a lesson."

Johnny took a swig from the bottle then wiped his mouth on his sleeve. "And we shall do precisely that."

"What kinda lesson, Johnny?"

"That big old plantation house we passed on the way out here; that's his place."

The man with the tobacco breath tried to whistle but just blew out a wet spray.

"Hell," Johnny said, "that man has more lights in his driveway than we have in our entire house," saying the word 'entire' as thought it was two words.

"Ain't right," stink breath said, "him havin' all that when my place ain't worth a spit," which was what he did next to make his point.

Johnny took out a cigarette lighter, and as he held the flame under the rag hanging from the bottle his friend was holding, he declared, "There ain't nothin' like fire to burn the corruption out of a place."

After planting his feet unsteadily, preparing to heave the bottle, his friend said, "I'll throw it through that big window. That'll burn those brats, right quick."

"No," Johnny said, "just throw it at the front door. We wanna scare 'em, not kill 'em."

His friend held the bottle until the flames had climbed up the rag to the neck. It looked as though he was pouring a stream of fire from the bottle. Then he tossed the flaming bottle at the trailer, nearly falling down from the effort. A bright orange spray of flames splashed against the front door of the Damons' trailer then died down to a smoldering fire burning their front steps.

Moments later flames burst out of the smoke and began to climb up the doorway. When he saw them Johnny held his arms up toward the sky like a Sunday preacher and said in a booming voice, "The devil's disciples cannot hide from the flames of the righteous."

Johnny's friend took the whiskey bottle from him. "I'll drink to that," he said. "Yes sir, I surely will."

The blaze cast the clearing in a strange-looking golden light that pulsed as breezes fanned the flames, the flickering glow lighting the faces of Johnny and his friend. I saw Mary

Anne and Nettie watching from one of the windows. They would've seen Johnny's friend toss the flaming bottle at the trailer, but wouldn't know how fast the flames were spreading.

If I ran home for help. I'd have to wake my parents and get them to call the fire department. By the time the firetrucks to got here the trailer would be a ball of flames. I had to do something, and quick, or Nettie and her sister would be trapped in a burning trailer.

Backing into the tall field grass so I'd be beyond the reach of the firelight, I pushed my way through it toward the back of the clearing. The trailer had a back door, but Clayton hadn't put steps in for it so I couldn't reach the door handle. I pounded on the door and yelled Mary Anne's name.

When she opened it I told her, "You gotta get out of there," but she just stood in the doorway with one arm holding Nettie behind her.

Nettie peeked out from behind Mary Ann, her teddy bear dangling from her hand by its leg. I begged them to hurry. Then Mary Anne, who looked as though she'd just seen a ghost, yelled, "Run," and shoved Nettie out the door just as a big calloused hand grabbed the back of my neck. I recognized the smell of bad teeth and chewing tobacco immediately. While I struggled to get away from Johnny's friend Nettie disappeared in the field grass.

The man crushing my neck said, "Well, looky what we have here."

Johnny appeared then. He spit in the dirt. "We are the righteous doing God's work, but the law does not abide killing children."

"You mean I gotta let him go?"

Johnny shook his head. "No, I mean we can't have any witnesses. Hell, we could get the electric chair for torching the trailer with them kids in there, and the boy there saw you do it." Johnny pointed at Mary Anne. "So did she." Then he pointed toward the field, "And that little girl out there did too, so you'd better go catch her. I'll take care of these two."

After Johnny's friend pushed me to the ground he ran into

205

the field after Nettie. I saw Mary Anne turn around. I think she planned to hide in the trailer but Johnny grabbed her by the leg and yanked her out of the trailer before she could move.

We'll never know what Johnny would've done to us because his friend burst out of the tall grass yelling something senseless as he half-ran, half-staggered toward the truck. We watched him climb in and slam the door.

With a look of disgust Johnny shook his head, telling me, "Lucky for you that little girl got away, 'cause now there's no point in killing you," before he dragged Mary Anne to his truck. He forced her into the cab then climbed in, telling her, "You sit there real quiet like or I'll let my friend have his way with you."

Johnny gunned the engine so hard I thought it would explode. The tires squealed when the truck caught the pavement at the road. I watched them until there was nothing left to see but flashes of the truck's lights through the trees as they raced toward town.

By then the fire was so intense the air rushing in to feed the flames ruffled my hair, and even standing two car lengths away from it the heat was too much for me. If the girls hadn't gotten out they'd be dead for sure.

With Nettie nowhere in sight, I was alone, surrounded by fields where shadows flickered eerily at the edge of the firelight's reach. Somewhere in the tall grass a monster with glowing yellow eyes waited. And Poor little Nettie was out there all by herself.

I knew I'd be safe as long as I stayed near the fire, and I hoped Nettie would come back before the flames died. I yelled her name and watched the field grass for movement. When I saw something coming out of the field, I held my breath and backed up closer to the fire in case it was the wolf.

I felt dizzy with relief when Nettie stepped out of the grass, but barely had time to catch my breath before the monster appeared behind her. With it behind her, Nettie looked tiny. I watched in horror as she walked toward me with that monster right behind her. I must've looked scared, because she stopped and looked back. She didn't run, or yell, or scream. She held her hand out to it. It went to her, sat next to her then stared at me, its eyes glowing bright gold in the firelight.

Nettie held her hand out to me. I shook my head. She came to me holding her hand out. I took it warily. I trusted her, with my life I guess. The beast turned around then and walked back into the field.

When I asked Nettie, "What's with the dog?" she just shrugged her shoulders.

Little Nettie looked at me with tear-filled eyes, as though she wanted me to fix everything that had broken in her world, the same way I suppose I looked to my parents when I wanted help. And even though she wanted more from me than I could possibly do. I had to try.

I told her, "I'll take you to my house, if you want. You'll be safe there while you wait for your dad. But I heard Johnny say they're going to Judge Madison's house next so that's where Mary Anne will be. If you're not too scared, we'll take the railroad tracks through the woods to his house. If we hurry we might get there before they leave.

I can take you to my house if you'd rather, but here's the trouble with that; if we go to my house and tell my parents what happened, they'll call the sheriff, but he might not get to Judge Madison's house before Johnny leaves with Mary Anne."

Nettie's answer was to take a step toward the road then tug on my shirt sleeve. I took hold of her hand and we hurried toward the road with Nettie's little legs working twice as hard as mine, just to keep up.

We took the turnoff for Clayton's still, following the dirt road until we came to the railroad tracks then on into the woods. Afraid Nettie might fall running on the railroad ties, I let her set the pace. But then I worried we might be too late to catch Johnny at Judge Madison's. And I wondered what I'd do if we did catch up with Johnny.

When I spotted the lights from the Madisons' place, I led Nettie through a pasture then across their back yard to the house. As we neared the house I heard Johnny and the judge talking, and the talk was angry. From behind a bush at the corner of the house I saw Johnny standing at the foot of Madisons' front steps holding a bottle with a rag hanging from it, like the one his friend had thrown at Nettie's house.

Mr. Madison stood on his porch holding a rifle pointed at Johnny. Donna and her brother Peter stood behind him in the open doorway.

With the bottle in his left hand, an open cigarette lighter near the rag in his right hand, and his thumb on the flint wheel, Johnny told the judge, "I've got the bootlegger's daughter in my truck."

The judge glanced back at Donna and Peter. "You kids go inside and close the door."

"I'm warning you, Madison," Johnny said, waving the bottle at him. "I'll toss this right in her lap."

I wondered what Johnny's friend, who was sitting in the truck next to Mary Anne, thought of that.

The judge told Johnny, "Go ahead. She means nothing to me."

"You lied to us," Johnny said, sticking his chin out like an angry kid. "You said you'd let us go free if we took care of that old woman, but that was just a lie to get us to do your dirty work, wasn't it?"

"Leave now or get shot, it's your choice," Madison said.

I whispered to Nettie to stay out of sight in the bushes then stepped out into the open.

When Johnny saw me he said, "I should've knocked you silly and dumped you in that trailer to burn."

Madison told Johnny, "You've got till the count of ten," then started counting.

Johnny threatened to tell the sheriff that Madison had hired them to burn down Mrs. Miller's house.

Madison counted. I held my breath.

When the judge said, "Nine," Johnny tossed the bottle on the lawn unlit, said, "This isn't over, Madison" then stormed off toward his truck.

I yelled to Johnny to stop but he ignored me. He got into his truck and gunned the engine, his tires spraying gravel at Madison's house as he spun the truck around in the driveway.

I'd wasted my one chance to help Mary Anne. When Clayton got home, he'd find his place in ruins and both of his girls missing. I wondered what he'd do to me when he found out I'd put Nettie in danger by bringing her with me to Judge Madison's.

Pointing his gun at me, the judge asked, "What the hell are you doing here?"

"Those men set fire to the Damon place, twice."

"So what?"

"You got them to burn Mrs. Miller's place too."

"If you know what's good for you, you'll keep your mouth shut about that."

I'd never get another chance to say it. "Jessie heard you and Quinn arguing about Mr. Ford getting shot."

Him saying, "And you can't prove it without her," meant that Jessie did know something important, and that the judge probably knew what had happened to her. But it didn't matter because in a few seconds Madison would go inside and it would be game over.

Then as Madison reached for the doorknob, I remembered something the sheriff thought was important. I told Madison what Thelma told the sheriff. "Mrs. Ford heard four shots the day Mitch was killed."

With his hand on the doorknob he glanced back at me. "So there were four shots, so what?"

I had stopped him, which meant that the number of shots was important. I gave it some thought and things began to fall into place. "My friend Dalton brought a gun with him that day. We each took one shot at a tree. That's two shots. Mitch heard them and came looking for us. Just before he found us we saw the 'Wolf's-Head Man,' and it scared Dalton so bad that, when he heard Mitch on the trail behind us, he spun around and fired his

209

gun. That's when Mitch fell."

"That's right, kid. Your friend shot old man Ford."

"But that's only three shots. Mrs. Ford heard four. I did too. I thought the forth one was just an echo. But it wasn't an echo, was it, Mr. Madison? It was another shot, the one that killed Mitch."

Madison had turned to face me again. His fingers were white where they gripped his gun. And even though he said, "Doesn't matter what you think," I knew it did, because he looked unsure of what to do about me. He was probably wondering how much more I knew, and I had just figured out plenty more.

I told him I'd seen both Quinn's and Clayton's car there that day, and that, "Clayton pretended to be the 'Wolf's-Head Man.' He does that to scare people away from his still, and if he'd had a gun I would've seen it. So it must have been Quinn who fired the other shot, the one that killed Mitch."

By saying, "No one's gonna believe a snot-nosed Yankee kid over me," he was admitting that I was right. Unfortunately, he was also right – just knowing that's what happened didn't do me any good. He opened the door to go inside.

Out of desperation I told him, "I saw your wife and Quinn doing things the preacher said they shouldn't do."

As Madison spun around I told him, "And she's there now," out of desperation. I had no idea if it was true.

He came at me in a rush, wild-eyed as a crazy man, I thought for sure he'd hit me, but he rushed past me, as though I wasn't there. He got into the Chrysler. The big engine screamed and the tires spun. I put my arms up to protect my face from flying gravel.

"HE'D BE JUST AS DEAD."

I sat on the top step and watched my last hope driving away in that Chrysler. It didn't matter that I'd figured it all out on my own, something the grownups couldn't do. Because no matter what I did, it didn't work, and I was out of ideas. I would have gone home if Nettie hadn't come and taken my hand. She looked at me expectantly, as though I should know what to do next.

Since the trouble had started with Quinn I figured it had to end with him. So I decided to go to his house. If I found Jessie there maybe I could help her, and maybe the sheriff would believe her in spite of what Thelma and Judge Madison thought. And I didn't know what else to do.

I could follow the railroad tracks which ran straight as an arrow right past Quinn's place. But Nettie would be a problem. She'd slow me down, and I didn't know what I'd do with her when I got to Quinn's. Even though Donna hated her she'd be safer at the Madisons'. But when I told Nettie I planned to leave her there she shook her head defiantly and started to cry. It was a stupid thing to do, but I took her hand and promised her I wouldn't leave her.

We hurried back through the pasture behind the Madisons' then followed the tracks toward town. The woods we passed through on the way to Quinn's were so thick and dark and close against the tracks my imagination started to run wild again. Several times I was sure I heard something big crashing through the brush behind us.

Once when poor Nettie began gasping for breath I stopped to let her rest. While I waited for her to catch her breath I heard more rustling in the woods behind us, in the direction of the Madison place. I spun around to look and saw the demon dog's bright yellow eyes.

If Nettie hadn't come and taken my hand and led me away, toward Quinn's house, I might still be out there, too scared to move. All the way to Quinn's house I heard it moving in the woods, pacing us, and I wondered why Nettie wasn't afraid of it. If I asked her about it, she'd just shrug and pull me along.

When we got to Quinn's I saw Judge Madison's Chrysler parked in the driveway. I whispered to Nettie to wait behind the garage then gave her little hand a squeeze. I looked in the garage window and saw the Thunderbird. I wondered if Judge Madison had caught Quinn and his wife doing something they shouldn't.

I heard a gunshot then, and there's no mistaking the sound of a gunshot. I had expected the judge to be angry about his wife and Quinn, but I hadn't expected to hear a gunshot.

When I got back to Nettie I told her to stay there a little while longer then snuck across the yard to Quinn's bedroom window, and pulling one of the crates out from under the house, I stood on my tiptoes to look over the windowsill.

I saw Mrs. Madison sitting on Quinn's bed, leaning back against the headboard. Her face looked as white as the sheet she had pulled up to cover her. Quinn was sitting on the side of the bed in his underwear looking down at the judge. He was lying on the floor and with a big, red stain on his chest. Quinn had a strange little smile on his face, as though he'd heard a sick joke.

He told Mrs. Madison, "I knew it was only a matter of time before he caught us. Now I'll have to leave town."

"You didn't have to kill him, Joe?"

"Are you crazy? He couldn't live with us cheating on him,

212

not with that monster ego of his. If it wasn't today it would've been some other day and he'd be just as dead. Luckily no one else knows about us. I'll dump his body where no one will ever find it and he'll just be a missing person."

I moved the crate over to the next window to look into the other bedroom. Through a crack in the curtains I saw a girl lying on a bed. Her hands and feet were tied to the bedposts and she had a rag tied over her mouth. It had to be Jessie. Something bad would happen to her now that Quinn was leaving town.

It seemed as though everything that had happened to me since I'd arrived in Tuscumbia had been leading up to that moment. If I helped her I'd also be helping Nettie, and Dalton, and Clayton. It was all or nothing, and with Quinn leaving it was now or never.

I jumped off the crate, ran around to the front of the house, and jumped up onto the porch to look in the front window. Lights were on but I didn't see anyone. After I took my shoes off I tried the front door knob. It turned so easily I had already opened the door and stepped inside before I had decided if it was a good idea. I heard Quinn and Mrs. Madison arguing about him leaving.

I held my breath then tiptoed past the kitchen doorway. If the floor squeaked I'd be dead. The door to the first bedroom was open. I saw Mr. Madison's body on the floor. Jessie would be in the next room.

The moment I stepped into the room Jessie thrashed against the ropes holding her. I remembered Mom standing in our bedroom doorway to say goodnight to us. With light from the hallway behind me I would just look like a dark shape to her. I rushed over to the bed so she could see my face then put a finger to my lips to quiet her. But no sooner had she stopped struggling than she began shaking her head frantically, looking past me, as though she'd seen something terrifying behind me.

I turned around and saw a black figure outlined in the doorway. The bedroom light came on. It was Quinn and he was wearing his gun belt. He said, "You put me in a real bad spot, boy," but he was grinning when he said it.

Mrs. Madison appeared at the door behind him. She put her hand over her mouth and gasped. "What the hell have you done. Joe?"

"Now darling," Quinn said, "don't go soiling your panties. I only did what the late Judge Madison told me to do."

She shook her head. "He wouldn't."

"Oh yes. He would. And he did. Hell, your husband deserved to die for all of the terrible things he did."

Still shaking her head, Mrs. Madison asked, "Is that why you killed him, Joe?"

"You know," he said, "for the wife of a judge, you're not real bright. Neither of these kids saw me shoot your husband, but now that you've told them I did, I have to make sure they can't tell anyone."

Mrs. Madison started to turn around to leave, but before she finished saying, "I'm calling the cops," Quinn's hand shot out, fast as a snake, and grabbed her hair.

He yanked her back and turned her around to face us. "You should tell these kids you're sorry, seeing as how it's your fault they have to die."

"You're not gonna kill 'em," she said. "Not even you would do that."

Hearing her say that I felt a glimmer of hope, but only until Quinn said, "Thanks to you, my dear, it's the only way I can keep the noose off my neck."

I felt lightheaded and unsure of my bladder. I must have looked as bad as I felt because Quinn's lips curled into a smile. He said, "You don't look so good, kid. But don't worry about messing yourself, 'cause dead people don't embarrass as easy as live ones."

He yanked Mrs. Madison's hair, pulling her head back so his mouth was next to her ear. "I can't very well leave you around either, now can I?"

While she struggled with him I watched for a chance to get past them and run for help. Quinn gave her a hard shove into the room that sent her sprawling on the floor. She got to her feet slowly then backed away from him.

He pulled his gun out and pointed it at me. "I think I'll start with you."

It felt like one of my nightmares, but not the kind you wake up from. Things couldn't possibly get any worse, but they did. It started with a noise in the hall. Quinn spun around. Nettie appeared in the doorway.

I yelled, "Run Nettie."

Quinn grabbed her before she could move. He was pulling her into the room when I heard another sound in the hallway. Quinn turned to look just before a big dark blur slammed into him. As it drove him into the room his gun went off. Then it got very quiet.

Quinn was lying on the floor with the big demon dog on top of him. Quinn pushed it aside and stood up. The beast's chest was heaving. It wasn't moving otherwise. Dropping her teddy bear, Nettie ran over to the dog and sat on the floor next to it. She cradled its head it in her lap. Its tail twitched.

Quinn took a step toward Mrs. Madison. She had picked up his gun. I figured he must've dropped it when the dog hit him.

Pointing it at his chest, she said, "Try me, Joe." He didn't.

She told me to untie Jessie, and when Jessie was free, said, "You kids get out of here."

By then, blood oozing out of the half-breed's chest had left a red stain in Nettie's lap. I held my hand out to her and said her name. Nettie shook her head. When I reached for her arm she pulled it away.

Mrs. Madison told us to hurry. "I'm not sticking around while she plays nursemaid to that thing."

With the Dog's head still cradled in her arms, Nettie's tears streamed down her cheeks and dripped on its face, but the thing's eyes were closed and its chest had stopped moving. Nettie stopped petting it. She knew it was dead.

"Last chance," Mrs. Madison said.

I picked up Nettie's teddy bear. Jessie helped me pull Nettie away from the dog and guide her out of the room. From Quinn's front porch we saw lights on at the neighbor's and went there to get help. I stood back with Nettie while Jessie knocked on the door.

Somewhere inside a man yelled, "Yeah, yeah, hold your water, I'm coming."

The barefoot old man who opened the door was wearing pants and suspenders without a shirt. We must've gotten him out of bed. He held the screen door closed and looked us over. He made a face when he saw the blood on Nettie's dress.

Pointing at Nettie he asked Jessie, "What happened to her?"

"Quinn shot her dog."

"What do you want me to do about it?"

Jessie pointed at Quinn's house. Judge Madison is there. He's dead. Quinn killed him. Mrs. Madison is there now and she has his gun."

The man made a sound like a groan. Then I heard another gunshot.

"YOU'RE THE WOLF'S-HEAD MAN"

For as long as it takes to count to ten I didn't see or hear anything at Quinn's house. Then I heard his back screen door slam shut. Right after that I saw Mrs. Madison run to his garage and pull the doors open then disappear inside.

As the Thunderbird's engine roared to life an old woman with curlers in her hair came to the door wearing a bathrobe and stood behind the man and asked, "Was that a gunshot, Verne?"

Verne didn't bother to answer her. Mrs. Madison backed the Thunderbird into the street then drove away in a big hurry.

Peeking out from behind Verne the old woman looked the three of us over suspiciously. "Who are they, and why's she got blood on her?"

Verne told her, "I'm going over there. You'd better call the police." He told us to wait inside with his wife. As Jessie walked past him he told her, "Make sure she doesn't get any of that blood on my furniture."

After a while I heard sirens off in the distance and knew we were finally out of danger. A young policeman with a big square face came to the door a few minutes later.

I'd kept so much in for so long I couldn't keep it in any longer, so when he looked at me the dam holding it back burst. "Quinn kidnapped Jessie because she knew he's the one who shot

217

Mr. Ford, not Mr. Damon. And tonight Quinn shot Judge Madison 'cause the judge caught him in bed doing things to his wife. And he was gonna shoot all of us, but then the wolf knocked him down, so he shot the wolf instead, and...."

"Whoa, there young, fella," the policeman said, putting a hand up to stop me, like my dad did. "You kids had better come with me to the station. I'll have the dispatcher call your parents, and while we're waiting for them you can tell us what happened."

Jessie and I sat in the back of the cruiser with Nettie between us. At the station they asked us for our names and phone numbers and showed us a bench to sit on. A tired-looking man wearing a gray suit who said he was a detective came and asked us a lot of questions. After we told him what had happened at Quinn's house, I told him about Quinn shooting Mitch. He called and talked to the sheriff.

Even though I knew it would get Dalton in trouble with his dad, when the detective hung up I told him, "Dalton brought his dad's gun when we went looking for the 'Wolf's Head Man.' We thought he shot Mitch and we lied about it so he wouldn't get in trouble."

He asked me what kind of gun we had.

I shrugged my shoulders.

"Rifle or pistol?"

"Pistol."

"The sheriff told me they took a .30-06 slug out of your friend. That's from a hunting rifle. He says he never suspected you kids of shooting Mr. Ford. But he wondered why you were lying."

So all the time we'd spent worrying and feeling guilty had been for nothing. I swore I'd never do that again.

A few minutes later two policemen brought in a man in handcuffs. His face looked dark and full of creases, but maybe it was the way the bright ceiling lights cause shadows on his face. The shaggy brown hair hanging down over his ears matched the color of his eyes.

Nettie ran to him and put her arms around his neck. I knew it was Clayton then. He knelt down and put his arms over her head so he could pick her up with the handcuffs on.

After they whispered a bunch of stuff to each other, Clayton looked at me. I expected him to scold me for taking Nettie to Quinn's house, but instead he thanked me for looking after her and for trying to help Mary Anne.

"You dress up like the 'Wolf's-Head Man' to scare people away from your still, don't you?"

He asked me if I'd figured that out all by myself.

"Yes, sir."

He smiled then told me, "I got the idea from Nettie's pet wolf. I knew it would scare people away from my still if they saw it, but it wasn't always around. Then I remembered the legend and decided to make my own wolf."

I told him that Quinn had killed Nettie's dog.

He told me, "That'll hard on Nettie. She loved that thing, even though it was part wolf. Must've been someone's half-breed pet that ran away. When I saw it lurking around my still I told Nettie to stay away from it, that it was dangerous. But she was never scared of it. When it came around begging she'd pet the thing and share her food with it. I caught her sneaking food scraps out of the house for it. It's been following her around like a puppy."

I never saw Nettie or Clayton again after that night. A policewoman came and took Jessie away while I was talking to Clayton. I never saw her again either.

When my parents finally got there, I couldn't tell if they were mad at me or not; I don't think they knew. I fell asleep on the bench while the sergeant told them some of what happened. I woke to having my foot wiggled by my mother who said it was high time we went home.

When I stood up Mom grabbed me and gave me a really tight hug then started sobbing. She pressed my face against her chest so hard I could barely breathe. I wished she'd waited until we were outside, because it embarrassed the hell out of me. And to make things even worse, she told the sergeant that it was past my bedtime then asked him if she could take me home.

On the way to the car she asked me what I was doing at Quinn's house.

"Mr. Quinn shot Nettie's dog."

"That's not what I asked."

"Mr. Damon told me it was part wolf. That's why it was so big. It's what I saw in the field behind our house the night Star got so scared. I thought it was some kind of monster but I was wrong. It only looked like one."

Dad frowned, said, "Buster, your mother asked you a question."

"I know, and I'm telling you what happened. Nettie's dog followed us to Quinn's house. I told Nettie to wait outside, but just when Quinn was going to shoot me Nettie came in looking for me, so Quinn grabbed her, and that's when the dog jumped on him. So you see, Nettie and her dog saved my life, and Jessie's, and Mrs. Madison's too."

Mother said, "Oh dear," several times while Dad asked me why Quinn was going to shoot me.

"Because we knew he killed Judge Madison. He shot the dog when it jumped on him, and that's when he dropped the gun and Mrs. Madison got it, and Nettie held the dog it while it died...."

Dad held his hand up. "Whoa there, Son, slow down."

Mother asked me "why on earth" I went to Quinn's house in the first place.

"To help Jessie, so Nettie wouldn't end up in one of those terrible places where they put kids who don't have parents."

Mom asked me who Jessie was.

Sometimes explaining things to my parents is just about impossible. "She's the Madisons' maid. She knew what really happened to Mitch. I thought if I could get her to tell the sheriff what happened, Clayton wouldn't have to go to jail and Nettie wouldn't have to go to one of those orphan houses."

"Oh, dear Lord," Mother said. "You went to Quinn's house

because I told you they'd put Nettie in an orphanage?"

"And because Sis told me what happened to that Oliver kid, the one in her book."

Mother slumped against some stranger's car like a blow up doll with a hole in it. "Oh, Billy," she said, "that book was written a hundred years ago. Orphanages aren't like that now. Lisa shouldn't have told you that."

Dad said, "I'm sorry they're going to put your friend in an orphanage, Billy, but the sheriff said Clayton killed Mr. Ford and he has to go to jail for that."

When I said, "He didn't neither," my mother told me to watch my grammar.

My parents could be downright exasperating. "One day, Jessie overheard Quinn tell Judge Madison that he shot Mitch, and they found out she heard them. That's why Quinn was gonna kill her."

We had gotten to the car and Mother had just opened her door when I told her, "Quinn was gonna kill me because I heard him say he killed Mr. Madison."

"How do you know he was going to kill you?"

'Because he told me so, and he pointed his gun at me."

Mom squeezed the handle on the car door so hard her fingers turned white. "Oh Billy," she said. "Promise me you won't ever do anything like that again."

Dad shook his head. "Then why did people think Clayton killed Mr. Ford?"

"Because you can't tell from the shell."

"I don't know what that means, Billy."

"It's something Mitch told me."

Dad shook his head again. "That's not much help, son."

"I learned it from him one day when we were eating pecans. You can't tell if a pecan is rotten just by looking at the shell, and people are like that too. Like Mr. Madison; he was rotten on the inside, but you couldn't tell by looking at him. And people think the Damons are bad because they look bad, but that's only on the outside. Clayton is like one of those pecans with a black spot on the shell that tastes good anyway. And you know what else?"

"I know you did a very foolish thing, and that you've upset your mother terribly."

"But, Dad, Clayton was the 'Wolf's-Head Man.' He stole dead bodies from cemeteries and put wolf masks on them to scare people away from his still."

Dad and Mom both said, "What?"

"Clayton and Quinn were both there the day Mitch was shot. Clayton put on a wolf mask to scare us away, but I think Quinn knew it wouldn't work on Mitch. That's why he shot him."

Dad asked me how I knew about Clayton stealing dead bodies from cemeteries.

"I got the idea from one of those Midnight Monster Movies. We watched one at Dalton's house about an evil doctor who bought dead bodies from grave robbers."

Mother said it was late, that I'd had a big night and should be in bed. Dad patted me on the head, something I hated almost as much as Mom licking her hand to fix my hair or hugging me in public.

Dad said, "We'll talk more about this tomorrow" then got in the car, and that was the end of that.

As we pulled into our driveway, Mom told me to take the dog outside to do her business. "Then it's straight to bed for you."

The poor dog was so eager to get outside I had trouble holding her still while I hooked the leash to her collar. As soon as I unlatched the door she forced it open with her muzzle and ran out, yanking on her leash so hard I almost tumbled down the steps. As she frantically sniffed the yard for a good spot to leave a mess for me to clean up, I looked at the fields behind the house and thought about the half-breed and the first time I'd seen it.

Star found a spot she liked and squatted facing me. She always looked at me with her ears back, like she was embarrassed. It made me uncomfortable, so I looked away until I heard her scratching the dirt. In all the years I took her outside I never actually saw her bury any of the messes she made. She just scratched the dirt with her back paws once or twice. Sometimes she got dirt on her mess by accident, but mostly she missed it by a mile.

She came over to me and rubbed against my leg, offering me a chance to scratch her back, but I just wanted to crawl into bed. When she realized I was headed inside she took off for the door, pulling on the leash like a sled dog.

FOR EVER AND EVER

While Mom made breakfast for Sis and me the next morning, she danced around the kitchen singing that stupid love song from "South Pacific," the one about a guy who sees a woman across a crowded room.

Star came and sat down next to my chair to beg for a handout. She knew I was an easy target, knew I'd slip her something under the table if she stared at me long enough. If I found gristle or fat in my dinner I gave it to Star when no one was looking. And no matter what I gave her she swallowed it whole. We were so fast Mom never caught us, unless she happened to hear Star's teeth snap shut.

As Mother was putting plates of eggs and toast on the table for Sis and me I heard a car pull into the driveway. I looked at Mom. Mom stopped dancing to lean over the sink and look out the window.

I had just gotten to the door when she yelled, "Billy, you come back here and eat your breakfast," but I kept going, yelling to her from the driveway, "Mom, the sheriff's here."

She yelled back, "You get in here this instant."

I pretended I didn't hear her while I waited to see whether he was coming to our house or the Fords'. I ran back inside when his patrol car turned toward our house. Mother scolded me for letting my breakfast get cold, but it didn't taste any different. When she opened the door for the sheriff she gave him a big smile and acted surprised to see him.

224

He said, "Morning folks," as he took his hat off.

Mom asked him if everything was alright.

"I have some news, ma'am."

She offered him coffee. He thanked her but said, "No" which meant he wouldn't stay long, which was disappointing. He told her Joe Quinn was behind bars and probably never coming out.

Mom asked him about the two men who had kidnapped me.

"That would be Johnny Vail and his buddy Floyd Coffey. Luckily for Mary Anne, the state police caught them on the way to the coast. No telling what would've happened to her if they hadn't. Anyway, those two will be behind bars for a very long time."

When Mom asked him how long a long time was.

"Last time I arrested them, Judge Madison let them out early. But that won't happen this time. This young fella will probably be all grown up by the time they get out of prison."

I imagined a dusty black sedan parked on a dirt road, and a man wearing dark sunglasses sitting on the hood of the car with a shotgun in his lap, watching a bunch of men standing in a roadside ditch swinging scythes and chanting. And I pictured Johnny and his friend chained to them in leg irons.

I asked the sheriff what happened to Clayton.

"The police let him go after they talked to Mrs. Madison and her maid. But you won't have to worry about stolen cars in your driveway anymore."

I asked him why.

"The state police dropped Mary Anne off at my office this morning. I took her home before I came here. Clayton's car was packed. He said they were moving south. I imagine they're gone by now."

I wished I'd had a chance to say goodbye to Nettie.

The sheriff said to me, "Going to Quinn's house like you did was a dangerous, foolish thing to do, but no telling what would've happened to Jessie or Mary Anne if you hadn't. And as for Clayton; well, he'd be on his way to prison."

I told him I thought Nettie and her dog were the brave ones, but before he could say anything to me about it Mom asked him what was going to happen to Mrs. Madison.

That made him smile. "I reckon she'll get to stand in front of the same bench where her husband used to hand out justice. There is some irony in that, although I don't suppose she'll do much time since she shot Quinn in self-defense, and I don't think she had anything to do with the bootlegging, or with Mr. Ford getting shot."

The sheriff left after that and Mother went back to dancing and singing, only this time it was a song about a woman washing a guy out of her hair. I went outside to get away from it. I found a cool spot to lay down in the shade of an oak tree.

I thought about sitting with Mitch on his porch and how I felt like a grownup when he and I were talking, and about how good that made me feel. And I thought about the first time Thelma brought us pecans and how Mitch could break them with one hand, and about eating the rotten one and Mitch saying, "You can't tell from the shell."

That night, I'd taken Star out to do her business, and was bringing her back in when I spotted Nettie's teddy bear on our front steps. I'd stepped right over it when Star dragged me outside.

After I took Star off her leash I took it to the bedroom. I wanted to put it where I could see it from my bed. To make room for it on the dresser Sis and I shared, I pushed some of her junk out of the way, being extra careful not to knock any of it on the floor.

Lisa and I had to take turns using the bathroom to brush our teeth and change into our pajamas, and Mom always sent me to bed first, so I was already in bed when Sis came into the bedroom.

She noticed the teddy bear right away and made a face at it. "Billy, you get that thing off of my dresser right now."

I told her it was our dresser and that I had a right to put

226

something on it.

"Not if it's ugly."

"It isn't ugly."

"Is too. It's filthy and its stuffing is falling out."

I told her I wasn't moving it and she couldn't make me. She yelled for Mom, and when Mom didn't answer right away, she yelled again. Mom appeared at our door right after that to ask what was wrong.

Sis said, "Tell Billy he can't put that dirty thing on my dresser."

Mom picked it up and looked it over. "This is Nettie's, isn't it, Billy?"

"It's the only thing she had in the whole world."

Lisa said, "Please, Mom, please tell him he can't put that on my dresser."

Mother told her to be nice to me, that I'd been through a lot lately.

Sis flopped down on her bed, said, "You always take his side" then rolled over.

Sis had fancy horse bookends holding up a row of her Nancy Drew books on the dresser. Mom propped the teddy bear against one of the bookends so it was sitting up and I could see it from my bed. I thanked her.

She smiled one of the big fake smiles she used with strangers then told us, "Now go to sleep you two."

"Mom?"

"Yes, Billy."

"Nettie saved my life and I didn't thank her."

She told me not to worry, that Nettie would understand.

"But she only had one thing in the whole world, and she gave it to me. I don't think I could do that."

"She must have really liked you. Now go to sleep."

I decided right then and there that I'd keep it for ever and ever.

227